Raven's Widows

ALSO BY VINCE KOHLER

Rainy North Woods
Rising Dog
Banjo Boy

For Ruth —
I hope you enjoy my crazy
Alaska Book —

RAVEN'S

VINCE KOHLER

WIDOWS

Best wishes —
Vince Kohler 10/18/97

ST. MARTIN'S PRESS NEW YORK

Library of Congress Cataloging-in-Publication Data

Kohler, Vincent, date

Raven's widows: an Eldon Larkin mystery / by Vince Kohler.

p. cm.

ISBN 0-312-14714-7

I. Title.

PS3568.O358R355 1997

813'.54—dc20 96-25576

First edition: June 1997

10 9 8 7 6 5 4 3 2 1

This one is for Mary Joan, as are all of them,
past and future; for she is my past and future

AUTHOR'S NOTE

Raven's Widows is a novel. Its people and events are imaginary. Klinkatshut, Alaska, like Eldon Larkin's home base of Port Jerome, Oregon, is fictitious. The Klinkatshut Indians are fictitious, as well. Their folklore, traditions, and totem poles are based on those of actual Pacific Northwest tribes and on works by Alaskan and Canadian artists; but these have been melded and distorted to suit the story's needs.

The following works were sources of Indian legends and totem lore: *Alaska's Southeast: Touring the Inside Passage* by Sarah Eppenbach (Seattle: Pacific Search Press, 1983); *The Wolf and the Raven: Totem Poles of Southeast Alaska* by Viola E. Garfield and Linn A. Forest (Seattle: University of Washington Press, 1948); and *The Legacy: Continuing Traditions of Canadian Northwest Coast Indian Art* by Peter McNair et al (Victoria: British Columbia Provincial Museum, 1980).

The citations from Rainer Maria Rilke are from *The Migration of Powers: French Poems,* translated by A. Poulin Jr. (Port Townsend, Washington: Graywolf Press, 1984).

ACKNOWLEDGMENTS

Raven's Widows was completed with the help and encouragement of many people, some of whom have been reviewing Eldon Larkin's antics for a long time.

Foremost among them is my wife, Mary Joan O'Connell, who as usual patiently edited the manuscript, helped with Eldon's French, and touched up his fishing skills. Other friends whose advice was invaluable include Steve Perry, author of *The Digital Effect* and many other novels; Phillip M. Margolin, who wrote *The Burning Man;* and Jim Lane, Bill Robins, and Foster Church. Greg Mandel, author of the mysteries *High Hat* and *Dead Ringer,* and Seward Whitfield, who wrote *The Adventures and Sufferings of C. S. Elliott,* were living databases of Southeast Alaska lore. John Dean gave advice on mountain climbing. Brian McCullough and Bridget Madill of Brightstar Communications, Kanata, Ontario, Canada, aided by Suzanne Gervais, kept Eldon's French on track. Special thanks go to the Reverend Matthew Tate, pastor of the Orthodox Church of the Annunciation in Milwaukie, Oregon, for advice on the practices and beliefs of the Russian Orthodox Church in America.

Thanks also to Keith Kahla and John Hall of St. Martin's Press, and to my agents, Sharon Jarvis and Joel Gotler, for their sustained efforts on my behalf.

There is no murder; there is only art.

—John "Big Head" Leonard,
in conversation, about 1974

RAVEN'S WIDOWS

1

Eldon Larkin clutched his fishing rod and yelled as the totem pole came at him.

Actually a section of a totem pole, his reporter's mind corrected as the canvas wrapping came off the stout plug of log to reveal bright Alaska Native carving. The totem, as big around as a hogshead barrel and squat enough to fit between the alley walls, was rolling straight for him. A shouting jug-eared Indian sprinted after the log, knees pumping almost up to his chest.

Eldon watched it happen through a cloud of driving Alaska rain. The flatbed truck skidded on the drenched street at the alley's far end. The big log bounced off the back of the truck, rolled across the street, and crashed down the wooden stairs leading into the alley. The Indian sprang from the truck and followed.

The totem pole rolled at Eldon, its huge bright gargoyle face rotating in and out of view. Yelling, Eldon turned and ran.

There was a wooden stairway at his end of the alley, too. Eldon skidded on the wet concrete and bounced off the alley wall. The totem pole was gaining on him. He screamed and threw his fishing rod back at the gargoyle just as he reached the stairway and his foot slipped on the rain-slick boards. He sat hard and bounced down the stairs. Fortunately, he was fairly well padded.

Welcome to Alaska, Eldon thought. A great start for my vacation.

The new graphite rod had cost a fortune. But he'd needed to

splurge. The whole fishing trip was a splurge. He'd had to get away from Port Jerome, Oregon, and Melissa Lafky and all the murders and especially his editor, Fiske, and Fiske's gout. But nothing was going right.

He heard a snap and a crunch as the log slammed to a stop at the top of the stairs, wedged against the alley wall. After a moment, Eldon sat up on the wet sidewalk at the foot of the stairs and tried to slow his breathing. Rain dripped from the brim of his sodden jungle hat and soaked into his coat. The seat of his pants was wet and cold. Ketchikan, Alaska, got one hundred sixty-five inches of rain a year, two and a half times the annual rainfall of Port Jerome. And the summer of 1979 seemed to be typical.

His fishing rod! He stumbled back up the stairs. A cold hand clutched his heart. The rod's splintered top half lay in the alley. The lower part stuck out from under the totem pole. The rod's butt had stopped the log like a chock thrust beneath a wheel.

"No." It was like gazing upon the mangled corpse of a loved one. Eldon grabbed the rod and tugged futilely.

"What'd you do to my totem pole?" the Indian demanded from the other side of the log.

"What'd you do to my fishing rod?" Eldon retorted.

The Indian glared. He was as thickset as his log, with thick black hair slicked down by the rain. He had intelligent brown eyes and a nose that looked as if it had been broken—more than once. But his salient feature was his huge ears. One ear stuck out like a jug handle. The other was so badly cauliflowered that it looked like a piece of gristle.

His head looks like a lopsided pot, Eldon thought. A grin spread across his face of its own accord as the idea lodged in his mind. The Indian's eyes lit with knowing anger and he hauled off to swing.

Eldon registered that the other man wore a heavy silver ring—an excellent knuckle-duster. Then a woman cried, "Jason! Don't!" The Indian dropped his arm. Eldon let go of the rod, suddenly too tired to fight or run. He clumped slowly back down the stairs and sat on the bottom step, staring at the street. His rump ached.

"Are you okay, cheechako?" the woman asked. Eldon looked and saw legs descending the stairs in snug jeans tucked into knee-high rubber boots. He started up painfully and slipped again.

"Careful!" Her voice was rich and low. She took Eldon's hand and half-pulled him to his feet. Her hand was slender despite its strong grip, its nails long and red, impeccably manicured. It was a left hand—no wedding ring.

Eldon clutched the hand tightly to verify the lack of jewelry. He reached his feet and looked into large gray eyes set in a face with a long nose and high cheekbones. The effect was elegant and distinctly feline. The eyes gazed out from beneath a thick knitted watch cap. They glittered with amusement and intelligence. They belonged to a slender, long-legged woman of about thirty, buried in a big blue quilted parka, her fair cheeks reddened by the cold.

Eldon instantly grew tongue-tied. He knew with dismal certainty what the woman saw: his fair, plump face with its ragged walrus moustache and big sad blue eyes—like a disillusioned choirboy's, as his ex-wife, Bernice, used to say. I'm thirty-three and I never manage to grow up, he thought miserably.

"Are you okay?" the woman repeated. "Jason's kind of hot-tempered."

"He ought to get that fixed," Eldon said bitterly.

"That's his totem pole," the woman explained.

"Yeah? Well, *that* was my fishing rod."

"That was brilliant, throwing it under the totem like that! Otherwise, the totem might've gone straight out into the traffic and hurt somebody." The woman went back up the stairs and returned to hand Eldon the upper part of the rod. "These graphite rods are great," she remarked as he looked away in pain. "I do some fishing myself."

"It was new," Eldon repeated sadly.

"We owe you another one. But right now, we've got to get that totem pole back on the truck. Hey, Jason, wrap the canvas around it first—!"

She turned and hurried up the steps to where Jason, still frantic, was single-handedly trying to roll the totem pole section back up the alley. He hopped around as if he were venting steam from some overheated internal boiler. Then he reddened like an abashed boy and rushed back up the alley after the tarp. The woman came down the steps as the onlookers wandered away.

"What was that you called me?" Eldon asked her. "It sounded like a Mexican word."

"What? Oh—a cheechako." She laughed. "That's not Mexican, it's Alaskan."

"What's a cheechako?" Eldon tried to pull out the wet seat of his pants while maintaining his dignity.

"A tenderfoot. A beginner."

"I'm no beginner. I fish a lot."

"I meant a beginner to Alaska. First time up here?"

"Yeah."

"Then you're a cheechako. Unless you want me to call you a puker, the way Jason would. Where're you from?"

"Oregon."

"Well, so am I! The Dalles."

"Port Jerome."

"That calls for a cup of coffee! Maybe with something stronger in it, Mr., uh . . ."

"Larkin. Eldon Larkin. Now, about my rod—"

"Pleased to meet you. Can we have your help? We've got to get this to the art gallery—"

Eldon wasn't letting this woman out of his sight until she'd paid for his fishing rod. And he wasn't about to turn his back on Jason. As he climbed the wet steps and joined in putting his shoulder to the log, he wondered how they were going to get it back up the steps at the alley's far end. But Jason laid boards along the stairs there, and the three of them managed to roll it up to the truck. Eldon was relieved to find that the flatbed was equipped with a hydraulic lift at the rear. Soon they had the totem pole section back in place, secured by a web of ropes.

"All right, let's get going." The woman swung behind the steering wheel, and Jason clambered into the cab's other seat.

Eldon saw that the center of the cab was piled high with canvas luggage. "There isn't room for three."

"Someone will have to ride in back," the woman told Jason pointedly.

"It's raining," Jason said. "Let *him* ride in back. Or *you*."

"Wotta man." She shrugged and gestured Eldon onto the back of the truck.

"Hey, just a minute," Eldon said. "Who *are* you?"

The woman beamed and handed over a slightly dog-eared business card. Eldon stared at it as she closed the truck's passenger door:

ANITA POVEY
Editor & Publisher
THE AURORA
Klinkatshut, Alaska
Job printing—Good rates

She's an *editor,* Eldon thought, his irritation giving way to shock. That explains everything. He hauled himself aboard the truck, braced himself against the back of the cab, and dropped the ruined fishing rod beneath his feet. The truck pulled away, water surging up and away from its wheels.

They moved slowly down the busy street. Traffic was bumper-to-bumper—pickups, cars, campers, big commercial rigs loaded with logs or fish, their windshield wipers slapping as the rain pounded down and their wheels splashing big gouts of water like ships cutting rough ocean. Waterfalls sluiced off the eaves of buildings. Rain whirled through the cool air. Huge cold raindrops bounced off Eldon's shoulders. People in rain gear jostled along the sidewalks beneath bright thunderbird motifs. Here and there through the downpour Eldon glimpsed a totem pole, its paint weathered and rain dripping from its wings as it kept watch over the city.

Oregon's rain is a joke compared with this, Eldon thought with a shiver. This is incredible. How am I going to get any fishing done? Rain seldom daunted him. Rain was Eldon's security blanket; but now he felt as if he were drowning.

They crawled uphill, past staircases leading to houses that seemed to float among low clouds. The truck pulled into a parking lot and around to the rear of a low commercial building. AURORA ALASKAN ART—KETCHIKAN—NO PARKING was stenciled on the building's wide metal doors. Anita jumped from the truck, unlocked the doors, and went inside.

Eldon fumbled with the wet knots securing the totem pole's ropes. "Hey, Jason, come out here and gimme a hand!"

Jason climbed from the truck with a bottle in his hand. Tokay. He stood in the downpour, defiantly swigging from the bottle and glaring as rain dripped off his nose.

Eldon's stomach turned over. Next would come the attack. But he couldn't run. No, dammit, he *wouldn't* run. He glared back and pulled out the new clasp fishing knife Melissa Lafky had given him. He snapped it open and had the satisfaction of seeing Jason's eyes seem to contract in a sort of subliminal flinch.

Eldon slashed the ropes and started viciously kicking the totem pole toward the rear of the truck, an inch at a time. Jason hurled the bottle aside with a curse and climbed aboard to help Eldon wrestle the totem pole onto the lift. Eldon made a show of closing his knife and putting it away. Anita returned, pushing a big, low industrial cart. They got the totem onto the cart and rolled it into the darkened building.

Anita followed, carrying the wreckage of Eldon's fishing rod, shut the doors, and threw on the lights. Eldon saw that they were in a storage room filled with boxes and flat wooden crates that he guessed contained framed pictures.

"Gallery's closed," Anita said. "It's Monday."

"I try to forget what day it is when I'm on vacation." Eldon accepted the mangled pieces of the fishing rod and dropped them onto a table.

"Anyone ever tell you you're fast on your feet?" Anita asked.

"Thanks," Eldon said. "I guess it could've been worse."

Jason was already stripping the wet canvas from the totem. He was hyperventilating again. The odor of Tokay on his breath filled the room like a spreading cloud of doom. "Yeah—this log could've split."

"It would've been easier to get it off the truck in two pieces," Eldon said.

"A year's work—," Jason started up with an angry snort, but Anita stepped between them.

"We have to check this," she said quickly. "Then we'll talk. Have a look around, Eldon."

"Will they mind?" Eldon asked.

"Hell, I'm a part owner and Jason's agent."

But not his girlfriend? Eldon's spirits lifted and he wondered if Anita was free for dinner, even as he quailed at the thought of Alaska's horrendous prices. Maybe she'll buy *me* dinner, he thought.

The notion slowed his thumping heart. So did the gallery's pleasant ambiance. The display area was warm and carpeted, with track lighting aglow and white walls covered with Alaska Native art. Eldon examined paintings, statuettes, and carvings of thunderbirds and whales, hunting scenes, winter tableaus, and auroras. Pottery, stone carvings, and gleaming cast silver filled display cases. Eldon wished that there were such galleries in Port Jerome.

He went to the front window and looked out over the rainy city. Down near the harbor, boxy, peak-roofed buildings hung out over the estuary on pilings. Fishing boats and pleasure craft filled the basin as if huddling for shelter from the storm. Beyond, a tug bucked through the choppy white waters of the Tongass Narrows. Rain fell in unrelenting sheets, giving the view a submerged, greenish cast, and all around, the limitless Alaskan forest seemed to drift through clouds. The trees looked flat against the white sky, like a backdrop on the stage of an enormous theater.

How am I going to get any fishing done in this? Eldon wondered again. He had flown into Ketchikan the day before and had found a hotel room at a sky-high price. The cost of a fishing charter was as appalling as the weather. He should have done more research.

He had a month ahead of him—all the time off he had been able to wangle out of Jimbo Fiske, editor of the *South Coast Sun*. He had headed for Alaska on impulse, without reservations or proper plans, to go fishing in a place as wild and remote from Port Jerome and its violence as he could practicably reach. Now his wallet threatened to go flat and send him home to Oregon before he had properly escaped.

"Hey, Eldon, it's okay." It was Anita. Eldon admired her long legs as she strode up. "There's some chipped paint and a gouge, nothing that can't be repaired. Totems are sturdy—all-weather stuff, y'know."

She guided him back to the storeroom. Jason, now considerably calmer, was still inspecting the totem. "It could've been worse—could've been teeth marks or something." Eldon blinked, mystified. Jason stood and stuck out his hand, throwing his arm straight out like a clumsy punch: "Jason Baer."

He relates real good, Eldon thought sourly, and he warily shook the hand. "Eldon Larkin." He feared a bone-crushing grip as they shook, but Jason's handshake was rather slack, withdrawn a little too quickly, as if the artist had touched something unpleasant. The silver ring, Eldon noticed, was the figure of a totem bird.

"I got excited out there," Jason said. "This thing was a lot of work."

"It sure gave me a scare," Eldon said.

"You sacrificed your fishing rod to save my totem," Baer said, almost formally. "I'm in your debt."

Eldon replied carefully: "Replacing my fishing rod will do."

Jason glowered and fidgeted and was silent. Eldon realized with sympathy that the man was at a loss for words. With some it was women, and with others it was accidents with their totem poles.

"Nice ring," Eldon said.

Jason spread the fingers on his ring hand and smiled. "Thanks. That's Raven. Raven's a trickster."

"And what's this?" Eldon asked, pointing at the totem. "What's it represent?"

The totem had been carved into the semblance of a bearlike creature. Not a bear, but not a man, either. A big ring in its flaring nose hung over the grotesquely gaping mouth. Its paws were clamped to the sides of its head. No, not paws: hands. The effect was comic.

"Sasquatch," Jason said with a smirk.

"Doesn't look like any Bigfoot I ever met," Eldon said.

"Oh? You've met one?"

"Uh, kind of, yeah." Eldon wondered whether to tell about *that,* then decided against it.

"You should recognize him, then." Jason put his hand into a socket cut in the section's top. "This is a piece of a full-sized totem pole. It'll stand more than thirty feet high, all put together."

"I thought they carved 'em all in one piece."

"Usually. Depends. Not this one."

"Why not?"

"You're a nosy cheechako, aren't you?"

Eldon tried to keep his voice steady. "Guess so."

"Well, this one'll sell better this way."

"Isn't there a law about selling this kind of thing?"

"Old stuff's protected, yeah. But this is my own piece."

"Who buys it?" Eldon asked.

"People with big living rooms. That's why this one's in sections. Gonna be my comeback, too. Gonna make me a pile. They're gonna remember me—"

"There's a growing demand for Alaska Native art," Anita said, "from companies, institutions, and private individuals."

"The tradition's a thousand years old," Jason said, his face and tone relaxing as he warmed to his subject. "The Northwest peoples began developing art for white markets during the late nineteenth century—Charlie Edenshaw and others. Modern interest in totems only picked up about 1938 or '39, though, when carvers like John Wallace and Walter Kita brought back the craft."

"For the tourist trade?" Eldon asked.

"Art follows markets. I carve red cedar, mostly. I get some nice detail." Jason ran a hand over his work, and something like veneration entered his voice. "Red cedar grows tall and straight; it's easy to carve and cuts clean across the grain." He thrust his face against the carving and inhaled vigorously, running his nose over the wood like a vacuum cleaner. "It's aromatic, too. C'mere and smell—"

Eldon backed away hastily. "Reminds me of topiary."

"Topiary?" Anita asked.

"Shaping plants into figures," Eldon said. "It takes patience. I hadn't thought of a topiary totem pole, but I suppose it's possible."

"You've got quite an imagination," Anita said.

"No, I'm a newspaper reporter."

"You *are?*" Anita laughed with delight. "Which paper?"

"The *South Coast Sun* in Port Jerome."

"Well, well, a kindred spirit, Anita," Jason said, his tone turning unpleasant again.

"The *Sun* is a good little paper," Anita said.

"There are no good newspapers," Jason said.

But Anita's expression sharpened. "So how do you know about topiary? Are you the garden writer?"

"No, a general-assignment reporter—"

"See?" Jason asked. "He isn't really that smart."

"The topiary was part of a good story," Eldon persisted.

"Let him talk, Jason. Are you up here on assignment?"

"No, I just want to go fishing."

"I see *Sun* stories on the wire sometimes," Anita said.

"Maybe you read some of mine."

"Maybe I did. Such as what?"

"Well, there was the big drug raid last fall, in '78. And the murder of the radical environmentalist this spring—"

Anita shook her head. "I guess not."

"The topiary murder case was my latest big story," Eldon said a little desperately. Maybe he could impress her by talking about fishing. . . .

Anita snapped her fingers. "Just a minute. 'Eldon Larkin.' The *elephant lynching!* You took that incredible picture!"

"Well, no. But I wrote the story."

"I saw that on the wire. That was *good copy*. I thought I knew your name!"

"Thanks." Eldon gave an embarrassed grin. "But I was just at the right place at the right time."

"In other words, you're a good reporter." Anita had an eager look. "How about that coffee? I want to talk to you."

"What about?" It was Jason.

"Maybe about getting you some Stateside ink!" Anita said.

"Yeah, I'll bet," Jason said nastily. "You go on. I'm gonna touch up my totem. Have a good time at the potlatch, white boy."

Anita led Eldon past Jason, back into the storage area and out into the rain. They crossed the parking lot and went down the street. They passed store windows full of cheap Alaskan souvenirs, nothing like the quality of the work in the Aurora Gallery. Here were row on row of garish plates, varnished wooden plaques, and ranks of identical, crudely carved little totem poles. "Made in Japan," Anita said over her shoulder.

She ducked through a pair of glass doors with *Sluice Box Saloon* etched upon them. "Welcome to Alaska!"

"I'll say." Eldon looked around. The place was an overdone Gold Rush fantasy. The knotty pine walls were decorated with crossed shovels and picks, gold pans, and other mining equipment and with mounted heads of moose, deer, and bear. A bartender who looked as if he trimmed his corns with a beartrap stood polishing glasses behind the bar. But what captured Eldon's attention was an immense king salmon mounted over the bar. "Oh, baby!"

"Like that?" Anita asked.

"That's why I came up here!"

"That's nothing."

"It must've weighed thirty pounds!"

"Try fifty," Anita said as they sat down at one of the tables. "Thirty wouldn't even get mounted—and that one up there wouldn't place at most salmon derbies. You should see 'em where I live. Spanish coffee okay with you?" Anita waved to the bartender. "Hey, two Spanish here." She opened her coat, pulled off her cap, and shook out long auburn hair. She is quite a dish, Eldon thought, even if she is an editor. And she fishes, too.

The Spanish coffee was served in white ceramic mugs heavy enough for doorstops. Eldon put his worries aside, blew on the coffee, and took a cautious sip. It was real Spanish coffee, all right, strong and hot. The bartender had even coated the rim of the mug with sugar. The whiskey instantly filled him with warmth. He realized how tired he was—and not just from dodging totem poles in the rain. Eldon dropped his hat on the table, shrugged out of his wet coat and hung it over a chair.

Anita watched Eldon with heavy-lidded eyes. Eldon noticed that she wore deep blue eye shadow despite her rough clothing. Eldon's heart skipped a beat as she appraised him. He worried that he had boasted unduly.

"So you're up here to go fishing," Anita said. "Long way from home, isn't it? There's salmon fishing in Oregon."

"Not Alaska kings," Eldon said. "I needed a break. I had to get away. Alaska seemed like a good place."

"Why's that?" Anita's tone was sympathetic.

Sympathetic women were Eldon's downfall. He found himself telling the story of the past few murderous months—the dead

Vietnamese and the lynched elephant, the mummified foot in the landfill and the dog that had risen from the dead, the enormous pimp, the deaths of a fishing comrade and of a piano player, the streetwalker who had nearly died, and how religion and topiary and tinfoil spaceships had figured in. Naturally, he did not mention the various women who had gotten him tangled up in all of it.

Eldon became aware that he was speaking too intently. He stopped and sipped his drink. "Sorry to bend your ear."

"Sounds like damn good copy."

"People got killed."

"Not your fault." Anita's big eyes looked straight into his and Eldon hoped against hope.

"I had to take this vacation," he said, "because of Fiske's gout."

"An editor with gout. I've heard everything now."

"You haven't met Jimbo Fiske," Eldon said. "That gout is all in his head. There's a lot of stuff in Jimbo's head. One time it was plate tectonics—he was afraid the news desk would slide out from under him. And the macrobiotic food—that's why he thinks he has gout. And he's hot on Bigfoot—"

"Sasquatch?" Anita smiled. "Well, you can tell him you saw one in the gallery. . . . How'd you like the artist?"

"Nasty," Eldon said, "and talented."

"Right on both counts. He's a client of the gallery, of course—one of the reasons I'm in Ketchikan."

"Business is off, though?"

"The market's down, but it'll come back. Jason's work is unique. He's brilliant."

"Does he change moods like that all the time?"

"He does when he drinks. He's flying back to Klinkatshut on his own, fortunately."

Aha, Eldon thought. "Why else are you in Ketchikan?"

"To pick up printing supplies . . . and have a good time."

"May I take you to dinner?" Eldon asked at once.

Anita gave a broad smile. "I was going to invite *you.*"

The pioneering spirit of Alaska surged through Eldon. He took another swig of Spanish coffee. "Accepted."

"How about salmon? I know a great little place."

"Uh, is Jason coming, too?"

"Jason's on his own. You really stood up to him, by the way. That'll save you problems later."

"I'm at a point in my life where I'm tired of being pushed around."

"I saw your move with that knife, out on the truck. Someone up here would've tried to carve him up. But you went one better—you shamed him."

"Well, I wasn't going to stick him. What was that crack about a potlatch?"

"Kind of Jason's way of admitting that you'd topped him."

"Do they still do potlatches up here? Give away everything they own?"

Anita grinned. "We'll talk about that. But first, let's find you a new fishing rod. The cost of which I will take out of Jason's commission on that damn totem pole."

"It's still raining."

"Southeast Alaska's like Oregon—you have to do it in the rain, whatever it is. Want another Spanish coffee?"

"You bet!"

Anita signaled the bartender. When the man brought the fresh drinks, Anita pulled out a thick roll of banknotes and paid for both rounds. "I may have a proposition for you," she told Eldon.

"Like what?"

"I'll tell you later. I'm still thinking it over."

Eldon decided it was his turn to tease. "How d'you know you can trust me? Do you always flash a big bankroll in front of strangers?"

"I can trust you." Another warm smile. She leaned back and tugged open the left flap of her coat, and Eldon saw why she hadn't taken it off. Anita wore a shoulder holster. It held a big blue revolver.

"Smith and Wesson Model 19," she explained. "Three-fifty-seven Magnum."

t I have had very bad luck with gun-toting women, Eldon thought, and this one's an editor. He took another sip of Spanish coffee. "Why the hell do you carry that?"

"For shooting bears," Anita returned serenely.

"This bear lives quietly under the name of Sanders," Eldon assured her.

"You don't scare worth a damn, do you, Larkin? And you read *Winnie the Pooh.* I like that. How'd you like a job?"

Eldon laughed. "No."

"I'm serious. I just made up my mind. How would you like a short writing gig?"

"Huh? I've got a month and I want to spend it fishing."

"Fishing included."

"Go on," Eldon said, thinking that something else might be included, too.

"I'm up against it on a special tabloid insert for the *Aurora,"* Anita said. "Hunting and fishing articles, features on local people. Tabloid format and lots of pictures. You know the drill—"

"Sure. We do the same kind of thing at the *Sun."*

"It's my paper's advertising gravy train for the year," Anita said. "I've sold a lot of ads, and I've got a big news hole to fill. I've got a pile of stringer copy to edit—and you know that means rewrite most of it—plus photos to be shot and stories to be written. The cover story will be the tribal potlatch a few days from now. It's the biggest deal around."

Potlatch! Eldon imagined beating drums, firelight on leering totems, treasures cast into vast fires. "You mean where they go broke burning stuff up?"

"That's nonsense. A potlatch is a serious affair."

"And good copy."

"And good copy, yeah. The tab's due at the printer in Sitka in ten days. With your help, I can make it. It's about a week's work, in some of the best fishing country in Alaska."

"How d'you know I can do it?"

"You can do it. I saw that elephant story."

"What's in it for me?"

"I fly you up to Klinkatshut and back to Ketchikan in my floatplane. You get room and board and all the fishing you can cram in. And I mean *fishing.*"

"I work all year. I don't want to 'cram in' my fishing."

"Then cram in the writing. Just get it done. You can practically walk out my back door and be standing on a fabulous salmon stream. Hit the fishing first thing in the morning, come in and crank some copy, go fishing some more. When the tab's done, there'll be three weeks of fishing and good times. And think of the money you'll save on provender and charter fees."

"I was worried about that. Things are pretty steep around here."

"You'll have use of a car, too."

"Where would I stay?"

"My place." Anita waited.

Eldon tried to appraise the situation coolly and logically, with professional aplomb; but the words *my place* seemed to burn before him in the air. Eldon realized that he'd jump at the chance to stay with Anita in a pup tent, in a lean-to . . .

"When your vacation's over, I'll fly you back down here," Anita added, "with regret, I'm sure."

Maybe the weather'll turn bad, Eldon thought. I could be marooned with her. I could send Fiske a telegram—*Snowed in, home as soon as possible, ha ha. Eldon*—and there'd be nothing he could do.

"Will you do it?" Anita looked anxiously into Eldon's eyes.

Rain rattled against the windows. Eldon's gaze went to the king salmon over the bar, played along the frozen silver and purple arc of the fish. He looked through the streaming window, past the buildings and the cars to the white sky and the vast Alaska forest, full of fish for the taking. A free fishing trip hosted by a beautiful, gun-toting woman, just for turning a few puff features. . . .

Oh, boy!

"Okay," he said, ignoring the alarm bell in his mind, "it's a deal."

2

"People in Ketchikan have a saying," Anita said the next morning as she opened her preflight checklist. " 'If you can't see Deer Mountain, it's raining. If you can see it, it's about to rain.' The mountain's over there."

Eldon nodded happily. He sat next to Anita in the cockpit of her floatplane near the Ketchikan docks, enjoying the vastness of the setting. Across his knees, resting in sections in a canvas container, was his new nine-foot-long, 10-weight graphite fishing rod. The storm had blown over. It was a dazzling morning.

Ketchikan gleamed in the sun. Light glittered on the Tongass Narrows as white gulls wheeled above the waves. The sky was a pure, vivid blue and the forest a vivid green. The mountains descended steeply to meet the water, cupping the city like a chalice.

Flying made Eldon nervous. He had fidgeted all the way to Ketchikan on the flight from Seattle. But today he sat in happy anticipation, listening to the gulls' cries and smelling the water's briny odor. The plane was loaded with photographic supplies, groceries, fishing equipment, and mail, lashed down with rope, bungee cords, and nylon belts. He fantasized that he was aboard a relief mission to the far north. He turned and carefully placed the fishing rod with the other cargo.

"Great flying weather," Anita said. "We'll be home in a few hours. I have to be antisocial now, so be quiet."

She moved the control column and checked the elevators, rudders, and ailerons, then began reading off the preflight checklist: "Magnetos, throttle, oil pressure and temperature, fuel . . ."

Her competence impressed Eldon. He was relieved that she could be so meticulous after their night on the town. They had bought the fine new fishing rod and then gone out for a splendid salmon dinner and several drinks. Then it had been disco dancing until after midnight, in a club with walls plastered with John Travolta posters. All of it was paid for from Anita's big roll of bills.

Anita had danced like a wraith. Eldon had never before danced with a woman wearing a concealed revolver and had to admit that it had spiced the occasion. He had been amazed that Anita could move so gracefully while packing the weapon; then he had wondered how many others in the disco were armed as well. Alaska was quite a place. He had ended up sleeping alone in his own hotel room—she had slipped from his grasp like a wraith, too, after a quick, brushing kiss. But Eldon had awakened rested and buoyed with hope, a little afraid that it had all been too good to be true.

Anita had been downstairs awaiting him as promised. And after breakfast, here they were, ready to fly away together.

Anita called the airport tower for clearance, got it and said, "Hang on. Flaps."

She moved the throttle. The engine revved, its heavy vibration building to a roar. They began to move on the water, sluggishly at first, then more smoothly. They surged away. The climb felt like an elevator. Eldon looked out his side window and watched the water fall away. *"Whee-ooo!"*

Anita looked over at Eldon with a grin. "You're all mine now."

"Be good or I'll jump out."

"Not with all that fishing ahead, Larkin. I've got you scoped."

"Maybe you have." Eldon reached over to stroke Anita's shoulder.

She pulled a bulging manila folder from a seat pocket and thrust it into Eldon's hand. "Don't distract the pilot. Here—you may as well start work."

Eldon took the folder with a sigh as the plane continued to climb. He knew a stack of assignments when he saw it. He waited until their climb leveled out, then asked, "Did you fly that Sasquatch totem down here?"

"What? No, it wouldn't fit in the plane. Jason shipped it on the ferry and then flew down after it. He took off for home early today. He's probably almost there by now."

"How'd you get to be editor of the paper?"

"Got it in a divorce settlement."

"He's not still around, is he?"

"God, no. Klinkatshut's too small for that. He's back in The Dalles. The *Aurora* was just an investment to him."

"He must have loot."

"Are you out to marry me for my fortune?"

"It's just the reporter in me," Eldon said.

"He's into cattle and shipping. I'm the one who had the journalism degree. I never got to use it after we got married."

"Sorry."

"Don't be. He used to hit me. You aren't married, are you?"

"Divorced. Bernice is in Australia or the Far East somewhere. I haven't heard in a while."

"Any kids?"

"No kids."

Anita smiled. "You'll like my daughter."

"You have a daughter?" Eldon was uncomfortable around children. This could spoil everything.

"Cassandra. She's nine. Cute as a button, smart as a whip." Anita reached into a jacket pocket and handed Eldon a billfold.

He opened it. Behind the Alaska driver's license, the pilot's license, and the credit cards, he found a color snapshot of a little girl. She was a small replica of her mother—somehow graver, with a rounder face but the same big feline eyes. The cat's kitten.

"She might give you some competition when she grows up," Eldon ventured. "But that'll be a while."

"She likes books." Anita took the wallet back. "Reading's good for a child—not a lot else to do when the weather's bad. I ration TV. The shows up here are all at least two weeks old, anyway."

"Are there a lot of fishermen around?"

"Don't worry, Eldon. You'll think you're back in the Pleistocene."

He believed it. Below was a trackless green forest cut by shining channels of water forming a flat, lustrous highway northward. It was as if people had never come into the world.

Eldon stared out the window while he collected his thoughts. He'd have to be urbane with a kid around . . . maybe read her bedtime stories or something. Or teach her to tie flies.

Fishing, that was it. You were never too young to learn to fly-fish. The idea of teaching a child to fish made Eldon feel warm, somehow paternal. As if to head the feeling off, he wondered absurdly if Cassandra packed a gun the way her mother did. He imagined the nine-year-old with a short-barreled .22 revolver in a shoulder holster, ready to draw down on a bear. Or on Mama's new boyfriend. He'd have to play it cool.

"Uh, does she carry a gun, too?"

Anita laughed. "Not yet. But she's quite a little gun nut, knows a lot about them, especially rifles. Most kids up here do. When she's a little older, I'll get her a .22." Anita dropped a folded newspaper atop the folder. "Here's the *Aurora.*"

Eldon unfolded the paper. The nameplate bore bold blue Alaska flags. Beneath the paper's name was the legend *The Weekly Journal of a Free Alaska.* Eldon scanned the front page in shock.

ANOTHER TAX PLOT IN JUNEAU!! screamed the banner. The story was about a rally at the state capitol in Juneau calling for Alaska to secede from the United States and become an independent country. The story carried Anita's byline. It wasn't very well written. An overexposed photo showed rough-clad men and women carrying signs denouncing high taxes and proclaiming Alaska a free nation.

Anita was watching him sidelong as she flew. There was a merry glitter in her eye that made Eldon wonder if he wasn't being led on, at least partly. "How're you going to run a country without taxes?"

"Alaska's so rich in natural resources that it can be an independent country without costing its citizens a dime—"

"And I've got a bridge in Brooklyn you can buy." Eldon

squirmed with the kind of irritation that he felt when talking with Bible-thumpers or flat-earthers, or with Fiske when the editor's imagination was freshly roiled by the latest issue of his favorite magazine, *Sasquatch and UFO*. "What'll you have once you've strip-mined everything?"

Anita slapped Eldon on the knee. "Good for you! I can't stand mealymouthed men!"

"Who took this photograph?" Eldon asked. It was shot from an oddly low angle, as if the photographer were a dwarf or had been intent on recording the insides of the demonstrators' nostrils.

"Cassandra. I let her help out. I told you, she's really smart."

Eldon took a deep breath and opened the paper. He saw with relief that inside was straight small-town news—features about high school students winning scholarships and good deeds by the Elks. Big play for a basketball tournament. But here was the editorial page: ". . . a gun-totin', rip-roarin' Alaska Republic, a linchpin nation, hub of a wheel of North Pacific prosperity whose spokes are the United States, Canada, Japan, and Siberia . . ."

"Siberia?" Eldon asked.

"The Communists have to fold up sometime," Anita said with confidence. "Siberia's our natural market."

Has anyone told Brezhnev? Eldon wondered. He shuddered at a sidebar headed JOIN CANADA? HELL, NO! He put the paper aside and opened the folder.

Here was more familiar ground. The folder was stuffed with notes and photographs, a typical newspaper's grab bag of stories to be done. Nothing political—just stories about people and their doings. Fair enough, he thought. It might even tell me something about the fishing.

On top was a photograph of a beefy man in traditional Alaskan

Indian dress. "It's Oliver Hardy—with a ring in his nose."

Anita laughed again. "That's Ed Katlean, chief of the Klinkatshut."

Eldon studied the picture. Katlean wore a red cape decorated with gleaming white trim and a feathered wooden headdress with a prow. A thick collar like a Hawaiian lei made from yarn lay over Katlean's shoulders. "What's the tribe again?"

"Klinkatshut. Same as the town. Small town, small tribe."

"He doesn't always dress like this, I assume."

"Of course not. That's ceremonial dress. That was taken at a potlatch in Angoon."

"What's the snout on the headdress?"

"That's Raven. That's his beak. I've seen Raven masks with five-foot beaks that open and close. Raven stories are a favorite theme for totem poles."

"What about Sasquatch totems?"

"That's a parody, actually. It got Ed kind of riled. Did you notice how it kind of looks like him?"

"So Ed's not jolly like Oliver Hardy?"

"Ed's got responsibilities."

"I'm not touching political stuff. You should've told me."

"Don't worry. I just want you to grind out features for that tab. That was our deal."

"You're sure they'll let me fish?"

"They'll let you fish. Trust me."

"Then you'll be collecting Alaska Newspaper Publishers Association awards off my stuff long after I'm gone."

"I think so, too, Eldon. I know I'm not the greatest writer in the world. But I want to put this paper on the map. Just keep it upbeat, okay? I have to *live* here. Come winter, when the dark sets in, you'd better be on good terms with your neighbors."

"Is Jason Baer on good terms with his neighbors?"

"Sure—which is to say, he gets drunk and fights with them

all the time." Anita studied Eldon for a moment. "They're all friends of mine. I have a position in the community to uphold. Sometimes it's tough. You need to understand that."

"Of course," Eldon said. "The light touch." He went back to the folder as they flew northward. He noticed with unease that dark clouds were beginning to gather ahead.

The clouds were massing in a gloomy vault above the forest by the time they approached Klinkatshut. Eldon was grateful when the plane began to descend. It was then that he saw the glint of ice, a white stripe on the horizon.

"Mandel's Glacier," Anita said.

The glacier looked like a gray-white sea that wound back up into the indigo mountains. The clouds parted for a moment and the glacier sparkled as the sunlight splashed across it like a wave. The ice glared with impossible brilliance before the clouds again hid the sun.

Anita looked down toward the water. "This is good timing. I don't relish flying in bad weather. We lose light aircraft up here all the time. I hope Jason got in okay. Here, take a look at Klinkatshut before we land."

They swooped lower and passed up the tree-lined coast at an altitude of about five hundred feet. The town sprang out of the forest: a weathered collection of structures lining a narrow beach where a dark pier jutted into the water. Farther up the beach was another pier and a long, low building like a warehouse: KLINKATSHUT FISH PROCESSING CO. was painted on its side in big yellow letters. Buildings wandered around the point of the island and back up into the forest. Fishing boats and a blue floatplane were moored along the pier.

"Jason's plane," Anita said. "He's home."

Eldon was struck yet again with the immensity of the setting—a forest stretching as far as he could see, glittering water now turning steely with the approach of the storm. Eldon saw that

Klinkatshut lay on one of a cluster of small islands fitted together like pieces of a jigsaw puzzle.

"Sitka's out that way." Anita gestured. "Easy run by boat, quick hop by plane."

A flat-fronted building decorated with Alaskan Indian motifs stood a short distance up the beach. Before it were canted totem poles facing the water.

"The big building's the Klinkatshut clan house," Anita said. "That's where the potlatch'll be."

Eldon looked back, fascinated, as the village receded. Anita made a wide turn and they entered their final approach. As they descended, two big brown-and-white birds rose from the beach. Eldon realized with awe that they were bald eagles, all but extinct in the lower forty-eight states. The scenery rushed up, and then they were skimming along level with the beach as if they were a skipping stone. Anita chopped the throttle. The floatplane dropped into the water and slowed with a jerk and a brief explosion of spray. A woman and a child stood on the pier. The child wore a bright pink parka and had a Roleiflex camera slung around her neck. The woman's long blond hair blew in the breeze.

"There's my baby girl," Anita said happily as they taxied to the pier.

Eldon saw that the child was aiming the camera at the plane. "Who's that with her?"

"Maggie Frame. She teaches school. She looks after Cassandra sometimes, now that school's out for the summer."

Anita cut the prop as the plane coasted up to the pier. Maggie threw a mooring rope; Anita caught it through the open side window. Maggie pulled the plane in and secured it.

"Smile, Mom!" Cassandra cried and snapped a picture as Anita popped open the door. Anita climbed out onto the pier and scooped Cassandra into her arms. The little girl clutched her mother, looking over Anita's shoulder at Eldon as he got out of the plane. "Who's that?"

"This is Eldon, honey."

Eldon thought Cassandra seemed small and young for a girl of nine. He recalled that someone had told him kids of that age were all over the map intellectually and physically. He gave a bow. "Hello, Cassandra. Eldon Larkin, at your service." He doffed his hat.

"That's a silly hat," Cassandra declared.

"It's a serious hat," Eldon said. "These are fishing flies."

Cassandra sighed. "Is this your new boyfriend, Mom?"

"Eldon is a reporter," Anita replied as Maggie snickered. "He's going to stay with us for a little while and help out with the newspaper."

The child peered at Eldon. "Yeah? Can you turn *good copy?*"

Eldon was startled. "You bet."

"Yeah? Like what?"

"Well, I met Bigfoot once."

"You *did?*" Cassandra's eyes widened. Then she caught herself and her expression grew mistrustful once more. "Did you do a story about it?"

"Er, no."

"You shouldn't have let that interview get away," Cassandra said.

"Well, I was being chased by pirates and I couldn't stop and talk," Eldon said.

"Pirates?"

"Yeah. But maybe I can interview him now. It might even be the same Bigfoot."

"Maybe he followed you up here," Cassandra said, brightening a little as her mother put her down. Her expression was unnervingly shrewd.

I've seen that look before, Eldon thought, but where?

"Eldon, this is Maggie Frame," Anita said. "Maggie—Eldon. He's going to write about the Button Club."

"Well, high time." Maggie stuck out a hand. Eldon appraised her as they shook. Maggie was of medium height, slender, with fair skin and green eyes that delivered a direct gaze. She wore a tan windbreaker and jeans. Her clothes fitted her nicely.

"Hello," Eldon said, thinking that he could do worse than get friendly with Maggie if he struck out with Anita.

"Don't squeeze the merchandise too hard, Maggie," Anita said. "I'm gonna keep Eldon busy."

"I'll bet," Maggie said. There was something acerbic in her reply. But Eldon decided she'd been merely teasing Anita when Maggie gave a big smile and waved toward the end of the pier. "I brought your car."

"That's our Amphicar," Cassandra told Eldon. "It goes on the water if you want. It's half car and half boat."

The rusty, dented convertible parked at the end of the pier looked like a cross between a Willys sedan and a stubby mid-'60s Thunderbird. The top was down; it had small decorative fins and four doors. Once it had been blue. The car sat oddly high on its wheel bed. Anita led Eldon to the rear and pointed under the bumper. He stooped and saw twin screws like motorboat propellers.

"Works fine for going salmon fishing," Anita said.

"That's a laugh," Maggie said.

"Where'd you get it?" Eldon asked in dismay. "It's like something out of *Popular Mechanics.*"

Anita shrugged. "Cassandra's father was a great one for gadgets. Anyway, it runs. And around here, you've got to have a boat."

Eldon realized that this was the car he had been promised. It figured. He always had terrible luck with cars. "Maybe I'd better fish from shore."

"I think you should," Cassandra said. "They're lousy cars and lousy boats. Jason always says so."

"Shush," Anita said. "Seen Jason, Maggie?"

"He flew in pretty early," Maggie said, "and went out to his place. He was in a foul mood. I think he lost a fight in Ketchikan."

"Yeah, with Eldon."

Maggie laughed with delight. "There's not a mark on you!"

"Only metaphorically," Eldon said with a smile.

"Let's get the plane unloaded," Anita said.

"It's high time that the press in the lower forty-eight discovered the Klinkatshut Button Club," Maggie said. "I hear you're a big gun down in the real world, Eldon."

"News travels fast," Eldon said. Apparently Jason had been talking—Eldon wondered to what end. "We'll get your club together with their buttons and do a story. Should be some good pictures."

"Okay." Maggie helped them wedge the Amphicar full of supplies. They left some of the stuff on the plane to pick up later. "I'll walk home," Maggie said when they had finished. "Got to stop at the store. Later, Eldon—the buttons."

"The buttons," Eldon said, watching Maggie go.

They climbed into the Amphicar and started out, Anita behind the wheel and Cassandra nestled among the supplies in the back seat. The white-and-blue candy-striped vinyl seat covers were grubby, but Eldon was more concerned with how to operate the car. This rattletrap had an ordinary steering wheel and, as far he could tell, standard automobile instruments and a stick shift. It ground along Klinkatshut's gravel streets, banging and rattling like a tank back from a hard campaign. What's Anita been doing in this thing? Eldon wondered. Drag-racing submarines?

"The weather's hard on cars up here," Anita explained, "but it still goes. German-made, runs on regular gas. Has a Triumph

Spitfire engine in the rear. You can get up to six or seven knots in the water. The Germans take them out into all kinds of rough water. Has bilge pumps and everything."

Eldon knew that the waters of the Inside Passage were sheltered by the archipelago. Still, he resolved to stick close to shore—assuming that he went out in the Amphicar at all. "What's the range? How far can you go?"

"Oh, gosh, all the way to Sitka. But I gas up before I start back."

Klinkatshut was a collection of cabins, trailers, and boxy houses unadorned by landscaping and mostly in need of paint. Muffled sounds reached them from the houses as they journeyed down the street—furniture breaking and drunken shouting, female and male. The sounds rose and fell as they passed. Eldon realized that major quarrels were going on in house after house. It was like driving past a row of soundstages in which riots were being filmed.

"They're all fighting again." Cassandra looked gloomy.

"Maybe we can go out tonight and see the northern lights," Eldon suggested.

The child sneered. "You can't see 'em in the summer, cheechako."

"Mind your manners, young lady," Anita said.

"It's okay," Eldon said. "Why's that, Cassandra?"

"Because of the midnight sun. It's got to get *dark* before you can see the aurora. It's got to be winter. Are you staying for all winter?"

"Only for a month." Eldon could tell that a month or all winter were equally measureless to the nine-year-old. "Have you seen the aurora?"

"Lots. The first time was when my daddy showed me when I was small. He got me out of bed and bundled me up and took me outside and showed me. It was really cold."

"How old were you?"

Cassandra thought it over. "Three."

"And what was it like?"

"Like fire. But it was cold. Our newspaper's named the *Aurora,* you know."

Rain started falling as they reached the house. Eldon had half expected a log cabin or a Quonset hut, but Anita and Cassandra lived in a split-level house, larger and better than most in Klinkatshut. Tall firs sheltered the house, and there was a deck that formed a carport. Her ex left her fairly well fixed, Eldon thought. Too bad he didn't leave her a decent car.

"The office is downstairs," Anita said as she pulled in under the deck. "The guest room, too. That's yours—you sleep behind the print shop like Ben Franklin. Eat upstairs with us."

"Which way's the fishing?"

"Behind the house a ways. Not far."

The rain hit hard as they unloaded the car. It drummed on the deck overhead. Cassandra insisted on carrying Eldon's new fishing rod and led the way into the *Aurora*'s office. For a moment Eldon was homesick for Port Jerome and the newsroom of the *South Coast Sun.*

The office was a single cluttered room with two old wooden rolltop desks and goose-necked lamps. The black upright typewriters looked forty years old or more. But there was an artist's table equipped to make page pasteups for modern offset printing and a little buzzing news teletype machine in the corner identical to the one behind Fiske's desk at the *Sun.* Next to that stood an older piece of machinery, a big gray metal console with a keyboard. It looked like a clumsy cross between a piano and a typewriter.

"Telex," Anita said. "Comes in handy in an isolated place like this."

"I haven't seen one in years," Eldon said. "Where'd you get it?"

"Listen, we're just starting to get live TV up here," Anita replied. "Technology in Alaska moves slow."

"They took our telex out about the time I joined the *Sun* in '73," Eldon said. "It's stored in back someplace."

"You could send your editor a message on this over the news wire."

"No, thanks. I'm on vacation."

The guest room was finished in cedar. Greenish light filled the room from a window looking into the rainy forest. Eldon checked out the place as Cassandra carefully leaned his fishing rod in the corner.

There was a double bed—a *double* bed!—covered with bright-edged Hudson's Bay Company blankets. There was a bathroom with a molded plastic shower. A night table with a lamp stood beside the bed.

Eldon switched on the light. It was adequate for reading in bed. "Thanks—I hate bedrooms with little tiny lights."

Miscellaneous books were piled on the night table's lower shelf. Eldon saw that they were mostly mystery and science fiction paperbacks. Among them was a small red hardback. He picked it up and glanced at the title—*Sämtliche Werke* by Rainer Maria Rilke. He opened it. "Hey, the title's German but the poems are in French! *Parlez-vous français, mademoiselle?"*

"I don't," Anita said. "Some other, uh, visitor must've left that." Cassandra started to pipe up but Anita interposed: "Do you speak French?"

"Pretty well, in fact."

"They speak French in Canada," Cassandra said. "It's over there about a hundred miles." She pointed in a direction that Eldon guessed was east. "Why don't you go to Canada?"

"Maybe some other time," Eldon said. If he didn't stand his

ground with this kid, it would be a miserable four weeks. *"Tu es certainement une petite fille intelligente. Est-ce que tu veux apprendre à parler en français?"*

Cassandra giggled. "What did you say?"

"I said, 'You certainly are an intelligent little girl. Would you like to learn French?' "

"I might."

"Here's your first French word—*une fille.* A girl."

"Une fille," Cassandra repeated.

"Very good. More words later." Eldon flipped the book's pages. "I've never read Rilke."

"You can have it," Anita said.

"Thanks. I'll take it with me when I go," Eldon said, as much to Cassandra as to her mother.

"Let's let Eldon get unpacked," Anita said. "Dinner about five, Eldon."

"Want help with the rest of the supplies?"

"I can get them," Anita said.

Cassandra looked back as Anita guided her from the room. The child's eyes glinted. That expression again, Eldon thought. Where had he seen it before?

3

"Eldon."

His eyes popped open. Cassandra stood by the bed wearing her pink parka and holding a small fishing rod. "It's time to get up," she said.

"It's—what time is it?"

"Five-thirty. Time to go fishing!"

Eldon sat up. It was rainy daylight outside, as if the sun had never gone down. And of course, for most of the night it hadn't.

"How do you say 'going fishing' in French?" Cassandra asked.

"Uh—wha'? *Allez à la pêche—*"

"Is that what you call a fish? A pesh?"

"No. *Un poisson.* Do you always get up this early?"

"We do when we go fishing," Cassandra said. "And when there's copy to turn."

" 'Copy to turn'? Where'd you learn talk like that?"

"Mom talks that way. Why shouldn't I?"

"If you're not careful, you'll turn into a reporter. Is Anita—is your mother up?"

"Sure. She said to tell you she's making coffee."

"Clear out while I dress, please."

Cassandra darted from the room and thundered upstairs, yelling, "He's awake, Mom!"

Eldon rubbed his eyes. His first day of fishing in Alaska and he'd almost overslept! He had lain awake for some time the night before, listening to the rain and fantasizing about Anita slipping into his bedroom. Finally he had opened Rilke and read in French until he had corked off:

> If with my burning hands I could melt
> the body around your lover's heart,
> ah! how the night would be transparent,
> mistaking it for a belated star . . .

It had knocked him out quickly enough.

He stumbled out of bed and went to the window. It was still raining—but that had never stopped him. He shaved and took a quick, invigorating shower. He was dressed and was assembling his new fishing rod when Anita came in with mugs of coffee. She wore jeans and a snug red turtleneck that set her figure off nicely. "Ready to hit that stream? Here's a wake-me-up special. Breakfast when we get back."

"Thanks." Eldon accepted a mug and sipped. "Hey, there's whiskey in this—"

"Warm ya up," Anita said. She winked and took a swig from her own mug.

Eldon raised his eyebrows but took another swallow and enjoyed the whiskey's added warmth. He felt too much like a kid at Christmas to worry. He locked the reel onto his new rod and got his tackle box from his luggage. "I hope the fish are biting."

"They are," Anita said. "It's the height of the season."

"The salmon are returning from the ocean," Cassandra explained, obviously reciting a lesson from school, "running up into their ancestral streams to spawn and die. You just scoop 'em up!"

"Maybe I'll catch a king for dinner." Eldon put on his coat and hat and slung his waders over his shoulder.

Anita went back upstairs and returned with her own equipment. She carried her rod and waders and wore her knit cap and coat. Eldon noticed the bulge of Anita's shoulder holster beneath her coat and wondered about bears.

They stepped out into the drizzle. Cassandra led the way, trotting down a path into the woods, waving her fishing rod. "This way, Eldon!"

The forest was thick. He looked back and saw smoke rising from the chimney of the house. He thought for a moment that he heard bells, borne faintly on the wind; but the sound vanished.

"You could come and go around here and nobody'd ever know," Eldon said.

"That's the truth," Anita said. "Cassandra, honey, you're going too far—the stream's over that way. . . . Oh, well! She's leading us down to the beach."

Eldon heard waves lapping. Sure enough, they emerged from the trees onto a graveled beach before a narrow channel. A small island lay no more than four hundred yards away. There was a concrete boat ramp with a motorboat tied up to it.

"Jason lives on that island," Anita said. "He's got it all to himself because the water supply is limited."

"I'll go see him today, get that interview out of the way," Eldon said.

"I admire your courage."

Eldon shrugged.

"Over here!" Cassandra waved from up the beach, where the stream disgorged. Eldon and Anita started toward her.

The stream proved to be fair-sized. They reached it to find Cassandra with line already in the water. She stood with her feet apart, gripping her rod and watching the gushing water.

"These salmon are big enough to pull her in," Anita whispered. "I've never had time to teach her to fish properly."

"Has she ever caught anything like that?"

"Just little fish—her hooks are too small for anything else. Look out that the salmon don't pull *you* in."

"I'm ready for that." Eldon sat and opened his tackle box. He'd tied two dozen flies before leaving Oregon, using a pattern he'd learned from a man who had fished for kings in Alaska. It was nothing like the delicate, intricately colored flies that he used in Oregon to catch rainbow trout, black bass, or spring chinook salmon—fish that he now was pleased to think of as the "small stuff." The new pattern was a No. 4-0 gold hook with a gold body, gold tail, and red hackle. "It's not much to look at, but I'm told it catches salmon."

"It might at that," Anita said. "Kings don't feed after they leave salt water, so you need something flashy."

"What do you use?"

"Anything they'll strike at. Today, a triple-barbed plug with some bright yarn on it. But I'm going to wait so I can coach you."

"Okay." Eldon raised the fly. "I dub thee the Golden

Cheechako. Bring me luck." He tied the fly to six feet of twenty-pound test leader at the end of his line, set the rod aside, and began to don his waders. He savored the ritual of removing his shoes and pulling on the high, thick woolen socks and then the thigh-high rubber waders.

Anita sat next to him and pulled on her own waders.

"Fishing for kings is *slow* and *deep,*" she said, making it sound suggestive. Eldon wondered whether it was the whiskey talking. "See that hole upstream? Throw your fly in there, at the head of the hole, and let it sink and bump along the bottom."

"Okay. What's it like when they hit?"

"Very subtle. The strike is usually just a pause in the line. Lots of times there's no feeling at all transmitted along the line or the rod. So stay alert."

"C'mon, Eldon," Cassandra said. "They're getting away!"

Eldon got to his feet. "You can't catch 'em if you're not in the right place."

"Where's that?" Cassandra demanded.

"How about out there on that big rock? I'll take ya there!"

Eldon scooped Cassandra up and stepped into the rushing stream. He felt the water's crisp cold right through the heavy rubber boots and woolen socks as he sloshed out and placed Cassandra safely on a big table-shaped rock in the middle of the stream. "Try that for size. And don't fall in." He turned to go back for his fishing rod.

"Hey! You're not gonna leave me out here, are you, Eldon?"

"I'll be right back. Gotta get my rod."

Cassandra watched with a worried face until Eldon made his way back out into the stream. "See?" he said. "I'm back."

"I thought you and Mom were gonna leave me."

"No way. I'm going to teach you how to really fly-fish. *Pêcher à la mouche.*" He prepared to cast. "Now, watch how I hold the rod. Get a nice, relaxed, underhanded grip—"

Cassandra was clumsy but no more so than some ham-handed adults. Eldon did not imagine that she would catch anything with her puny rod and line. He tested his new rod's spring and then cast, watching with pleasure as the line sailed out and the hook plunked into the surging water close to the top of the hole. He let the current carry the line along, then retrieved, stripped the line, and cast again. Cassandra mimicked him. "You might make a fisherman some day," Eldon said.

"Fisher*person,"* Cassandra said with a growl.

"Fisherperson. Let's not argue."

"No. Too many arguments around here."

"Yeah? Like who?"

"Oh, like Jason and Chief Katlean. And Jason and Maggie. And Max Renner. He's kind of like Jason—he fights with everybody."

"Who's Max Renner?"

"He owns the store. And my mother and dad used to fight, too."

"I don't want to argue with anybody."

"Me, neither. But as a reporter you need to know." That strange look again, then the solemn caveat: "This is on background."

"On background," Eldon agreed. "Totally off the record. You're casting pretty good. Watch me now."

Cassandra smiled hopefully, her expression again a child's.

Eldon cast again. He enjoyed the graphite rod's flex. A good cast was like a good punch, except that there was no crunch at the end. He fell into the familiar rhythm, grinning down at Cassandra as she mimicked him. He cast again and again, aiming at various parts of the current as he got to know his new equipment.

A strike! Eldon swore and hung on tight as the rod bent and

the line ran out. He'd subconsciously expected nothing more than the tug of a two- or three-pound Oregon trout or black bass. This was something else—his first king salmon, and it was *big*.

"Eldon's got one, Mom!" Cassandra yelled. "Don't let it get away, Eldon!"

Anita came down to streamside. "Work him, Eldon—tire him out. You can't just haul a salmon out of the water. You have to play the game first."

"It feels like I've snagged a submarine!" Eldon worked his way back toward shore, playing the line. He braked the buzzing reel, letting the rod bend sharply to stop the salmon's rush. He played out more line, then reeled in, holding his elbows tight to his sides. Then a struggling dark torpedo shape leaped from rushing green waters and turned somersaults.

I've really got a fish! Eldon thought. He let line buzz out, then braked and let the fish sweep back and forth in the water. His quarry began to tire. At last, at Anita's prompting, he reeled the salmon in.

"I'll help you land him." Anita waded into the stream.

"Got a net?"

"Too much trouble. We land 'em by hand."

Anita caught up with the salmon as Eldon hauled it into the shallows and pushed the big struggling fish toward shore with her hands and feet. At last she forced the creature onto the rocky beach. "Nice little fish," Anita remarked as she watched the salmon flop.

"Little!"

"Twenty pounds. A peewee." She picked up a stout stick and clubbed the salmon twice, then tied a nylon lanyard around its tail and hoisted it up. "But nice. Cheechako's luck."

Eldon freed his hook from the salmon's mouth and took the lanyard. The fish weighed on his tired wrists. The king was a rich, dark reddish black. Eldon's mouth watered as he imagined the flavor of the steaks. "Should make dinner for three, anyway."

"Three, easy," Anita said.

There was a plaintive call from Cassandra. "Hey, you're not gonna leave me *out here,* are you, Eldon?" She watched, brows knitted, as Eldon sloshed back out to the midstream rock.

"I'm back."

"My casting's getting better." Cassandra held up her rod. A dripping black disk swung on the end of her line.

Eldon peered, then realized that it was a visored cap.

"It was in the stream," Cassandra said. "I caught it."

"Well, good shot." Eldon freed the hat, turned it over. A little plastic window inside the crown held one of Jason Baer's business cards. "Look at this—it's Jason's hat."

"We should take that back to him. He likes that hat."

"Maybe the wind blew it off into the water and it floated over here."

"Or it could've been when he was out in his boat."

Eldon lifted Cassandra from the rock and carried her back to shore. Cassandra showed Anita the hat. "Let's take it out to him, Mom."

"It's much too early," Anita said.

"No, it's not," Cassandra said firmly. "Jason gets up early." Anita blushed at that. The tangled webs we weave, Eldon thought. Klinkatshut, Alaska, was seeming more and more like Port Jerome, Oregon, except that the fish were bigger, which counted for a lot.

The pleasure of the catch had energized Eldon, and mischief formed in his mind. Bearding Jason in his den bright and early, demanding an interview, might be just the thing to keep the sailing smooth between them. Show him who's boss when it comes to the news copy, he thought. "Yes—let's drop in."

"He's probably up," Anita admitted. "I'll call—"

"No. Let's just go over."

Anita eyed him. "We'll use the Amphicar."

Eldon's stomach tap-danced at the thought of committing the Amphicar to water but he said nothing. This was Alaska, after all, where men were supposed to be men. He'd handled enough small boats during years of fishing to let him handle an Amphicar, too. "Okay."

They hiked back to the house. There Anita partly filled an outdoor industrial sink with water and set Eldon's salmon into it while Eldon put the fishing gear in the house and got a notebook and the Rolleiflex camera.

"You drive," Anita told him when he got back. "Time you learned. And mind the driver's door—you have to really slam it. Then throw that lever down there, or the car's not watertight."

They pulled off their waders and climbed into the Amphicar. Eldon had trouble getting his door closed and sealed but finally managed it. He got the strange little car started and into gear, backed it out, and guided it away from the house and down the gravel road as Anita directed him. It handled like any other car—on dry land, anyway.

A turnoff led down to the beach not far from the stream where they had fished. "Now what?" Eldon asked.

"Slow down and shift into first gear," Anita said. "Drive into the water until we're floating—"

Eldon did as she said, feeling as if he were about to plunge from a diving board. They rattled down onto the beach until the wheels were awash. Eldon inched the Amphicar into the channel, grinding along over submerged gravel. Suddenly, there was no more traction; the car wallowed and dipped. Cassandra laughed as water sloshed across the hood. "Go for it!"

Eldon was ready to jump out and swim when the hood rose once more and he realized they were riding safely in the water at about the level of the Amphicar's headlights.

"Okay, depress the clutch," Anita said. "Put 'er in neutral and keep your foot on the clutch. Now, here's the water gear lever—push it forward. Now, step on the accelerator while you slowly release the clutch—*slowly,* I said—and, there! Now we're a motorboat."

There was a shudder as the props engaged. The Amphicar surged forward. Eldon found that it steered in the water just as it had on land.

He gunned it and they trundled through the water. The car rode straight and steady, but Eldon sensed that it was nautically inefficient for its weight. He felt as if he were riding in a barrel toward Niagara Falls. "Christ, what's it like in high seas?"

Anita laughed. "Don't take it into the ocean unless you're fleeing imminent arrest."

The Amphicar showed no sign of sinking. Eldon aimed for Jason's boat ramp. As they approached the concrete pad, Anita had Eldon engage first gear once again. The car's rear wheels started slowly spinning as the twin screws propelled them forward. At last they rolled up onto the boat pad. "Put the water gear into neutral," Anita said.

Eldon did so, then hit the brakes and killed the engine. "I need a little more practice."

"You did pretty good," Cassandra said.

They got out and walked up the ramp to a straight dirt track that after a few hundred yards led into a clearing. There stood a cubical house with black tar paper siding with a light on in the front room. Eldon saw no one inside. Then he noticed the television set through the front window—tuned to a dead channel, the screen like a white, streaked eye.

Eldon felt a queasy rush. Something was wrong.

He strode to the front door and knocked. No response. He peered through the front window. No one—just a sofa and some other furniture and the TV. He turned to Anita. "He wouldn't have left it on all night."

"Well, he might've if he tied one on."

Eldon rapped on the door again. No response.

"Maybe he's in the workshop around back," Anita said.

They went around the house.

There was a toolshed to one side and a covered work area where a partially finished totem pole lay across trestles. A heavy orange electrical cable stretched across the ground from an outside outlet on the house and ended in an industrial work lamp that lay, still alight, on the ground. Another totem pole lay there, toppled off its own trestles, its carved faces staring across the yard at them under the white Alaskan sky. The totem pole had arms and legs at its middle. Real ones.

4

Eldon stared in disbelief. Human arms and legs stuck out stiffly on either side of the totem pole's middle. Whoever owned the limbs lay squarely beneath the totem's length, pressed by its weight into the soft Alaskan earth. It had to be Jason Baer.

Anita took a sharp breath and ran from the yard, scooping up Cassandra on the way and carrying her to the front of the house. Eldon heard the door open. She's phoning for help, he thought as the protective feeling of separation, so familiar from covering accident and murder scenes, settled over him.

Eldon recognized the Raven ring on the clenched left hand—it was Jason beneath the totem pole, all right. His body was neatly in line with the pole, his arms and legs flung out as if their owner were about to do battle. Not robbery, he thought. They didn't take the ring.

He stooped and gingerly touched a finger to Jason's hand. Cold. He snatched his finger away.

"I called the state troopers." Anita had returned. Her face was chalky. "We've got to get that log off him."

"Yeah—"

The impulse was irrational; Jason was as stiff as the carved log. Yet the thought of rescue seized them both. Eldon and Anita threw themselves against the totem, frantically rocking it until they heaved it away.

"Oh . . . God." Anita let out her breath in a rush as the log rolled aside.

Jason Baer was not just dead—he had been murdered. A big red stain covered his chest, with a black hole in the center of it. Jason's eyes were half-closed, his once-pugnacious jaw slack and skewed, as if the weight of the log had dislocated it. His nose looked flatter, too. He looked like something lying in a skillet.

Anita stepped back, staring from side to side, back and forth. She held her arm across her midriff, hand in the air with the fingers half-curled. Eldon thought she was going to grab her stomach and throw up, then realized that she was ready to reach for the gun in her shoulder holster.

He scanned the surroundings but sensed nothing. "It's okay. It's clear. . . . He's been dead awhile."

Anita nodded and dropped her arm, started blinking back tears. "Someone shot him. Then—then crushed him . . . under his own totem pole."

"You're right. It couldn't have fallen that neatly."

"He had enemies—but not like *this.*"

"Let's go back around the front," Eldon said, "get away from the crime scene. We're disturbing evidence."

"Is that Jason?" It was Cassandra. She spoke in a squeaky

voice. She had come up behind them and stood staring.

"Don't look," Eldon said sharply. "Go back around front and stay there."

Anita reached for Cassandra, but the child fought her off, still staring. "He's *dead*—isn't he?"

"Yes," Eldon said.

"He's *dead,*" the child repeated in amazement, her eyes flooding with tears as Anita scooped her up and carried her away. "Get the story, Eldon! You gotta get the story!"

The words kicked Eldon's mind into gear. She's right, he thought. And I don't even have to interview him. The irreverent thought started his legs working. He lumbered after Anita and Cassandra to the front of the house.

"You two go home," he said. "I'll stay and meet the troopers at the boat ramp. And I'll get the story."

"We can't get scooped, Mom," Cassandra said, still weeping.

"Just get going," Eldon said. "I'll turn the copy, Cassandra."

Anita pulled her out of the yard, heading for the boat ramp.

Eldon let them get out of sight and then returned to the backyard. He picked up the camera and started photographing the scene, working his way around the spot where Jason lay. He kept back from the body and stepped carefully, trying to keep from obliterating anything that looked like a footprint or a clue. His professional side told him this was a rare opportunity—he seldom got a crack at a crime scene before the police.

He inspected the workshop. There was sawdust everywhere, but most of the tools were neatly racked. An adze lay on the grass where Jason clearly had dropped it. No sign of a struggle.

An ambush, then, Eldon thought. Or somebody he knew—and trusted. But who the hell would Jason Baer trust?

He checked the back door to the house, carefully grasping the handle through a handkerchief. Locked. Eldon moved around to the front of the house. Anita had left the front door ajar. He stepped into the living room to the hiss of the television, still on its dead channel.

Eldon walked through the house. There was nothing to suggest a robbery. The place had a bachelor sloppiness to it, but it had not been ransacked. An extensive record collection was on shelves along one wall. Eldon found an enviable array of jazz and classical titles and recordings of Native American music from the Smithsonian Institution. But there was shit-kicker stuff, too. Just as I was starting to find something to like about the guy, Eldon thought, wrinkling his nose at a Waylon Jennings album.

He started to slide the album back into its place when he caught a glint of light on something behind the records. Eldon pulled out several albums and found a bottle of Old Granddad. There were marks in pencil along the side of the label. Eldon returned the bottle and albums to their place.

In back was a bedroom with a big, low queen-size bed, unmade. A punching bag hung from the ceiling in one corner above a rubber floor mat. A pair of light boxing gloves lay on the dresser. Eldon strolled over and tapped the bag. He stopped it with his hand on the backswing and felt something sticky. There were faint rectangles of adhesive-tape residue on the bag, spaced as if Jason had taped something to it. A paper target?

Eldon rummaged further, unsure of what he was looking for and wondering if he would find any pornography. He turned up another fifth of bourbon in the night table, next to a box of condoms. Both containers were partially empty.

A second bedroom had been turned into a studio. Its window looked out on the backyard. On an easel was a partially completed pastel drawing of a totem-pole face. Eldon admired Jason's skill. It seemed to be a woman's face, huge-eyed, mouth agape, hair like waves streaming down the sides of the image. There also was a folder containing smaller pencil drawings of totem designs on graph paper—Raven, Salmon, Sun, according to notations penciled on the sheets. Presumably Jason converted the images into full-size blueprints or tracing patterns when he felt ready to carve them in wood.

Eldon picked up one of the pencil drawings by the edges and carried it back into the master bedroom. Sure enough, the drawing fit neatly inside the tape marks on the punching bag. That's one way to work out your artistic conflicts, Eldon thought. I wonder what Fiske would do if I set up a bag in the newsroom and taped my stories to it? Probably make some joke about punching out the copy. . . .

A voice spoke urgently in the front room. Eldon jumped. Moving fast, he slipped back into the studio and dropped the drawing atop the others, then crept carefully down the hall, expecting to confront the cops.

But it was merely the television. The dead channel had come to life, broadcasting a Montreal Expos baseball game. Eldon watched bemusedly until he realized from the announcer's remarks that the game was two weeks old.

This is really the forest primeval, he thought, stepping out onto the porch just as a group of uniformed men walked into the clearing.

Eldon took out his spiral notebook and ballpoint pen, set his jungle hat squarely on his head, and marched out to confront their leader, a red-haired state trooper who looked like a freckled version of Sergeant Preston of the Yukon, complete with a thin and unbecoming mustache.

"I'm Eldon Larkin from the *Aurora,*" he announced.

"You and Anita found the body," the trooper retorted.

"Yeah—"

"And you're a reporter?"

Eldon smiled and shrugged. "It's my other hat."

"Did you touch anything?"

"No . . . well, we rolled the totem pole off him. But he was dead—"

"Show us."

As Eldon led the way into the backyard, another trooper came up beside him. He was a big, square-faced man with happy hazel eyes and an air of deadpan good cheer. "Hi."

"Hi. Eldon Larkin."

"I'm Trooper Potter. Suppose you tell me about this."

Eldon started telling the story as they approached the body. But he never reached it. Potter unobtrusively maneuvered him into the work shed and gently backed Eldon against the shed's rear wall while he took notes in a leather-backed policeman's notebook. His fellows examined the body and cordoned off the property with yellow crime-scene tape while Potter stood in Eldon's line of vision, asking the same questions over and over in different ways.

Eldon had to weave and hop to see around Potter and keep tabs on the work going on around the body. He realized he was being grilled. They couldn't suspect him! Back home in Oregon, Eldon could have talked his way into the crime scene or at least lingered at the tape, picking up scraps of information until a sheriff's deputy shooed him away. He felt a surge of homesickness as he thought of how the Port Jerome cops had tolerated him. Without his familiar contacts he felt helpless.

At last the troopers began zipping Jason into a gray plastic body bag. "Hey, look," Eldon said, "I've got to take at least one picture. You guys at work—'police in action,' you know?"

Potter closed the notebook and called to the red-haired trooper. "Hey, Mike—okay if he takes a picture?"

"No."

"Why not?" Eldon demanded.

Mike marched over. "Suppose you hand over the film in your camera. Evidence."

"Always glad to oblige an investigation. Get a warrant and it's yours."

The big trooper chuckled. "Knows his business, Mike."

"I need a statement, too," Eldon said.

" 'No comment,' " Mike said. "You know what we know."

"No, I don't. You wouldn't let me back over there while you worked."

"That's so we wouldn't have to comment."

Eldon sighed. He had the same sort of conversations with Detective Art Nola back in Port Jerome.

"I didn't know Anita had anybody working for her," Potter remarked.

"I'm summer help," Eldon said.

"You're a witness," Mike said.

Potter chuckled again. "You better talk to him, Mike. He's gonna write it up anyway."

"You going to buy an ad in the *Aurora* or something, Potter?" Mike asked.

"Yeah, I got that boat I want to sell. I want a rate."

The other troopers laughed and that broke the tension.

"Okay, okay," Mike said. "It'll be all over the wires in a little while anyway."

And I'm going to put it there, Eldon thought, getting out his notebook. "Thanks. How'd Jason die?"

"Shot—with a rifle, looks like. Bullet through his chest. Then the totem pole went on top of him."

"Why would anybody do that?"

"Did I say anybody did? To pin him down, maybe."

"He wasn't dead first?"

"There was blood in his nostrils and mouth—like he was still breathing after he was down. The totem smothered him, pressing on his chest like that."

"Jesus."

"Maybe it just fell over on him somehow," Potter put in, "but it fell kinda neat."

"That's what Anita and I think, too," Eldon said, partly to get Anita's name back into the conversation. "Was he shot up close or from a distance? When was he killed?"

"You write about this kind of stuff a lot?" Mike asked.

"Quite a lot, yeah."

"He died last night," Mike said. "From the positions of the tools on the ground, he was working on the totem pole when someone shot him from at least medium range—there were no powder burns on the body. Which makes sense if it was a rifle."

"Somebody shot him *at night* with a rifle and then managed to roll a totem pole—" Eldon stopped. "Oh, yeah, I forgot. It's never night here."

"You're from the lower forty-eight," Potter said, as if that explained everything. "In summer, the sun only goes down here from maybe eleven or midnight to two or three."

"I'm from Oregon." At least he didn't call me a cheechako, Eldon thought.

"Nice state," Potter said. "Been fishing down there. Nice fishing, but you have to like small fish."

"The autopsy'll have to establish the time of death," Mike said, "but he'd been under the totem pole for some hours when you found him. The back of his clothes were soaked—"

"And there are little teeny bugs on him," Potter said.

"What kind of rifle was it?" Eldon asked.

"I'd guess a .30-30 or a .30-06," Mike said.

"The kinds of rifles everybody around here has got," Potter added.

"How about suspects?"

"Well, we don't suspect *you,*" Potter said. "Your only motive in life is fishing. We could tell from your hat. That hat of yours kind of gets you off the hook, ha ha."

"Potter's a regular Sherlock Holmes," Mike said. "It could've been anybody."

" 'Anybody'? We're on an island."

"Lots of people come and go," Mike said. "The Inside Passage is a regular aquatic highway."

"Venice Northwest," Potter said.

"Jason quarreled with lots of people," Eldon said.

"Everyone in Southeast quarrels," Mike said.

"Fights are Alaska's idea of fun," Potter said. "Domestic disturbance calls are a blast."

"How about robbery? The place hasn't been tossed."

"Oh?" Mike said. "You've been inside?"

"Just to call you guys."

"No comment, then," Mike said.

"And we were doing so good!" Potter said.

"Might've been a hunter," Mike said after a pause. "Are we still on the record?"

This guy must be Art Nola's pen pal, Eldon thought. He closed his notebook and said, "Okay, off the record now."

"Never hunt alone," Mike said.

"Why is that?"

"Because there are people who go out every hunting season to hunt people—I'm convinced of it. We find five, six hunters out in the woods dead, every year. Shot."

"Somebody came by hunting artists?" Eldon asked.

"Could be," Mike said.

"Remember, this is off the record," Potter added solemnly.

"Lemme get your last name, Mike," Eldon said.

"That's off the record, too," Mike said.

"It's Atkov," Potter said. "A-T-K-O-V."

"And *his* first name is Clarence," Mike said with a scowl. "C-L-A-R-E-N-C-E."

"Clarence is a manly name," Potter said. "Not like Atkov. His brother's a priest. Now, which one would you say turned out better?"

Mike reddened in what Eldon sensed was real annoyance, then looked back at the other troopers. They had set up a gurney on its collapsible chrome legs and were getting ready to hoist the gray plastic body bag onto it. "Okay, Larkin, one picture."

"Thanks." Eldon stepped out into the drizzle, shielding the Roleiflex's open viewfinder with his hand. He focused hastily and snapped off one shot and then another as the men hoisted Jason's body onto the gurney.

"That's all," Mike said.

"Okay. . . . Hey, I need a ride back to town."

"You do? Our launch is just for police business."

"Aw, you fish from it all the time," Potter said.

"I oughta leave you," Mike told Eldon. "But that'd just give you more freebies at the crime scene."

"Anita won't give me a rate," Potter said, "if you leave her star reporter to get eaten by bears. Or killed by snipers."

"I don't want the criminalists to have to watch you," Mike said. "They'll have enough to do dusting the house. Let's go."

Two of the troopers headed for the house carrying tool kits while the others secured the body bag to the gurney with straps. Eldon, Mike, and Potter fell in behind them as they wheeled it out of the yard. The troopers conversed casually among themselves while they bumped the gurney along the path to the boat ramp. The rain picked up, tapping on the body bag.

The troopers rolled the gurney down the ramp to the launch. They rechecked the straps, collapsed the gurney's legs, and hoisted it into the launch.

"We'll leave you at the pier in town," Mike said, "unless you want to wade ashore over there on the beach."

"The pier's fine," Eldon said. "I left my waders home with my rod." The ride would give him a chance to ask a few more questions.

But Mike didn't give him an opening. He left Eldon with Potter in the stern of the launch, sitting close to Jason's head, and went up into the bow to smoke a cigarette. They rode in silence down the channel, Eldon peering into the thick forest that came right down to the green, rain-pitted water.

One of the other troopers bummed a cigarette from Mike. Another dozed. That property of easiness . . . Eldon had seen it often at the scenes of murders and dreadful traffic accidents and usually shared it. But he had never been the one who'd discovered the body. This time he was a participant, not just a spectator.

Eldon peered into the enormous forest as if it somehow held answers. But there was nothing save the shadowy growth and the swish of the wind. It seemed deeper than an Oregon forest. For a moment, he thought he heard the tinkle of bells but was distracted by a reddish brown flash in the trees. "Black-tailed deer," Potter said. Eldon listened for the bells again, but the sound, if it was there, was lost in the patter of the rain and the engine's stutter. One more bit of strangeness.

A group of people waited on the Klinkatshut pier, taut-featured and muttering among themselves as the launch pulled up.

Potter turned to Eldon. "Cap'n'll have Mike's balls for husky food if that crazy sniper theory of his sees print."

"I won't say a word. But, hey—is it safe to go fishing alone?"

"Don't worry about that. Fishermen they gotta throw back."

Eldon stepped onto the ladder and the launch drifted away. "Thanks for everything, guys. We'll talk again."

He clambered up onto the pier and watched the launch head out into the steely waters. Shooting a totem-pole carver for sport sounded like an Alaskan joke, a tall tale spun to get him off the track and out of the way of the police investigation. A thrill sniper wouldn't have pushed the totem pole atop his victim . . . except that Eldon had once heard a similar theory about thrill hunting from an Oregon state trooper.

If it was a passing hunter, I'm out of luck, Eldon thought. But who else might've gone hunting for artists?

He looked over the spectators on the pier. Whom had Baer fought with? Cheated? Committed adultery with or against? Some of them? Most of them? All of them? It should be a simple process of elimination. But he hadn't the slightest idea where to start.

I'm on vacation, Eldon thought. I don't have to cover this story. I'm damned if I'll spend a month untangling the incest in some Alaska Panhandle town. I'll write the murder story, because it's good copy. And I'll write the features. Then I'm going fishing, and Anita will just have to be satisfied with that.

Anita . . . Eldon thought of her big eyes, long legs, and sensuous mouth. It might butter her up if he wrote a dynamite obituary for Jason Baer. Baer had been a leading citizen of the town. A few words from the chief wouldn't be amiss.

Eldon snagged the sleeve of a skinny little man who was gazing after the launch. "Hey, where do I find the chief?"

The man turned and Eldon started. There was a huge swelling on his forehead, a bruise like a big black-and-blue loaf of bread rising between his eyes. He had a face like a stomped-on rat. "Katlean? Ed's place is over there, behind the clan house."

"Thanks." Another recreational fighter, Eldon decided. Wouldn't guess it from his size. He gave what he hoped was an authoritative nod and waved after the launch; by good luck, someone in the stern waved back. Potter. Eldon smiled as he sauntered off the pier. It wouldn't hurt if people thought he was with the cops somehow.

Chief Katlean's house was a dark brown box with peeling sides and a hand-painted sign on it that said "TV Repair." Eldon climbed the porch and rapped on the door. No answer. He peered through the rain-streaked window and saw a cluttered little shop. There was a workbench covered with electronics parts and tools, a gray metal government surplus desk littered with papers, a swivel chair with padding coming out of the arm cushions, and a couple of old dark-green file cabinets. A huge set of moose antlers and a Lions Club plaque hung on the wall. Some throne room, Eldon thought.

He climbed off the porch and headed for the front of the clan house, running a hand along the gray weathered wood of one wall. The drizzle had lapsed and the sun peeked through the clouds; the damp wood was warm to the touch.

The clan house was a big square building with a sloping roof and great figures carved and painted on the front wall. Leaping whales flanked a squatting creature with big ears, its arms or forelegs thrown up as if in surprise. A bear? A Sasquatch? There was a door in the creature's belly. Eldon opened it and stepped into darkness.

The door swung shut. A huge animal hurled itself upon him in a flash of glowing eyes and a rush of halitosis. Eldon screamed and was slammed to the floor.

5

"Down, Woody!" a man ordered from the darkness. "Knee him in the chest. I'm trying to break him of jumping."

The creature gave a comradely whine. A tongue like a huge wet rug slapped across Eldon's face. It was the biggest dog he had ever encountered.

"Woody!" the guttural voice repeated. "Here, boy."

The dog barked and sat down as Eldon got painfully to his feet. He made out a white mound about the size of a small bear. It had a black dot for a nose and smaller dots for eyes. Woody's tongue lolled out of the side of his mouth, seeming to hang halfway to the floor.

"He likes ya," the voice said. "Here, Woody."

The dog didn't move.

"Woody! C'mere, dammit! *Here!*"

The dog rose at last and trotted into the darkness. Presently there was a gnawing sound, as if a beaver were at work chewing on a log.

Eldon squinted in the direction of the sound. "Chief Katlean?"

"And my royal mascot. Welcome to the belly of the beast."

"I'm Eldon Larkin. Can you turn on a light—?"

"Hang on. They failed just a second ago. You police?"

"No police. I'm writing Jason Baer's obituary for the *Aurora.*"

"You're that hotshot reporter Anita imported. Ah—there!"

Track lights flashed on at the far end of the hall. Eldon found that he was in a big square room with a central fire pit and tiers of wooden risers around the walls. A smoke hole in the roof was shuttered against the rain. Immense carved posts filled each of the room's corners, the totemic figures seeming to shoulder the weight of the roof. The room smelled of smoke and cedar.

A man who looked like Oliver Hardy with a ring in his nose sat on a folding chair before a great carved wooden screen that stretched across the back of the room. Eldon's gaze fixed on the nose ring. Good God, Ollie, where's your derby? he wondered and started forward.

Katlean was splicing bright electrical wiring with a pair of pliers. Woody lay before him, gnawing vigorously on a thick piece of wood; Katlean's bare feet rested on the enormous dog's woolly back. A toolbox lay open on the wooden floor among coils of wire and scattered tools. Katlean put the pliers aside. "The lighting needed the king's healing touch. Pull up a chair. Call me Ed."

Eldon took a folding chair from a stack leaning against the screen and sat down. The chief unclamped his nose ring and dropped it into the toolbox. "Got to get used to wearing that thing again," he said, briefly rubbing his septum. "Potlatch coming up. Damned if I'll get my nose pierced, though."

Eldon watched Woody. The dog was *eating* the stump of a two-by-four.

"Samoyed," the chief explained, pronouncing the word as "shamoyed." "The biggest, dumbest Samoyed in Alaska and maybe on the whole Pacific Coast. Woody's the kind of dog other dogs would have for a dog."

"He's huge—"

"That's why I keep him. A king should think big. It sure isn't because of his brains. You know how when you point at food or something, and a dog looks where you point? Woody looks at your finger. They gave him to me at a potlatch in Angoon. It must've been an act of revenge."

Eldon's ears pricked up at the slurred S's in Katlean's speech.

They were most pronounced at the ends of words. "Shamoyed" for Samoyed, "poleesh" for police, "looksh" for looks. Was the chief drunk? No, it was an accent.

"I'm writing about the potlatch for Anita—"

"We're not going to postpone it because Jason got himself killed, either," Katlean said. "Be sure to put that in the paper. . . . What've you found out about it?"

"The killing?" Eldon pulled his gaze away from the dog. "Someone shot him with a rifle, then rolled or pushed the totem pole on top of him."

"As if they were trying to make some kinda point."

"Jason had enemies, I gather."

"He wasn't a popular man. He picked fights. Fighting is good, clean Alaskan recreation, but you should choose your bouts. Jason didn't discriminate."

Eldon nodded.

"Jason had a special way of fighting," Katlean went on. "He was a real son of a bitch." The chief's eyes twinkled and he looked more like Oliver Hardy than ever. "Don't worry—I'll talk nice for the newspaper. 'The chief speaks.' It's my job."

"Did *you* fight with him?"

"Fists? Beneath my dignity as an electrician, not to mention as chief. Anyway, that's not the way Jason liked to fight." Katlean indicated the great pillars in the corners of the room. "Know about these?"

"They're totem poles."

"Kind of. They're house posts. They show the Klinkatshut royal lineage, Eagles and Ravens. The Alaska Native answer to banners and shields. The descent of the chiefs of the Klinkatshut from the beginning of time, see? Bigger tribes have a clan house for each lineage, but we just have this one."

"Right."

"Well, I'm not on there. Jason is. When he and I ran for chief, he made something of that. But I won the election."

"You outsmarted him."

The chief grinned. "Katlean is about the most famous name in Alaska—Chief Katlean fought the Russians in Sitka in 1804. He wore a Raven helmet. You can still see it in the museum there. I let people think I'm from that Katlean."

"Don't they read their own house posts?"

"The old ways are fading. And the ANB backed me."

"ANB?"

"Alaska Native Brotherhood. Any Indian who's anybody is a member. But Jason ran out of friends there. He runs—ran—through friends pretty quick."

"Jason was a Raven," Eldon said. "Does that make you an Eagle?"

"How do you know about that?" Katlean asked.

"Jason wore a Raven ring. Just a guess."

"You're a good guesser. Yeah, I'm an Eagle."

"It's like two political parties?"

"Naw, just tribal subdivisions. All the Pacific Northwest tribes have 'em, broken up into a potful of clans. You have to marry into the opposite side—Eagles always marry Ravens. A child goes with its mother's side."

"So Eagles and Ravens are all intermingled."

Katlean nodded. "Connections are very intimate. And Jason picked too many fights."

Eldon nodded. "He seemed pretty tough to me."

"You like to fight?"

"Hey, I'm a marshmallow."

"What d'you do when you want to nail a guy?"

"Well, I don't take a swing at—" Eldon saw that Katlean was looking pointedly at the notebook and pen in his hands. He thought of his plan to corner Jason in an interview. "I see your point."

"You write a newspaper article," Katlean said. "Jason carved totem poles."

"I thought his poles were famous—"

"There's a tradition known as a 'ridicule pole,' " Katlean said. "The ancestors used to put them up to show what they thought of deadbeats and sons of bitches. A guy could lose a lot of face because of a ridicule pole. Ridicule poles are rare; Jason revived 'em."

"People still take that stuff seriously?"

"There's a ridicule pole in Ketchikan commemorating William Seward's visit to Tongass Island in 1869," Katlean said. "Seward's on top, looks like a real geek. He didn't reciprocate tribal hospitality with proper gifts. The secretary of state's reputation has not recovered."

"Seward committed a potlatch faux pas."

"You catch on quick for a cheechako."

"So how did Jason ridicule you?"

Katlean's face darkened. He took his feet off Woody's back, sat forward, and scratched the big dog's ears. Woody left off chewing for a moment; much of the two-by-four was gone. "Okay, fair enough—I brought it up. He did a pole with me on it and *put Woody on top*."

"Aw, c'mon, chief! So what?"

"And then he sold off the pole! To an Anchorage bowling alley!"

"Well, it could've been a cigar store—"

Katlean snorted. "I wouldn't've been surprised. That was Jason—always coming on holy about the good old days but profiting from the new. Part of the joke was that white customers don't understand what the poles mean or don't care. Jason sold a lot of poles. Selling out, some called it."

"So you think it was someone with a grudge who killed Jason?"

"That's obvious. Problem is, he had a grudge with everybody."

"A state trooper I talked with said maybe a hunter shot him."

"Red-haired guy? Mike's seen snipers in the corners ever since Vietnam. Everybody around here's a hunter anyway, so back to square one."

"Do *you* hunt?"

"Sure I do. But *I* didn't kill him. It's beneath my dignity as chief." He chuckled and patted Woody. "And it wasn't necessary."

"In that case, how about your official statement?"

"Oh, yeah." Katlean intoned: "'The Klinkatshut tribe and all Alaska's people have lost much through Jason Baer's tragic, untimely death. His was a unique contribution to our state's culture and to Alaska Native tradition.' How's that?"

Eldon wrote it down. "That's pretty good."

"I'm good at being chief. Let me know what you find out."

"About the murder? I've told you what I know. This is for the obit."

"Obit, hell. How about the scoop? That's what you guys call it, right?"

"Yeah—in the movies. You've got the state police."

"And they've got the whole Panhandle to worry about. You can give this your undivided attention."

"Why me? I'm on vacation—"

"I thought you were helping Anita."

"Just so I can go fishing."

Katlean eyed Eldon and snickered. "Don't play the choirboy with me."

"Honest."

"You never met Jason—"

"Yes, I did. In Ketchikan."

"Level with me—did you like him?"

"No."

"I didn't like him, either. Neither did much of anyone else."

"So?"

"So this town is full of suspects. Lots of Indians."

"So?"

"So I'm afraid those troopers'll latch onto the first likely Indian and let it go at that. They could make life hard for some innocent people—my people."

"I've got no sources here."

"You're a hotshot reporter. You can get sources, especially if I tell folks to help you."

"I came here to go fishing."

Katlean leaned forward. "This is the chief of the Klinkatshut talking. I hate to impose on a guest, but I want you to *look into this*. I can't have murder in my village, no matter what I thought of the victim. Think of this as a royal commission."

Eldon saw that Katlean wasn't jesting. The huge images on the cedar screen behind the chief suddenly looked primeval. The carved house posts loomed like monsters. And Woody growled, suddenly not very friendly at all.

"What if I refuse?" Eldon asked.

Katlean's answer made Eldon's skin turn cold. "Then no fishing rights for you," the chief declared.

By Eldon Larkin
Special to the *Aurora*

KLINKATSHUT, Alaska—An Alaska Native artist who won renown and sparked controversy with his satiric totem poles has been found murdered beneath one of his own creations.

Jason Baer, XX, was shot to death while carving a

> totem pole, which the killer then rolled atop his body. Baer was shot in the chest with a rifle, according to the Alaska State Police.
>
> The slaying snuffed out the career of one of the 49th state's rising artists. Baer was carving out a name for himself creating totem poles that drew on the traditional forms of his Klinkatshut culture. Yet his work aroused bitter controversy . . .

"What are you doing?" Cassandra asked.

"Getting it on paper," Eldon said. "Makes me feel better. And we have to get this story on the wire. Give me that folder, please."

Cassandra handed Eldon the folder of notes from the plane. Eldon found Jason's curriculum vitae and looked up the artist's age—thirty-three. Same age as me, Eldon thought as he added it to the story, and what have I got to show for it? Well, at least I'm not dead.

Actually, Eldon didn't feel better. He was sulking over Katlean's blackmail. Usually when he wrote he felt airy and liberated, like a bird soaring through the infinite sky of language. Just now he felt like a turtle.

He saw that Jason's work had been shown not only in Anchorage, Ketchikan, and Juneau but in Seattle, Vancouver, Calgary, Portland, and San Francisco. His totem poles stood on private and public lands throughout the Pacific Northwest. Definitely a coming man—until he was murdered.

Eldon typed the names of Baer's major shows, then returned to the subject of the local anger that Jason's work had aroused. He balanced that with praise from a University of Alaska art professor that he copied from a brochure. He said there had not been a robbery but did not mention the mad-hunter theory. Then he put in Chief Katlean's quote.

That brought him to the bottom of the page. Eldon typed "more" and put the page in the copy basket. He rolled another sheet into the typewriter and continued writing. The machine's action was older and stiffer than that of his trusty gray Royal 440 at the *Sun*. Hitting the keys felt like driving nails with his fingers, but the ancient machine would have to do. His anger abated as he slammed the keys.

"This is going to be a news obituary," Eldon told Cassandra, attempting to put aside his mood. "You know about obituaries?"

"They're stories about dead people."

"Right. It's going to be a record of Jason's life, what he did and how it affected people and what happened to him. Kind of a monument."

"How do you say that in French?"

"Obituary? *La nécrologie.*"

Cassandra picked up the story's first page and began reading it. Eldon noted with approval that she did not move her lips when she read. He finished the second page and hesitated; it detailed the murder.

"Let me see it," Cassandra said.

She'll read it in the paper anyway, Eldon thought, and handed over the page.

Cassandra read it and looked up. Her eyes were sad, but a smile flickered across her mouth, a smile much like her mother's. "This is *good copy.*"

"Uh, thanks." Eldon's skin prickled.

Anita came downstairs, wiping her hands on a towel. "Well, Eldon, I cleaned your fish. Salmon steaks for dinner."

"Thanks. I'd have done it."

"I needed to do something." Anita studied Cassandra. "I think you ought to have a nap."

"I'm not tired! I'm helping Eldon. He's writing Jason's obituary." Cassandra enunciated the final word. "That's *nec—*, I forget what it is in French. Can't I wait till he's finished?"

"I'll be awhile," Eldon said. "You'd better do as your mom says. Anita, what's the wire service phone number? Do I call Sitka? Or Juneau?"

"We'll just type it right in on the telex," Anita said.

"Oh, right. You'll have to show me how—"

"I'll type it," Cassandra said. "I know how."

"Eldon can type in his own story," Anita said. "Now, upstairs—it's been a bad day."

"Can't I stay and help you, Eldon?" Cassandra was plaintive.

Eldon made a show of shaking his head. "The editor has spoken. Go catch forty. I'll see you at dinner."

Cassandra gave a big sigh and flounced up the stairs. Anita followed.

Eldon grinned and resumed writing. He found that the rest of the story was an airy coast; talking with Cassandra had cheered him up. He had typed "30" and was proofing the finished story with a soft lead pencil when Anita returned and set a fifth of bourbon on the desk. The bottle was half-empty.

"This is our second drink today," Eldon said.

"It's been that kind of day, don't you think?"

Eldon thought of where this might lead. "Like old-time, hard-drinking journalism."

"At least I don't keep a bottle in my desk." Anita got a couple of coffee cups and splashed liquor into each. She sipped from one and started reading Eldon's copy. "Good job, Eldon. This is service above and beyond." She read further. "So Ed filled you in on Jason's specialty."

"Yeah. I'm surprised you didn't explain it when we met."

"Would it have meant anything to you?"

"It does now."

"I'm surprised there aren't more murders around here than there are."

"We get one about every couple of months in Port Jerome," Eldon said. "That or a fatal traffic accident." He sampled his bourbon. "Ah, that *is* good. When we don't get one or the other on schedule, we get uneasy. It means there's going to be a multiple. It goes on like that all year."

"The murders here mostly happen during the winter. People go nuts."

"Winter here must be a bastard. What do people *do?"*

"Drink and fight . . . and screw."

Anita paused. Eldon hoped that she would lean down and kiss him. But instead she took her mug and Eldon's copy over to the telex, turned the machine on and began to punch in the story. She typed in a kind of slow motion, pausing briefly each time she struck a key. There was a moment's delay before the machine's clunking relays reacted and struck a character on the roll of teletype paper that fed up through the console's guts.

Port Jerome North, Eldon thought. Murder on Oregon's South Coast and murder in Alaska were much the same. They struck like a bolt from the blue—pure, angry energy discharged abruptly when someone's spirit snapped. "That totem pole that almost rolled over me in Ketchikan—who was it for?"

" 'For'? Nobody's bought it yet."

"I mean, who was it making fun of? Ed Katlean?"

Anita chuckled. "Ed as a Sasquatch? It would figure."

"The figure had a nose ring."

"Well, so it did."

"Well, that's a damned big dog Ed's got."

"Woody's great with children. Cassandra loves him."

"Woody's not exactly a dog rocket-scientist, though," Eldon said. "That Sasquatch figure was a lower section, right? It was notched at the top. It was a pretty good joke to put Woody on top of that and make a ridicule pole."

Anita smiled. "Very astute. Top man's not the most important on the totem pole, though. That's often just the owner's crest. An Eagle, in that case—Ed's crest. The largest figure is the most important in the story—usually bottom man. In this case, the Sasquatch figure. Jason had his reasons."

"Oh? And what'd Ed do to him?"

"Woody's name is very apt. He likes to eat wood."

"He likes to eat—oh, *no.* So that's what Ed meant."

"Oh, yes! Woody ruined one of Jason's works. Ed put Woody up to it."

Eldon had to laugh. "Woody's big enough to eat a whole totem pole, too. . . . Was it tough to be Jason's agent? And still live here?"

"I just treat those totem poles as art. I have to make a living. The paper doesn't completely do it."

Eldon thought of Anita's big roll of bills. "Sounds dicey to me."

Anita stopped typing and turned. "Southeast Alaska is very far away from everyplace else. And I mean *everyplace.* No one comes here from outside without a good reason. Anyone with brains or gumption who's born here leaves as soon as they can."

"Sounds like the Oregon South Coast."

"Without roads. Southeast is full of people who simply can't make it anywhere else or who aren't inclined to. The last frontier. It can get damned lonely here Inside, as we call it, so we hearty individualists have to rely on one another. We make big allowances, whether we admit it or not. Or we kill one another."

There was a ferocity behind Anita's words. He could guess it all—the abusive husband, the failed marriage, the child, the crazy little newspaper on the storm-swept edge of the world, where it just might be possible to earn a living and self-respect. Something like the way he'd been six years ago, when he had come to Port Jerome after Bernice had left him.

"You're a cheechako," Anita said. "How can you know?"

"Look, how do I move up from cheechako?"

"Put in your time in Alaska. That's the only way."

Eldon shivered. He was already running up the meter on Oregon's South Coast, where he had begun to feel like some kind of burrowing mammal: a big gray-rumped marmot with an Eldon head. "Ed Katlean wants me to investigate the murder."

"So do I."

"I'm not a private eye. I'm a newspaper reporter. I don't investigate cases; I cover stories. And I came up here for a rest."

"And to write for the *Aurora.* That was our deal."

"I remember our deal. I'll write about that potlatch and the other features, too. Meanwhile, I'm going fishing."

"Not without Ed's blessing," Anita said.

"You—you've been scheming with Ed!"

Anita smiled—that same heavy-lidded expression that Eldon had first seen in the saloon. "This is a prime fishing area. Fishing rights are an invaluable tribal asset."

"I am in no shape to cover a murder case," Eldon said desperately. "I'm tired."

"Too tired to walk back to Oregon? Because that's what you're going to have to do."

"You said you'd fly me!"

"I'll keep my part of the bargain if you keep yours. Eldon, what is the matter with you? This is news! Right in front of you! You sound as if you don't think you can handle it."

Eldon realized that he had taken more than a vacation. He was so far from Oregon that he need never go back. He could walk away from the *Sun* and Fiske and Nola, from his pal Frank Juliano and sniffy Marsha Cox, from Ambrose McFee, the trollish sports editor, and from Melissa Lafky, the foxy prosecuting attorney. He could disappear into the rainy forests of Southeast Alaska with his fishing rod and never go near the world of journalism again. Never go near the real world at all. Forget the whole comic opera Outside, make ends meet with odd jobs, and fish to his heart's content, up here in the pure vastness.

With the other losers, he realized. She's right—I don't know if I can still do it, if I still *want* to do it. But I found the body and I'm a witness. I'm trapped and I've got to see it through. "Okay, you've got a deal."

Anita clapped. "Bravo!"

"Just listen. I'll cover the story. I'll find out whatever I can. But if the case doesn't break before I go home, too bad. I report the news; I don't make it up. Fair enough?"

"Sounds like good copy to me, Eldon." Anita grinned.

"Okay." Eldon took a swig of bourbon and stood up. "Now let's seal the deal Alaska-style." He crossed to the telex, put his arms around Anita and kissed her.

She kissed back and then pushed him away, blushing. "Cassandra's upstairs."

"She's asleep. We'll be quiet." Eldon leaned in again.

"No!" Anita pushed harder this time.

"Hey, okay. I just thought—"

"I have a position in the community to maintain. How are you going to work for me if we're—we're—"

Editors, Eldon thought. They're all nuts. Fiske is nuts and this one's nuts. "It doesn't bother me to take orders, if that's what you mean."

Anita laughed a little. "That's gallant."

I knew it was too good to be true, Eldon thought, and then his thoughts took a brighter turn: Maggie Frame. Writing the feature about her Button Club would be a great way to get acquainted. If Anita didn't like that, she could lump it.

But Anita was musing. "You're going to put the *Aurora* on the map. Hell of a way to come to the world's attention."

"Yeah, well, that's the news business."

"I know. I want to catch the bastard who killed Jason. He didn't deserve to be killed. Not for a carving . . ." Anita broke off, her eyes swimming with tears.

"Did you have an affair with Jason Baer?" Eldon asked.

"No. With Ed Katlean."

6

Eldon walked on the beach, whistling tunelessly and looking at the totem poles. Raven . . . Bear . . . Wolf . . . They looked like weathered wooden Halloween masks to him. Raven's a trickster, Jason Baer had said, and it looked as if Raven had tricked Eldon, all right.

He was stranded on a foggy island hundreds of miles from Oregon, forced to cover a murder on behalf of a woman whose sometime boyfriend, the local king, could cut off his fishing rights anytime. What's more, the woman was the sales agent for her boyfriend's deceased enemy. . . .

Eldon shook his head to clear it. As long as he kept writing, he could keep fishing. Anita claimed that things were platonic now between her and Ed. If I actually could find the killer, Eldon thought, she might prove grateful, after all. And it would be *good copy* . . .

He should make a list of all the totem poles that Jason had created and find out which ones had offended whom. But he couldn't travel all over Alaska to interview them. And he didn't know what the totems meant. Maybe he could get a library book on the subject. . . .

Eldon studied the totem faces. These monsters had brooded sightlessly over the water for decades. They stood tilted in the ground, gray-white and weathered, paint faded, bearded with moss and fissured with vertical cracks, looking sightlessly out over the water. Eldon slapped a pole and thought about the weight of the one that had crushed Jason Baer. The wounded artist crushed beneath wounding images he had created. What an ironic death—

"Hey, Eldon, playing tourist?"

Eldon looked up to see Maggie Frame emerge from among the buildings that lined the beach. "Just taking in some culture," he said.

"Nice stuff, huh?"

"How old are these?"

"The one you're leaning on dates from about 1950."

"Only thirty years? It looks a lot older than that."

"It's the weather. Totems wear out like anything else. A lot of them are in terrible shape. There wasn't much restoration until the late 1930s, and there's almost nothing left that was carved before about 1880. The Indians tended to let things go. They even cut up old totem poles for firewood."

"I thought they were sacred."

"Being Indian was not exactly hip. Over in Canada, potlatches were even illegal for a time."

"Not in Alaska, though?"

"The USA didn't give a damn about potlatches *or* Indians. I find Indians fascinating. Look at the figures on that totem of yours, for instance. It's unusual—Raven's on the top *and* the bottom."

"Raven's important, I know."

"Raven was the founder of the world. You can tell Raven by his wings and by his long, protruding beak."

"The classic totem-pole Thunderbird."

"No, Thunderbird's different, got a hooked beak. Raven's bill is straight. And on this pole, Raven's bill is on his chest. He's looking downward."

"It looks like a mosquito's proboscis. Or like he's drinking an ice-cream soda through a straw."

Maggie was delighted. "Like he's really working the bottom of the glass, making that sucking sound—"

"—that your parents used to hate," Eldon said.

"Right, right!" Maggie laughed. "See how Raven's feet are elongated, too? He's looking downward, all right. The middle figure on the pole is a man, upside-down—he represents the imagination. And here on the bottom is Raven again, also upside-down."

"A mirror image," Eldon said.

"Raven's reflection in the water. Raven looked in the water, saw his own image, and was afraid that he represented all the evil in the world."

"All this is on the pole? In just three figures?"

"No. Totem poles are a kind of shorthand. They remind people of the legends. Oral tradition takes it from there. . . . With some of the oldest poles, the significance has been lost. You can identify the figures but not the context."

"Raven top and bottom," Eldon said. "The Raven was Jason's mascot."

" 'Mascot' might be a good way to put it, in Jason's case."

"What'd you think of Jason?" Eldon asked.

Maggie shrugged. "Sometimes he was hard to take. Damn good artist, though."

"His art was one big spiteful joke, the way some people tell it."

"It was good art. He was serious about it." Maggie looked stubborn. "But Jason was always so damn sure that he was right."

Eldon nodded, wondering where Maggie stood in Klinkatshut's tangle of personal involvements. Well, he'd soon find out—it was amazing what people would tell a newspaper reporter. "When can we get together about the Button Club?"

"Ha! How about right now, in the clan house? We're hard at work on our buttons. That's what I came to see you about. I heard you were down this way."

"Klinkatshut knows my every move."

"Eldon, you don't know the half of it."

The clan house cut off the view of modern buildings as they approached. Eldon braced himself as he stepped through the clan-house door, in case Woody fell slobbering upon him. He was relieved to find the lights on and no sign of Katlean's tremendous dog or of the chief. Women sat sewing at a long metal table set up before the great screen. Bolts of red and blue cloth lay on the table. Scissors, thimbles, and bowls of white buttons gleamed under the lights. A couple of Indian tots sat on the floor, playing with plastic toys.

"Welcome to the Klinkatshut Button Club," Maggie said.

"It's a sewing circle? I thought you collected buttons."

"The buttons are used to decorate potlatch robes—button robes, they're called. Step right up, Eldon."

An old Indian woman rose as they approached the table and proudly held up a robe for them to see. It was dark blue with a great-eyed Raven design in red, set off with rows of glittering buttons closely set together. They reminded Eldon of mother-of-pearl.

"The nineteenth-century white traders found a big market for buttons," Maggie explained. "Ladies, this is Eldon Larkin. He's doing a story about us for the *Aurora.*"

The women greeted him cheerfully. They were Indians and

Caucasians, ranging from teenagers through middle age to older women. Eldon learned that they were the wives or girlfriends of fishermen or loggers, women laid off for the season and mothers of small children. Eldon thought that Maggie certainly was the prettiest one there. But the ancient Indian woman who had displayed the robe held his attention. Her deep brown face was as seamed and weathered as a Klinkatshut totem pole, but her large eyes were bright.

"This is Kate Taylor," Maggie said. "She's our oldest member and a source of a good deal of our lore."

"Hi, Kate. How long ya been at this?"

"Shixty, sheventy years. They call me Peaches." Her speech had the same blurred S's as Katlean's. She was so old that Eldon wondered if English had been her first language. She was the perfect hook for the story he would write. Eldon turned on the professional charm. He went into a little act he had perfected for feature assignments, beaming and bowing and making much of drawing out his notebook and pen, playing on the somewhat comical appearance lent by his fly-studded hat and his tubbiness. The other women laughed, immediately at ease. Kate Taylor smiled, too, showing gapped and darkened teeth. There was something merry about her and yet sly, even sinister. Eldon knew he didn't fool her a bit.

That didn't matter. Eldon knew that almost anyone was willing to discourse at length on a favorite subject. Such interviews could be treasure troves of unintentionally revealed information. He asked questions all around the table—how many robes the club made annually, how many buttons they used, who wore the robes—some of which, he learned, were sold in Sitka. But he always came back to old Kate.

"Why do they call you 'Peaches'?"

"Because I'm a vegetarian." Kate gave a dry chuckle.

"What? Why?"

"Got tired of eating salmon, is about the size of it." Kate kept grinning. Eldon wondered whether she was putting him on. "Got tired of bear, got tired of deer, got tired of eating all that stuff. You eat too much meat, you get crazy. Never gotten tired of sewing buttons, though."

She held up the robe once more. "I like to have fun like Raven. Raven created the salmon streams. Raven discovered fire and liberated the moonlight. He transformed the world from the time when people had no light. And do you know something else, young fella—?"

Eldon stopped scribbling. "What?"

"Raven was poor. He was immortal and he knew everything and he was always poor." Kate laid the robe aside. "The village isn't as poor as it was. Our button robes bring good prices in Sitka. We keep the best robes, though."

A business angle, Eldon thought, swiftly revising his plans for the story. "How'd you start selling them?"

"Jason Baer helped us," Maggie said. "He got art dealers in Sitka and Juneau to take the robes. And Anita has some of them in her gallery down in Ketchikan."

"I saw them." Eldon jotted that down. "I thought Jason didn't get along with a lot of people around here."

"He helped the Button Club," another woman said. "He said we were fellow artists."

"He was good enough to some of you girls, that's for sure," Kate said. "Pushed your buttons, all right." A couple of the women glared, but Kate ignored them. "We call ourselves 'Raven's widows' sometimes. Everybody's in on the joke."

Aha, Eldon thought, carefully keeping a straight face. He wondered if most of Jason's enemies weren't male. It's a wonder it took this long for somebody to shoot him, he thought.

"Poor Jason," someone said.

Kate nodded and picked up the Raven robe again. "This will

be worn at the potlatch in remembrance. Jason was a Raven."

"What's the potlatch for, anyway?"

"Ed called it to celebrate the anniversary of his election as chief," Maggie said. "But the mur . . . Jason's death makes it a less happy event."

"Why not postpone it?"

"White men don't understand potlatching," Kate said, "but there's nothing to it. You hold potlatches when the seasons change. You hold one when someone launches a boat. Or you hold one to have a good time. You hold a potlatch when somebody dies. You can hold a potlatch for just about any reason. But it won't work without everyone's goodwill. So Ed's potlatch will be for Jason, too."

"Did Jason ever throw a potlatch?"

"Funny question!" Kate said. "He always said he would but he never did. Big talker." The chuckle again, like a dry wind. "One day Chief Ed got tired of hearing Jason talk. Ed said he'd throw one himself."

An election potlatch would be a way to put the knife into Jason that wasn't beneath the chief's dignity, Eldon thought. A potlatch could be a challenge, one man to another. He visualized Katlean, ring in his nose, squinting through the sights of a rifle. But why would Katlean gun down Baer when he had him where he wanted him?

"Maybe Jason was too busy carving to throw a potlatch," he said.

The women turned their eyes to their sewing. There was a silence. I'm not going to get anything more, Eldon thought.

Kate indicated Eldon's hat. "You're a fisherman."

"Yeah. I came up here after kings."

"I'll tell you a fishing story. It's about Raven and the Daughters of the Fog. You remember I said that Raven created the salmon streams?"

"Yes."

"Raven made the salmon streams when he stole water from Petrel," Kate said, "but the salmon refused to go up them, so the people couldn't catch the salmon to eat. Raven was wondering what to do about this when he noticed a beautiful woman sitting beside one of the streams. He decided to place her at the head of the stream so that all the salmon would rush upstream to look at her. That's just what the salmon did. And now the salmon travel up the streams to see the beautiful women, the Daughters of the Fog, who live there."

Kate stopped speaking and grinned, glancing at Maggie. This is a matchmakers' club, too, Eldon thought. Then Kate told him, "I don't know if Raven's really for you. Thunderbird's the protector of fishermen and of all good people. Got a hooked bill, like a fishhook."

"Why do you let the totem poles decay?" Eldon asked.

Another dry chuckle. "Why not? Nothing is permanent. The fortunes of clans change. Wealth and status go up and down. Even a single human being's spirit changes. And eventually everyone departs."

Outside again, Maggie said, "You made a hit with Kate."

"She's a real Alaska character—'Raven's widows.' " Eldon chuckled.

"Kate's been a fixture at the club since her husband died. It's been some years—he went out one night and got drunk and died of exposure. She still uses their two-seater kayak."

Eldon was sobered. "Is a potlatch really as catch-can as she says?"

"Don't let her kid you. In the old days, all the important social changes were made at the potlatch. Naming a chief, marriages, funerals, legislation. Demonstrating a family's ownership of names and crests—after all, there weren't any written laws or documents. You invited everybody so that there were plenty of witnesses and no disagreements later about what had happened."

"Kate must be a walking cache of legends."

"She's priceless—and a crack shot, too."

"Oh, yeah?"

"Still hunts her own game with the best of 'em—in season and out," Maggie said.

"I thought she was a vegetarian."

"She *sells* the meat, Eldon. People up here get by as best they can. Principle has to take a back seat. As for the legends, a lot of that stuff is dying out. For a long time, the younger people weren't interested in it. Now they're trying to save it. But it isn't the same."

"Kind of like Jason's totem poles," Eldon said. "Is any of Jason's work around here?"

"Yeah, but not here in town. It's on one of the other islands around here."

"I'd like to see it. Maybe you could show me."

t "Maybe." Maggie's eyes sparkled. Eldon decided that her eyes weren't feline, like Anita's, or for that matter like anything animal. They were hard and bright, like gems.

"I hope Anita won't mind," Maggie said.

t "All in a day's work," Eldon said. Hot diggity, he thought. Lousy little feature about a button collection gets you a date with a real cute blonde. Talk about cheechako luck. "When can we go?"

"In a day or so?"

"Sounds good. Anita's got me working hard. And," Eldon added mischievously, "I've got fishing to do."

"I own a piece of a fishing boat," Maggie said. "Come ocean fishing, Eldon. That's *real* fishing. The really big kings are caught in the ocean, not in rivers."

Maggie's tone was almost hungry. Eldon glanced up and

caught the eye of Raven, the trickster, gazing down at him from atop the totem pole, and was inspired. A vision of a ménage à trois rose in his mind. It was a fabulous idea, as wonderful as the wild vastness of Alaska.

"It's a date." Eldon lifted his hat. Maggie bowed and went back into the clan house.

Full of optimism, Eldon walked back to Anita's. If he could charm Maggie, he could charm Anita. He hadn't counted on there being so many unattached women in Alaska. Raven's widows, indeed.

Cassandra burst from the house as he approached. "Eldon! There's a message!" She tugged his hand.

"A message? From who?" Was it a telephone call from Katlean? Or perhaps from the state police?

"You'll see." Cassandra pulled him along.

They entered the office to find an amused Anita reading the chattering telex. "It's for you, Eldon."

Eldon sat down at the machine. He scanned down rows of coding to the words:

> ELDON
>
> OBIT RE DEAD INJUN ARTISTE GOOD COPY WIRE IS SINGING PORT AUTHORITIES IN PORT JEROME AND PORTLAND BOTH COMMISSIONED BAER TO DO TOTEM POLES PLAN TO MAKE OREGON TOURIST MECCA THRU WORLD CLASS POLES NOW IN TOILET FRANK DRESSED UP OBIT WITH LOCAL REAX BUT WE NEED FOLO FIND OUT WHO KILLED BAER AND WHAT ALASKA THINKS OF PORT JEROME HOW'S THE FISHING
>
> JIMBO
>
> PS CASSANDRA'S REAL SHARP IS SHE YOUR ALASKA GIRLFRIEND

Goddammit, he's found me, Eldon thought. I'm trapped.

"I told your paper about Jason's obituary," Cassandra said proudly. "I didn't say I was nine."

"I told you she was smart," Anita said. "The message carried on the news wire."

"Fiske must've hauled our old telex out of storage to reply," Eldon said. "Why doesn't he just use the phone—?"

The telex chattered again, briefly.

> PPS MY GOUT IS BETTER THIS TELEXING IS LIKE OLD TIMES

"Jimbo knows a lot about Bigfoot," Cassandra said.

Eldon stared, recognizing her expression at last. He had seen the same cagey, glint-eyed look countless times in the newsroom of the *South Coast Sun*—in the eyes of Jimbo Fiske. This kid's a baby editor, he thought as the hairs on the back of his neck prickled. A proto-Jimbo. And now she's in touch with the master himself.

" 'Find out who killed Baer,' " Eldon said. "Just like *that.*" He snapped his fingers.

"Well, you're going to do that anyway," Anita said.

"I'm going to cover the story. Any 'finding out' is strictly gravy."

"This story *will* put us on the map," Anita said happily. "Who owns the *Sun*?"

"What? A California outfit—"

"Would they like to buy an Alaska weekly?"

"I don't know and I don't care."

"They might if it's the right paper," Anita decided. "Hard-hitting and with an advertising base throughout Southeast Alaska—"

Eldon scowled at Cassandra. "I'm on vacation. You had to tell Fiske where I was—"

"Hey, take it easy, Eldon," Anita warned.

But Eldon went on, resentment welling up in him, propelled by the pent-up stress of the past months. "I've been shot at, beaten up, chased, and conned. I've wrecked two cars and had another one blown up. I've had three love affairs, two of them unrequited, and through all of that I've been hounded by that man Fiske. I came here to get as far away from him as I could, and you've loused it up—"

Cassandra's expression collapsed. Tears splashed down her cheeks. *"I hate you!"* She bolted from the room.

Eldon half rose to go after her, thought better of it. "I'm sorry. It was her expression—"

"Her what?" Anita demanded.

"I'm sorry."

"Don't be sorry. Just do the work you said you'd do." Anita tossed the folder of assignments into Eldon's lap and went upstairs after Cassandra.

Eldon nearly threw the folder after Anita. The hell with this, he thought. I'll hitch a ride over to Sitka and fly home.

But he didn't throw the folder. Not with this story staring him in the face. It would have been easier to do if Fiske hadn't found him. But now what? Return to Port Jerome and say, "I didn't get your story, Jimbo"? He'd never done that before. He might as well not go home at all. But staying in Alaska was a fantasy.

Trapped. Eldon knew the feeling well. He felt sick about bullying a nine-year-old kid. He opened the folder and looked at the photo and the note on top. Next assignment, Max Renner, the storekeeper. Eldon sighed. He rolled a sheet of paper into a typewriter and started writing the Button Club story.

7

The interior of Max Renner's store looked like the burrow of a pack rat that had overdosed on geometry. The long, narrow room was crammed to its low ceiling with groceries and supplies stacked with absolute precision. They looked like fortifications. The cans, boxes, and jars were so carefully aligned along the central aisle that they exaggerated perspective from Eldon's viewpoint in the doorway. The man behind the counter at the room's far end seemed to sit at the end of a precisely ruled tunnel. Fluorescent tubes threw ghastly illumination; the only natural light leaked in through small windows flanking the door.

Eldon recognized the rodentlike little man he had seen on the pier. "Hi," he called. The man didn't answer. Eldon started down the aisle, shoes clumping on the floorboards. He felt as if he were being squeezed farther through a funnel with every step.

That bruise on his forehead is incredible, Eldon thought. Like someone hit him across the forehead with a log.

A log. Eldon wondered where Renner had been the night Jason was murdered. He would've had to have gotten close to Jason to push the totem pole on top of him, Eldon thought. Maybe Jason put up one last fight.

Eldon reached the counter. The odor of mint seared his nostrils, so strong that he almost flinched. Cough drops? Mouthwash?

The man watched him like some Buddha or a man imitating

Calvin Coolidge, the silent Vermont greengrocer. He wore blue jeans, a red plaid shirt, and a worn store apron. Even the apron was neatly pressed. The only untidy thing about him was the bruise. A master's degree in business administration from the University of California at Berkeley hung framed on the wall behind the counter. Berkeley was Eldon's alma mater.

"Max Renner? I'm Eldon Larkin. I'm writing for the *Aurora.*" The man reached into an open tin of mints on the counter, placed one of the white disks on his tongue, and closed his mouth. When he didn't offer the tin, Eldon put his camera on the counter, plucked a copy of *Field and Stream* from the magazine rack that ran across the counter's front, and started thumbing through it.

"Take it easy! That's new."

Eldon paused. "I hate people who're rough on books, too."

The mint clicked on the man's teeth as he pushed it into his cheek with his tongue. "I don't know why I even let people come in here." He watched as Eldon closed the magazine and carefully replaced it on the rack. "I'm Max Renner. I was sizing you up."

"We met on the pier."

"When the police took Jason's body away. I heard that you were the one who found him."

"Me and Anita."

"Terrible thing. What do you think happened?"

"I think he pissed somebody off—"

"Me, too. It was winter."

"What? Who?"

"Who knows? Winter's when the grudges get started. They get settled in the spring."

"It's summer now."

"The killer must've planned very carefully." Max gave a little smile.

An interesting point, Eldon thought. And why's he smiling? "Any idea what the grudge was?"

"Could've been anything," Max said. "Little things get blown out of proportion during the winter. I never have that problem."

"Oh? Why?"

"I keep things under control." Max gave a grand wave around the store. "Stacked, inventoried, and arranged. Everything in its place. It takes nearly all my time."

"You married?"

"She ran off. Why?"

"Just asking," Eldon said. "Mine did, too."

"She did, huh?" Max warmed up a little.

"I went to Cal myself."

"Really? When? You weren't a business major, were you?"

"Journalism. In the sixties."

"Oh. You're a different breed, then."

"I'm here to do a story for the *Aurora.*"

The eyes narrowed below the bruise. The mint clicked. "About what?"

" 'The neatest store in Southeast Alaska,' " Eldon improvised quickly.

"So there's going to be some positive news in the paper, for a change! I can give you an interesting business story about my marketing strategy. . . . You're not going to put in that my wife ran off, are you?"

Would anyone be surprised? Eldon wondered. The freakish neatness of the place extended even to the nail bin. The nails lay in layered, aligned ranks, heads toward the rear of the wide metal bin, points toward the front. "I'll just say you went to Cal." Eldon got out his notebook. "How'd you manage to stack these nails?"

Max swept around the counter. He pulled out a shiny metal cylinder and thrust it under the nail bin. It stuck to the underside with a clank. A ring of nails sprang up on end. "I use a magnet." There was a scraping noise as Max slowly dragged the magnet across the underside of the bin. Nails rose and sank back like fur on an aggravated cat. "Nails are hard to keep neat. I massage them into exact alignment."

Eldon stared. "That must take a while."

"Nothing like it for a relaxing and productive afternoon."

"Suppose I want to buy some nails?"

"I pick the nails out for you one at a time." Max displayed a pair of tweezers. His tone became severe. "I don't let customers disturb the bin. I just wish I could keep them from pawing through the groceries. It's a disorderly world, but not in here. Not in my little corner of it."

"You must work long days."

"That's only good business. Proper stacking maximizes use of expensive space. People can't seem to understand that."

Max spun like a gyroscope and headed back to the counter. Eldon followed, jotting notes. "How'd you get into this, anyway?"

Max slid behind the counter again and placed another mint on his tongue. "I was with Safeway down in the States. I worked my way through college and was on my way up the corporate ladder. But I couldn't make them see the importance of a properly policed inventory. They let customers run wild. Why, an hour after opening in the morning, a Safeway store looks as if it's been sacked by a mob. The company forced me out. I came to Southeast to prove my theories—for bigger opportunities."

"Bigger opportunities?"

"Siberia will need a lot of grocery stores after we've nuked the Commies."

"This is the only store around here?"

"The only game in this town."

"Jason Baer shopped here, then."

"Shopped here? He was my business partner."

"You and Jason ran this store together?" Eldon was incredulous.

"Jason was an investor." Max clicked the fresh mint against his teeth. "It's shocking about him, but the store's on an even keel and that's all I care about. Does that offend you? It didn't offend Jason. He accepted his share of the profits."

"You don't sound as if you liked him, Max."

"Most people aren't likable." Max scowled in the direction of the magazine rack. "He split the spines of paperback books. I won't miss *that* little quirk."

"How'd Jason buy in?"

"He invested in my fishing boat, actually. He needed the boat to transport his totem poles. . . . Is this story about me or Jason?"

"You. But the more background the better." Eldon cast around for a temporary change of subject. "I'm up here to fish," he offered.

"I could tell from your hat. That's why I've decided to talk to you. I admire fly-fishing's precision—it's largely an import from the lower forty-eight, you know, reminds me of what can be achieved where there's real civilization. You have some very precise flies on your hat, Mr. Larkin."

"Thanks. I tied most of 'em myself."

"See? Most people value precision as much as I do, if only they'd think about it. . . . You're working with the police, aren't you?"

"Chief Katlean asked me to make some inquiries."

"Don't know why Ed doesn't make them himself. He buys enough from me on credit. Most folks around here run a tab all winter, pay off when they're working again. Especially the Indians."

"Jason, too?"

"Not Jason. He paid cash and was proud of it. He liked to rub that in."

"Well, what would I ask if I were Katlean?"

"You'd ask, 'Max, did Jason's death have anything to do with that fishing boat of yours?' "

"Okay, I'm asking that. What would you answer?"

" 'Nope.' "

Max smiled and Eldon grasped the game. It was the game that fishermen played to discover each other's secret fishing holes and positions of advantage along fishing streams. Secrets had to be worried loose. "What about the boat?" Eldon asked.

"A troller." Max spelled it. "Not to be confused with a trawler." Max spelled that, too. "She's a seaworthy craft, Mr. Larkin, but an unlucky one."

"Hmm . . . What did Jason have to do with your luck?"

"The boat's luck didn't change at all; in fact, it got worse. Jason changed the store's luck by investing in the boat." Max added proudly, "I think he saw the worth of my theories."

"Then why would Ed ask about the boat?"

"I was trying to use revenues from the boat to buy the store. But I'd had bad times and the mortgage was staring me in the face. I don't mind admitting it—the fishing was off that year. It was bad times for everyone in Klinkatshut."

"And Jason bailed you out."

"I prefer to say that he *bought in*. We hauled his totem poles all over Alaska, and it got this store out of the hole. Professional shippers handle most of that now, of course."

"What was the farthest place you hauled a totem pole?" Asking about distances was one of Eldon's stock interview ploys.

"Is this story about me or Jason?" Max repeated.

"You. But this is part of your adventure, the things that made you who you are. Part of the story angle."

"You have to have an 'angle,' don't you?" Max seemed pleased to know this bit of journalism lore. "The farthest, I guess, was Dutch Harbor, out in the Aleutians."

"And what was the toughest trip you ever had to make?"

"Dutch Harbor," Max said again. "We lost Mark on that trip."

Eldon waited, pencil poised.

"We caught a bad blow in the Gulf of Alaska," Max said after a moment. "The boat was like some crazy flying elevator. One second there was sky, the next second a wall of water—green and cold and *deep*. That green just goes on and on, Mr. Larkin. I've never felt more out of control in my life, I don't mind saying."

"Go on."

"Jason was going wild," Max said. "We had the totem pole lashed along the deck, alongside the pilot house. It looked as if we were going to have to cut it loose. Then Mark went overboard. He was trying to secure one of the lashings, or maybe he was trying to loosen it. Then he was—gone."

"Gone?"

"He just flew off during one of the plunges. I think . . ."

"Think what?"

"Sometimes I think Jason would've thrown me too if he'd thought that . . ."

"Thought what?"

Max shrugged, crunched up the mint and took another. "Thought that it would've saved the boat—and the totem pole."

"Mark was a crewman?" Eldon asked.

"An owner. Mark Frame."

"Mark Frame? Any relation to Maggie Frame?"

"Her late husband. You've met the Widow Frame?" Max's voice was a little dry.

"Yeah."

"Maggie's a partner in the boat now. She inherited her husband's interest, of course. She runs the boat these days, hires the crews and so forth."

Eldon nodded, digesting the information. "How *is* the fishing, by the way?"

"Good." Max gave a single, abrupt nod in the direction of a big freezer in the corner. The nod was like a doll's head dropping off its pivot. "Plenty of king salmon in there."

Max sprang to the freezer and opened the glass door. Cold air puffed out as he held up a frozen king salmon by the tail. It looked like a baseball bat. Eldon glimpsed frozen fish stacked in the freezer as precisely as manila folders. And in the freezer's refrigerator compartment was a frosty bottle of peppermint schnapps, half full.

"Interesting to think of these as worth a man's life." Max replaced the fish and closed the freezer door. "Commercial fishing's not like fly-fishing," he said as he reeled back behind the counter. "There's no precision to it. Fortunately, the Widow Frame was willing enough to take over." Max's eyes seemed to peer around the bruise. "So what did Anita tell you to write about me?"

"Nothing. I'm just here to do a business feature."

"I want to get my theories out to the world."

"They'll make a great story," Eldon said. "Can I have a mint?"

Max glanced into the mint tin, then slid it over to Eldon.

He's counting how many mints are left, Eldon thought. He took two, threw them into his mouth, and chomped the candy. Max winced and carefully rearranged the remaining mints with a fingertip that was definitely unsteady.

"That's a great little box," Eldon said, enjoying the peppermint's burn. The smell in the store wasn't so distracting now.

"They stack up nicely," Max said. "Boxes are sacred to the Northwest Indians, you know."

"So Maggie tells me."

"Jason made some boxes," Max said. "Fine work, but not many—they didn't pay the way totem poles do. But boxes are why I stayed in Southeast, what got Jason and me into business together."

"How so?"

"Boxes are important to my theories. Boxes can be inventoried and stacked. Jason used to say that Southeast is a universe of boxes, from the Indian viewpoint. That's how I knew this was the place for me."

Eldon wrote that down. "I ought to pick up an Indian box while I'm here. It would be great for storing my fishing flies. I keep 'em in an old cigar box right now."

Max regarded Eldon. "I like you in spite of everything, Mr. Larkin. I like those orderly little flies of yours. At heart, you understand my theories."

"They're quite unique."

"I'm going to give you a tip: attend the potlatch."

"Oh, I'll be there. We're planning a story."

"It'll be a better story than you think."

"How so?"

"It has to do with one of Jason's boxes. How's that for a hint?"

"Something's in the box?"

Max winked. "That would be telling."

"Thanks." Eldon picked up his camera. "But back to you. Let's get a picture of you here in the store."

Max shied, touching his forehead self-consciously. "Not now."

"Okay, we'll wait a few days for the color to go down. But we have to take a picture. How'd you get that bruise, anyway?"

Max stared at the freezer where the schnapps was stored. "I collided with a landed fish," he declared. "As I said, commercial fishing can be quite hazardous."

"You mean it jumped up and hit you?"

"Uh, yes. Fortunately, it was only a salmon. Halibut can run three hundred pounds or more. That would've been a lot worse."

It wouldn't have been as funny, either, Eldon thought, imagining a tipsy Max bumbling around the deck of his fishing boat and tripping over a flopping fish.

"What's in the box, Max? I can keep a secret."

"No, you can't. You're a reporter."

"I'll wait until it's time to open it. But I want to get my ducks lined up. I just want to know."

"That's right—you just want to *know*. That's why you're asking questions about Jason. That's why you do what you do."

"Don't you want to know who killed Jason Baer?"

"Not my business."

"He was your partner."

"The partnership will be dealt with in probate."

Tidylike, Eldon thought, surveying the well-ordered store and thinking of the wilderness outside. He noticed a candy rack to one side and picked out a Tootsie Pop. Eldon hated them, but lots of kids liked them. Maybe even Cassandra.

8

Woody gave a thunderous bark as Eldon opened the door to the *Aurora* office. Eldon leaped back in reflexive fear. "What the hell—?"

"Sometimes he comes over." It was Cassandra's voice. Eldon peered over Woody and saw her sitting at the telex.

"Where's your mother?" Eldon asked.

"Out."

"Whatcha doing?"

"Nothin'."

Wait'll she's a teenager, Eldon thought, easing through the door. Woody barked again and smiled, panting, but gave no sign of preparing to jump. Relieved, Eldon patted the dog's huge head, giving Woody's brow a good thumping to make sure that the message of friendship got through.

He held out the Tootsie Pop. Cassandra sneered at it. "You've been to the store."

"Max showed me how to stack nails with a magnet."

"He shows everybody that magnet trick. What did you find out about Jason?"

"Look, do you want this Tootsie Pop or not? Let's be friends. I'm sorry I got mad at you, but I came up here to get away from Jimbo."

"Don't you like Jimbo? Isn't he nice to you?"

"Jimbo's the best. But just because you like somebody doesn't mean you have to think about them all the time."

"I think about my daddy a lot," Cassandra replied. "Mom and Daddy didn't want to be around each other all the time. So Daddy left."

"Do you see him much?"

"Last Christmas, I did. But then I missed Mom."

"Well, like I told you, I don't want to fight with anybody. Certainly not with you."

"I'm sorry I told Jimbo where you were."

"It's okay. I guess I don't have to answer him, if I don't want to."

"Jason fought with everybody, and somebody killed him. You've got to find out who." Cassandra accepted the Tootsie Pop and slipped it into a pocket. "For later. After you get some *good copy.*"

She's put me right back on the spot, Eldon thought. My editor is a nine-year-old child. Or maybe all editors are like children. What was Fiske like at her age?

As with Fiske, when Jimbo gave him an assignment he didn't like, he put on a smile. "It's a deal."

Cassandra smiled back, but now it was a child's smile. Eldon felt his own smile becoming genuine in a paternal surge that he swiftly rationalized. The kid's right, he thought, this is a good story. "Where's your mom?"

"She's out selling ads."

"She just left you here alone?"

"Woody's here," Cassandra explained. "We're supposed to go over to Maggie's. But I've been watching the telex, in case Jimbo sends another message."

Maggie's place? Eldon thought, and saw a way to get a foot in the door. "Tell you what—let's drive to Maggie's in the Amphicar. Then I'm going to Sitka, to talk to the state police."

"Wow! I want to come!"

"Better not. Your mom wants you at Maggie's."

"But I want to fish from the car!"

"I'll troll a line behind the car," Eldon said. "If I catch anything, you can have it."

"Okay. But don't forget to take the camera. You can shoot wild art from the car. Mom always needs scenics."

"Yes'm. Get your coat and we'll go." Eldon tugged Woody's collar. "You, too, White Fang."

They lowered the Amphicar's top to make room for Woody and started out, the dog looming in the backseat like a fur mountain. His tremendous bulk made it impossible for Eldon to use the rearview mirror. Cassandra directed him down a winding gravel track that led away from town, crossing the gushing creek where they had fished on the day they had found Jason's body. Maggie's house was farther away than Eldon had expected. It seemed like a long walk through the forest for a child—but what could possibly happen, especially with Woody along as a guard? Everyone here knew everyone else, knew each other's children.

That didn't stop them from killing one another, of course.

"Aren't you afraid of getting lost," he asked, "or of meeting a bear?"

"The bears are at the dump," Cassandra said. "And I can always hear Maggie's house."

A breeze swept through the forest as Cassandra spoke, and over the sound of the motor Eldon heard a tinkling like hundreds of delicate, dissonant bells. He thought that his ears were playing tricks again, but the music grew more distinct. It was the music he had heard from the police launch.

They emerged into a clearing to find a low, wide cabin overlooking the water. The cabin was covered with wind chimes. Sets of chimes hung in every possible niche, under the eaves and on the porch, from brackets on the wall. They twisted and glittered in the sun, hundreds of them, tinkling gently. They made the stout cabin seem fragile, as if their glassy music could somehow cause it to collapse.

Maggie was digging briskly in a large vegetable garden behind the house. "Short growing season," she explained when they had parked and joined her. "Got to get on with it." Maggie's forehead shone faintly with perspiration, and she was breathing a trifle heavily; it set Eldon's imagination in motion. Maggie had planted lettuce, broccoli, and other greens. Peas grew up a little trellis at the back of the garden.

"I'll help dig!" Cassandra said.

"I'm all done for today," Maggie said. "How about a cookie?"

"Oh, that's okay." Cassandra looked disappointed.

"Why don't you take Woody down to the water, then?" Cassandra gave an elaborate shrug and ambled down toward the beach, the dog following.

"Come on back when you're ready for that cookie," Maggie called after her. She turned to Eldon. "She's pretty sensitive."

"It's the killing."

"And her parents' divorce."

"That was a while ago—"

"It sticks with a kid," Maggie said. "I know what it's like to lose somebody. . . ."

Her voice trailed off and Eldon decided to change the subject. "I ought to try something like this at home," he said.

"You've got a longer growing season to work with in Oregon," Maggie said. "Here, it's just a couple of months and—*pffht!* It drives Max Renner wild, of course, because growing your own vegetables cuts into his business. Max would make it be winter all the time, if he could. Come have some coffee."

"Delighted."

Maggie led Eldon through a back door arched with wind chimes and into the kitchen. It was compact as a ship's galley, with a woodstove and with every cranny packed with canned goods, jars, and tins of spices. Music was playing from a tape deck on one of the shelves—soothing New Age guitar that mingled with the music of the wind chimes. A prism hanging in the window caught the sun and scattered a spectrum across the square wooden table. It reminded Eldon rather pleasantly of his student days in Berkeley with Bernice. Maggie washed her hands in the square steel sink, got a glass carafe of coffee bean extract from the little refrigerator, and put water on to boil.

"Will Cassandra be okay?" Eldon asked.

"Sure." Maggie sat down. "Kids here are regular little woodsmen by her age."

"Suppose she meets a bear?"

"She knows to climb a tree. She also knows to keep a lookout, knows how a bear smells, knows to keep clear of one in the first place."

"What's a bear smell like?"

"Rank. You'll know one when you sniff it. If you meet one when you're fishing, throw it your fish. They like salmon better than they like you. And then get out of there."

The kettle on the stove squealed. Maggie took the pot off the fire, got two mugs and a shot glass. She poured shots of coffee extract into each mug and added boiling water.

Eldon regarded the shot glass. "No hair of the dog?"

Maggie frowned. "Pretty early in the day for that."

"No, no. Just a joke. It's just that Anita—"

"My husband drank. It did him in."

Maggie waited with an expectant look on her face. Eldon realized that she wanted to tell him about it. "I thought he was lost at sea," he finally said.

"That was why," Maggie said.

"How did it happen?"

"He was trying to taper off," Maggie said. "It was hard—he was a fisherman, the work came and went, and it's not any easier when your wife's working and you're not."

"That wasn't your fault."

"Kept us eating." Maggie got up and went into the living room, returned with a snapshot in a cheap gilt frame. "Here he is."

Eldon took the picture. It was a close-up of a man posing with a hunting rifle. "He looks intelligent." Eldon for some reason had expected a blond, square-faced Viking, a sort of male version of Maggie. But Mark Frame had dark hair and a long, solemn face with sharp cheekbones and nose and a mouth that suggested a V. Eldon thought of El Greco saints and Byzantine icons. Of totem figures.

"He was intelligent," Maggie said. "And strong."

Eldon glanced at the rifle over the fireplace. Relic of the departed husband. He let his reporter side take over. "Did he drink when you married him?"

"Oh, sure," Maggie said, "but it was a two-fisted kind of thing then, lots of recreation in it. I didn't think anything about it. I guess I should've; but this is Alaska, where men are men and women are women. People drink to get along."

"He was a fisherman then?"

"It's how I met him, in this very town. I was a student, working on the slime line at the fish cannery, and he was looking for crew. 'Let me take you away from all this.' " Maggie chuckled. "I knew what he was after, but it was a good line, at least for Klinkatshut."

"He had a boat."

"The very same boat. You might say I married the boat—or Mark's share of it."

"Were Max and Jason his partners then?"

"Max was. Jason came in later." Maggie took the picture back and gazed at it. "If Jason hadn't—well, Mark might still be alive."

"Hadn't what? Go on."

"Hadn't bought into the boat. Then they wouldn't have been hauling that totem pole." Maggie shrugged. "I talk like it was Jason's fault. But it was the breaks, I guess."

"Yeah."

Maggie studied the picture and her eyes misted. "No, damn it, it wasn't just the breaks. It was the drinking. Mark's fault, too. He shouldn't have listened to them."

"To who?"

"To Max and Jason—who do you think? He was tapering off, though he never did quit. Max kept him going. When Jason bought in, he really started going—even though business was better. Had to keep up with his partners, you know. And they didn't worry about money so much when they drank."

Lucky guys, Eldon thought. When I get drunk, then I'm just drunk *and* worried. "Did they drink on the boat?"

"Sure. Trail of beer cans like marker buoys, they used to say. . . . Drunk was the wrong way to be when they ran into that storm."

"Max said it was an accident."

"So did the FBI," Maggie said. "They investigated because it occurred more than three miles out at sea. . . . Could've been any of them washed over. Or jumped over, in some delirious miscalculation. But it had to be Mark."

Eldon felt a chill. *"Jumped* over?"

"Might've. And I wasn't there to help him."

"You couldn't have been."

"No, I couldn't," Maggie said with a wan grin. "I get seasick. I don't go out that much." Maggie picked up the photo and brushed a fingertip over Mark's lips, then took it back into the living room.

"I worry about Anita's drinking," Eldon said when she returned.

"She handles it," Maggie said.

"But Max Renner—"

"Smells of it, yeah."

"I don't mean to waltz in here and gossip about your friends and neighbors," Eldon said.

"It's good to learn what strikes an outsider," Maggie said. "What have you found out about Jason's murder?"

"Word gets around, doesn't it?"

"Straight from the chief."

"Well, I've learned that Jason didn't get along with anybody. That leaves a rather wide field of suspects."

"What's your next move?"

Eldon was about to tell Maggie about his plan to visit the state police but stopped. There's no reason I should hand out an agenda, he thought. "Oh, I've got this and that errand planned—"

"Confidential sources, eh? Like *All the President's Men*?"

"I wish they'd never made that film. Everyone thinks I have a romantic occupation."

"Don't you?"

"It's just a lot of legwork, mostly. I ask the same questions you'd ask."

"But you get answers." Maggie sipped her coffee. "You've got quite a reputation."

Eldon was aware that Maggie was watching him intently, her eyes wide. "Max told me about the fishing boat," he said. "About Mark. It just came up when we were talking about Jason."

"And what did he say?"

"Just what happened. . . . That was too bad about your husband."

"Yeah, Eldon, it was. It's been four years."

Eldon shook his head. "Commercial fishing is so hazardous. Max has that incredible bruise—"

"He didn't get that fishing!"

"Huh? He tripped over a fish—"

"I *hit* him with a fish. With a hard-frozen salmon in the store. Max tried to rape me."

"Max? He looks too scrawny."

"Max will surprise you. He'd been drinking, of course."

"So that's why Anita carries a .357 magnum."

"I didn't need a gun, not for Max. I picked a salmon off the stack in the fish locker and hit him square between the eyes. Knocked him cold."

Eldon winced. "And then?"

"I went on shopping. I had a long list. I stepped over Max several times while he lay there."

"And then?"

"I got a cup of coffee from his coffeepot in the back and sat down to wait," Maggie said. "He came to after about twenty minutes. I said, 'Ring up my groceries.' He said, 'You've killed me.' I said, 'Ring up my groceries.' I thought maybe I *had* killed him—caused internal bleeding in his little brain or something.

But Max didn't make any mistakes when he rang up my groceries, so I knew he was all right. Max is very careful about money."

"You didn't have him arrested?"

"Then who'd run the store?" Maggie asked.

"That's quite a bruise. Looks like a black-and-purple turtle shell hanging out over his face."

"You bet it does. And the story was all over the island practically before he woke up. No problems since." Maggie giggled but the laughter was cold. "Besides, he knows that next time I *will* use a gun."

A thought struck Eldon. "Can Max shoot?"

"What're you expecting? Me and Max at high noon?"

"Use a rifle, I mean. What's Max do nights?"

"He rearranges his store. You can tell when he's there because the light's on." Maggie's eyes narrowed. "You mean—?"

"Was his light on the night Jason got shot?"

"Well, I don't know, I was . . . No. It wasn't on. I was walking home from the Button Club and I noticed that."

"You were by yourself?"

"Yeah." Maggie laughed. "Sorry, Eldon, *I've* got an alibi." Then she frowned. "I can't say that Max doesn't, but . . ."

"Then don't mention it to anybody, okay? Just let me sniff around."

"Right. Not a word."

"You're sure about not seeing that light?"

"Well, pretty sure."

"Let me know if you hear anything. About Max or anyone else."

"Okay. It's hard for me to believe that Max would—even though he tried to . . ." Maggie's voice trailed off, and she watched Eldon.

"Rape isn't one of my hobbies," Eldon said after a moment.

Maggie set her coffee cup down in the spectrum glowing on the table. "No, I didn't think so." She reached across the table and petted Eldon's mustache with a fingertip.

Eldon reached across the table and caught Maggie's chin, drew her gently across the table. They kissed.

Eldon came around the table and they kissed again, hungrily. Maggie rose and threw her arms around Eldon's neck, backing him off-balance against the edge of the counter. Eldon's elbow dislodged a can of soup as he slipped his hands under Maggie's shirt. It rolled to the edge of the counter as Eldon ran his hands up Maggie's back, seeking the clasp of her bra. But it was the kind of bra that clasped in front. Damn, he thought, everything comes hard in Alaska.

The soup can rolled off the counter and hit the floor with a bang. Maggie leaned into Eldon, fumbling with his shirt buttons. Eldon staggered in his eagerness to get his hands over Maggie's breasts and slipped on the soup can. They fell to the floor together with a crash. Maggie landed on top of Eldon and knocked the wind out of him. He lay gasping for breath, seeing stars.

Maggie rolled off him and pushed her hair out of her eyes. Eldon's chest felt like a cave sucked clean of air. His ribs weighed a ton. At last he got his breath back and crawled unsteadily to his hands and knees.

Maggie caught his hand in a strong grip and helped him to his feet. It was the second time in Alaska that a woman had helped him up from ground level. "Cassandra's coming," she said.

They rushed back to their chairs, hurriedly rearranging their clothing as Cassandra clumped through the garden yelling, "Eldon! Maggie! I've found a clue!"

She burst inside with something clenched in her hand in a tissue. She stopped short and squinted suspiciously at Eldon, whose breath was still coming in gasps.

"A clue?" Eldon groped for his coffee cup and tried to act nonchalant.

"Look." They peered closer. The thing was a nail, mud-smeared but still bright. "There might be fingerprints," Cassandra said. "I didn't touch it."

"Put it on the table," Eldon said. The nail was new. "Where'd you get this?"

"Woody stepped on it up near the beach. He didn't hurt himself. I'll show you."

Cassandra rushed back outdoors with Eldon and Maggie following and led them down a path that skirted the beach. Woody sat dominating a small rise. "There," Cassandra said, pointing out an impression raked in the mud.

Eldon raised his eyes and looked across the water—and stopped. He could see over to Jason's island. In fact, he could see Jason's roof and Jason's backyard, because of the configuration of the trees. Someone with a rifle equipped with a telescope . . . No, that couldn't be right. Mike Atkov had said fairly close range—

But this *was* close enough, for a good marksman. It would make it unnecessary to go over to Jason's island in a boat, shoot him and then come home. Anyone who wanted to could steal down through the woods, do the deed while Maggie was at the Button Club, not at home to hear the shot.

Eldon decided to keep his conjectures to himself for the moment. "Good work, Cassandra."

"Good thing you thought of fingerprints," Maggie told the girl, making a thing of it. "Do you read Nancy Drew?"

"Sometimes," Cassandra responded coldly. "But I already knew about fingerprints."

She knows she's being patronized, Eldon thought. "I've got to go. Got some things to look into—including this."

"Take me with you!" Cassandra said.

"Nope. Your mom wants you here."

"Go up to the house and get that cookie," Maggie said.

"Okay. C'mon, Woody." Cassandra turned and ran back up the path toward the sound of the wind chimes. They got back to the cabin to find her munching a large oatmeal cookie and studying the photo of Mark Frame as one would study a picture book, her annoyance with Maggie apparently evaporated.

The nail lay on the table. "That nail looks new," Maggie said. "Let's see it."

"Give me a plastic bag," Eldon said. Maggie brought one, and Eldon put the nail inside, using the tissue. Fingerprints were unlikely, but he didn't want to handle it more than necessary. "Who'd be walking around here with a new nail in their pocket?"

"Someone who deals with nails a lot," Maggie said. "Can't you guess who? This came from Max Renner's store."

9

Eldon studied the bright nail through the plastic bag as he guided the Amphicar through the glassy waters toward Sitka. He had little doubt that if he visited the store again, he could match it to the hundreds aligned with demented neatness in Renner's nail bin.

It could belong to anyone who'd bought it at Max's store, but who else but Max would be walking around the Alaska woods with a single shiny nail in his pocket? And who would drop it in the act of committing murder?

Max would if he were drunk, Eldon decided. But hitting Jason would be pretty good shooting for a drunk with a rifle. And then who pushed the totem pole over on Jason?

Could there be *two* killers—one drunkenly spilling nails from his pockets while the other toppled a totem pole to perform the coup de grâce?

The Amphicar forged steadily through the water. Eldon was getting used to the weird craft, but he stuck close to shore as he worked his way among the forested islands toward Sitka. He had donned a life jacket for the trip—a sensible precaution in any boat. Eldon swam well enough, in a style something like the Little Tugboat That Could, but these waters were cold; swimming for it in the event of an accident was problematic. He kept glancing at the Amphicar's balky door, reassuring himself that he had closed the lower latch properly.

His fishing rod was wedged between the seat and the passenger door. The line trailed out to starboard, dragging through the fringe of the Amphicar's wake. Eldon turned to watch the small blue Alaska flag snap crisply as it flew from the light mast, thrust into its socket in the engine hood. The flag was Union blue like Oregon's. But where the Oregon flag had the state seal outlined in gold on one side and a golden beaver on the other, Alaska's showed the Big Bear constellation in gold, its pointer stars aimed at Polaris in the flag's upper right-hand corner.

Alaska's a hell of a place, Eldon thought, surveying the immensity around him, squinting at the bright shaft of the sun's reflection on the water. He felt relaxed and determined at last, the way he felt when he put his cares behind him and went fishing—or when he was chasing a good story. He'd turned some kind of emotional corner.

The sky was fading into gray, and a cold breeze was picking up. Eldon considered whether to put up the car's top, but there wasn't much farther to go. There were more boats now and more dwellings along the shore. Rickety private piers stood in the water above their wavering mirror images. There was Mount Edgecombe, a town resembling Klinkatshut, named after a spectacular snow-capped volcano that stood dormant on Kruzof Island, a few miles seaward. And there was Sitka ahead, on Baranof Island. He could see the high bridge and boats in the harbor. A huge white cruise ship was anchored near the bridge, dwarfing other craft.

A boat whistle sounded to port—a troller homeward bound, outriggers pulled up vertical alongside the center mast. She rode low in the water, no doubt gravid with troll-caught king salmon. Eldon's mouth watered. I'll have a salmon dinner in Sitka, he decided. I bet the restaurants buy 'em fresh off the boat. He grinned and sounded the Amphicar's horn in reply.

His odd little craft rated only amused glances from Sitka denizens as he drove out of the water at Crescent Harbor. But a group of tourists, obviously off the cruise ship, lined up with their cameras and started snapping pictures. The tourists were overweight people in bright windbreakers and polyester slacks. "You folks from the States?" Eldon asked.

"We're from Portland," a woman said. "We came in on the cruise ship."

"Portland, Oregon, or Portland, Maine?"

"Portland, Oregon."

Eldon shook his head. "Never been down there. Never been out of Alaska. You've got one hell of a newspaper, though."

"Oh, the *Oregonian*—"

"Hell, no! The *South Coast Sun*."

"Oh." The woman looked baffled. "What kind of boat is that?"

"It's an Amphicar," Eldon said. "Goes on land and water. You can't beat it for salmon fishing and for cruising the Inside Passage. You can outrun bears in it, too, on land. But it's no vessel for cheechakos, I warn you. . . ."

Eldon got a map at the visitors' information center and looked up the state police barracks. Not too far to walk, he decided. Walking was a good way to take in a new place, whether or not rain was coming. A little rain shouldn't stop an Oregonian. I'm getting used to this place, Eldon thought.

He put up the Amphicar's top, locked the doors, and set out. Shortly he came to St. Michael's Cathedral, Sitka's big wooden Orthodox church dating from Russian times. Its dome and spire poked up into a sky now turned bleak. It looks new, Eldon thought as cold drops of rain hit his face. They felt like icy rivets. It was going to be a pretty good blow, at that. Eldon hurried inside St. Michael's to wait out the storm.

Eldon was a thoroughly lapsed Roman Catholic. Yet he pulled off his fishing hat and absently crossed himself as he looked around. The church was empty except for a few people lighting votive candles. Icons hung on the walls. An ornate chandelier hung on a long chain in the room's center. Eldon's gaze followed the chain upward. The interior of the cathedral's dome was painted sky blue. Windows around the dome let in white daylight, suggesting in a curiously effective way that he was standing beneath the open sky.

A major difference from a Catholic church was the iconostasis, the holy screen running from wall to wall in front of the altar. It reminded Eldon of the screen in the Klinkatshut clan house.

Big icons flanked the doors. Eldon examined the tall oil-painted wooden panels. One depicted the Madonna and Child and the other a solemn Christ. A heavy silver gilt screen covered much of the Madonna and Child icon, although not the faces or hands.

"Theotokos, the Mother of God," someone murmured as rain rattled on the church's dome. "Sometimes called the Sitka Madonna. It dates from the eighteenth century."

Eldon turned to look into the face of a priest. The priest's long red beard obscured the lower part of his fair face and straggled down the front of his cassock. He resembled . . . someone.

"What's the metal overlay?" Eldon asked as his mind worked.

"That's called a *riza.*" The priest was American, though Eldon would not have been surprised by a Rasputin-like accent. "It honors and protects the image. The other icon is Christ the Judge."

"Who's the artist?"

"Vladimir Borovikovsky. You're interested in icons?"

"I like art. I don't know much about the Eastern tradition, though."

"The Sitka Madonna is the oldest icon in North America. These icons—really, everything you see around you—were saved when the original church burned in 1966. The cathedral was rebuilt three years ago, in '76."

"So that's why it looks so new."

"They used the original blueprints to rebuild. Let me show you around."

"Okay. Will this rain last long?"

"Do you have to get back to the cruise ship?"

"No, no. I came from Klinkatshut on business."

"Klinkatshut? My brother was just over there on . . . business." The priest paused. "There was a murder."

Eldon recognized the priest—but as clean-shaven and wearing a uniform cap. "Your brother's Mike Atkov, the state trooper. I'm in Sitka to see him."

"Father George Atkov." The priest thrust out his hand. "Mike's my twin brother."

Eldon peered as they shook hands. Shave off the beard and it was true. "I thought Potter was kidding when he said Mike's brother was a priest. He didn't say you were twins. Nice to meet you, Father. I'm Eldon Larkin."

"Are you a trooper, too?"

"I'm a newspaper reporter. I'm covering that murder for the *Aurora.* I was walking over to the state police barracks when it started to rain."

The priest's eyes twinkled. "A reporter? Come into my office. I'll save you a wet walk."

There was a dark wooden desk in the priest's office and a shelf of books in English, Greek, and Russian. A triple-barred Orthodox cross hung over the door. There was a coffeemaker on a table in the corner, next to a hat rack. Eldon was struck by the resemblance to Art Nola's nook in the Nekaemas County Sheriff's Office back in Port Jerome: ascetic, functional, religious.

But there was something else—a black Colt .45 semiautomatic pistol racked on a push-button desk telephone console. The pistol fitted into the console, balanced front to back, cocked and ready to grab. A coiled white telephone cord ran around the console and under the pistol's butt; Eldon didn't see a receiver.

There was a cardboard box on the desk next to the telephone. It was full of garish magazines: *Real Detective, Code Blue Detective, Detective Files. . . .* "Who Hacked Up the Hussy in the Minnesota Barn?" one cover demanded. "Huntsville Widow Wore a Railroad Spike from Ear to Ear!" roared another.

"Coffee?" George asked as Eldon stared into the box.

"Sure." He must've confiscated these from a schoolboy, Eldon thought. But what about the gun? He must get some heavy-duty sinners in here.

"Why do you want to talk to Mike about the murder?"

"There's something I want to show him. . . . I found the body, y'know."

"You did?"

"Yeah. I've seen a lot of that kind of stuff, but this one really shook me up."

"What was it like? Was he stiff?"

"Huh? He was getting that way—"

"You and Mike have exciting occupations. There must be nothing like being first on the scene."

"It's better to be a priest."

"Maybe." George went to the coffeemaker and poured coffee into plastic foam cups. "Sugar? Creamer?"

"Black, thanks." Eldon picked up a couple of the magazines and compared the covers. The same female model was on both, in about the same pose.

"How d'you like my collection?" George asked as he brought the coffee.

"These are yours?"

"You think it's a peculiar hobby for a priest?"

"Well—it's a way to study evil, I suppose."

George laughed at that. "I *write* for them!"

"What?"

"I've freelanced for the detective mags for years. Under pen names, of course. You ought to try it, pick up some extra money. The *Aurora* can't pay much—"

"I'm just helping out at the *Aurora*. I'm up here on vacation. I work for the daily paper in Port Jerome, Oregon."

"Port Jerome? I wrote about a great case down there. Let me see—" George rooted through the magazines. " 'The Hawaii Hacker' . . . 'The Newark Necrophile' . . . 'Who Stuffed the Utah Whore with Tar?' I've prowled America through my articles. Ah, here we are—'Oregon Landfill Mummy.' That was a good one! Just look at this photo."

The priest flipped open a magazine to a full-page photograph of a black dog holding what seemed to be a lump of wood—until you noticed the toes at one end. The caption: "Doggie Detective Dug Up the Dirt!"

The photo was pirated from the *South Coast Sun*. Eldon had taken it—Bouncer, the dancing mongrel raised from the dead at a landfill by a faith-healer seeking to make a comeback. The dog's discovery of the mummified human foot had been good copy all the way—and had nearly gotten Eldon shot.

He snatched the magazine. "How did they get my photo?"

"You took that picture?" George cried. "It's great. You wrote the news stories, too? They were really easy to rewrite."

Eldon scanned the article, shuddering at George's clotted prose. "It wasn't a mummy, it was a skeleton except for the foot."

"Poetic license," George said.

"The magazine never paid me for this photo."

"Sorry. But at least you had fun. You guys have all the fun while I'm stuck here in church."

"You don't like being a priest?"

"I like it fine. But writing these articles keeps me in touch with this country."

"With all the sex crimes, anyway."

George grinned. "The money goes into the poor box. . . . But let me call Mike."

George picked up the pistol and shoved the butt against his cheek with his finger on the trigger and the muzzle at his ear. The telephone cord came up with the pistol, and Eldon saw that it was attached to the butt. George punched out a number on the telephone console and pulled the pistol's trigger.

"Hi," he said as the hammer clicked down. "This is Father Atkov. Lemme speak to Mike. . . . Not in? When? Okay, tell him his big brother wants to talk to him. . . . Yeah, at church. Thanks. G'bye."

"You're older?" Eldon asked.

George racked the pistol once more. "By ten minutes. Makes a big difference. I'm a lot wiser."

"You're more talkative, too."

"Like I said, wiser. More coffee?"

"What is that thing? I thought I'd run into my first pistol-packing priest but it's a—"

George laughed. "A telephone. The guys at the state police barracks gave it to me. I'm a police chaplain." He turned the console so that Eldon could see a small brass plaque below the buttons.

FOR FATHER GEORGE ATKOV
THANKS FOR MANY A HELPING HAND

"Looks and feels just like an Army Colt .45. See?" George picked up the pistol again and thumbed the magazine release. A flat oblong metal container just like an ammunition clip slid out of the butt. But there were little speaker grilles cut in the clip's sides, and the telephone cord plugged into the base. "It's loaded, all right—with the electronics for the phone receiver and transmitter."

"That's quite a toy for a priest."

"Ain't it, though? Closest I'll get to being a man of action. Dodging bullets, digging up mummies, solving mysteries, and catching killers—"

"It's not what it's cracked up to be."

"Yeah, yeah, Mike says that, too." George reseated the clip and hung up the phone.

Eldon picked up the magazine. "What does Mike think about this?"

"My writing? He sneers at it. But he owes me. I did Mike a big favor once."

"How?"

"There's an Orthodox tradition that the oldest son in the family becomes a priest. Back in the Old Country, I mean. Dad came from the Old Country, but he was progressive. Mike and I were always fighting about who had to be the priest. Finally Dad said to flip a coin and whoever lost the toss would be the priest."

"And you lost?"

"I won. But I let Dad think Mike won—not so hard when you're identical twins. Mike played along. Or maybe the old man just didn't let on."

"Why'd you do it?"

"Oh, just an impulse. Same reason I told you about it just now. Anyway, that's why Mike's going to talk to you."

"Come on—why didn't you make *him* become the priest?"

"Because I'm the oldest. And because Mike's not tough enough to wear the cloth."

"Celibacy and all that—"

"Not for Orthodox priests," George reminded him. "I've got a wife and two kids. You Catholics oughta wise up."

"How'd you guess I was Catholic?"

"I watched you cross yourself at the church door. You went left to right. Orthodox sign right to left."

"Yeah, backward."

"No, Catholics do it backward."

They chuckled together over the ancient joke. Eldon reflected that George was not without powers of observation. Did the twins exchange work confidences? Two heads were better than one, he decided, and got out the nail. "What do you make of this?"

George lifted the plastic bag. " 'The game's afoot, Watson.' What about it?"

Eldon described how the nail had been found. He found himself telling rather more of the story than he had expected to.

"Sharp kid," George remarked. "Keep an eye on her."

"Cassandra's keeping an eye on me," Eldon said.

"I don't mean the little girl," George said. "I mean the big girls."

"Anita? And Maggie?" Eldon grinned. "I think I've got that part under control."

George cocked an eyebrow. "Well, then, let's consider what this nail could mean."

"Mike thinks the shooter was a mad hunter—"

"Spilling nails from his pockets, right!" George scratched his beard and mused. " 'Hardware Sniper Nailed the Totem Carver!' Mike should've been the writer and me the cop. Any footprints, cartridge casings, anything like that?"

"Not that I saw. Not that anyone told me."

"Nothing to connect the nail to anybody."

"Except maybe fingerprints."

"But suppose the nail was planted there?" George asked.

"Frankly, that sounds like *True Detective* stuff."

"Every crime in those magazines is authentic."

"But who'd plant it there? And why?"

"Somebody who wanted to frame the owner of the store where the nail came from," George said.

"That assumes that whoever did it expected the nail to be found. It also assumes that the store owner didn't do it."

"But you do suspect the store owner."

"Strongly. And that can't go any farther than you and me and Mike."

"Okay," George said. "What about this guy?"

"Max Renner. Strange man. Jason was his business partner. Max is not the kind of guy who mingles."

"That doesn't mean he killed Jason Baer."

"He might stand to gain from Jason's death," Eldon said. "Insurance, maybe. He told me that his store was on a shaky financial footing. Maybe it still is."

"How did they get along?"

"Neither one got along with anybody. I'm surprised nobody's shot Renner, too."

"Alaskans like things to fester," George said. "It'd be healthier if we had more fights. We ought to have fistfights every Sunday in church—"

"More crackerbox religion, George?" Mike Atkov stood in the office door in a dripping yellow raincoat.

"Hey, Misha." The brothers embraced. "I've been talking with Eldon here," George said.

Mike stared. "How the hell did you get over here?"

"I drove, like everybody else."

"How the hell did you get mixed up with Larkin, George?"

"Don't swear in church," George said.

"You swear all the time." Mike hung up his raincoat.

"I'm the priest," George said. "You're the sinner."

"So as the more hard-boiled of the two, I should do the swearing," Mike said.

"Who says cops are hard-boiled?" George asked.

The exchange between the twins seemed well-worn to Eldon, but Mike gave an unsettled smile. He nudged the box of detective magazines. "Birds of a feather, eh?"

George flourished the mummy article. "One of Eldon's greatest cases."

"He must be a real whiz at detection," Mike said.

"Eldon takes his work seriously," George said. "And he's got something for you on the Baer murder case."

"Oh? And what's that?"

"The nail there on the desk." Eldon pushed the plastic bag over to Mike and described how and where Cassandra had found it.

"Interesting—maybe." Mike took out a silver metal ballpoint pen and a leather-covered pocket notebook.

"Maybe?" George said. "It knocks your standard mad-hunter theory all to shit, Misha."

"That happens every season up here," Mike said defensively. "Happens in Oregon, too."

"My brother was deeply impressed by Vietnam, Eldon."

"While you were hiding in divinity school," Mike said.

"You shoulda told Dad you'd won the toss, Misha."

There was a silence. Eldon felt uncomfortable. At last Mike heaved a deep sigh.

"Eldon, tell him about Max Renner," George said.

Uneasily, Eldon laid out his suspicions. It was one thing to unveil information in the columns of a newspaper; it was another to use his status as a reporter to act as a police informant. But he wasn't going to hinder an investigation. He told himself that the *Aurora* wasn't a daily newspaper. He might send something out on the telex to Fiske and to the wire services, but it would be days before his story hit the street in Klinkatshut. By that time Max—or whoever the killer was—might've destroyed evidence or fled.

"If I was Max and I'd done it, I'd sit tight," Eldon finished. "I wouldn't call attention to myself by doing something stupid, like running away."

"You could ask if he owns hunting rifles," George said.

"We will," Mike said. "But who doesn't, around here?"

"But if a ballistics test matched bullets—" Eldon began.

"We don't have a bullet," Mike said. "It passed through the victim. The velocity a hunting rifle imparts to a bullet is twelve hundred feet per second, easy. Even more velocity in some rounds. A .30-06 or .30-30 moose or elk load will punch right through a human being. We'll never recover it."

"No other way to make a forensics match? No powder burns?"

"The shooter was much too far away."

"What about powder traces at an assumed firing point—say

where the nail was found?" Eldon asked.

"Larkin, you should write mystery novels or that true-crime garbage." Mike jerked a thumb at the rain streaming down the office window. "Even if there were traces, the rain's washed 'em away."

"You have one clue," Eldon said. "The nail."

Mike nodded. "We'll look into it. Thanks."

" 'Totem Pole Murderer Nailed,' " George intoned with satisfaction. " 'Exclusive Interview with the Cop Who Cracked the Case.' "

"That'll be a cold day in hell," Mike said with a snort.

"Mom would love it," George said. "She still saves those clippings about my JV basketball scores and that small print about you from the 'In the Military' column."

"Whoever shot Bear would've made a decent sniper," Mike said.

"There was a clear line of fire and Jason wasn't moving around," Eldon said. "He was standing over his totem pole, working."

Mike nodded. "Telescopic sight."

"Can you be sure?" George asked.

"Go figure," Mike said. "Low light levels and range and windage and all the things that lower the odds for a clean shot, yet it went right through his chest. That's either luck or a telescopic sight. Which also is common equipment around here."

George looked eager. "Now, if Renner has a rifle in the right caliber, with a telescopic sight, and if it's been fired recently—"

Eldon felt compelled to add, "Renner drinks a lot."

"So he wasn't drunk when he did it," Mike said. "Or not too drunk, anyway. . . . You say Renner stocks nails like these in his store?"

Eldon nodded. "I understand that Renner's store was dark on

the night of the shooting. He usually works late—counting his nails and such."

"Who told you this?" Mike asked.

Eldon hesitated at giving the name of a source to a policeman. But he had already told George about Maggie—and Maggie hadn't told Eldon not to identify her. "Maggie Frame. She was coming home from the Button Club."

"Button Club?"

"They make button robes."

"Oh, right. Indian stuff. I think we talked to her. No one remembers hearing any shots."

"She was at the club at the time," Eldon said. "Nothing to stop Renner from going out to her place."

"Could there be fingerprints on the nail?" George asked.

"Don't get your hopes up." Mike put the pen down and leaned over the desk on his elbows to study the nail. George did the same, his long beard flowing down onto the desk.

George picked up his brother's metal pen and pushed at the plastic-wrapped nail. When he pulled the pen back, the nail came along, too. "Look, Misha—it's magnetized."

10

The storm picked up. It was a cold, driving rain that slanted across Sitka's streets and sent the inhabitants scurrying. The weather seemed to enclose Sitka in a clammy glove. The mountains, the forest, the volcano offshore disappeared. There was no sky. The cruise ship in the harbor became a murky bone-colored shape brooding in the fog like a monster's skull.

"You'll never get back to Klinkatshut tonight," George said as rain hit his office window like pebbles. "You can stay with me."

"I'll sleep on a pew," Eldon said.

"Oh, bullshit," George said. "We've got a hide-a-bed. My wife'll love meeting a 'real' writer, anyway. Misha, come over for dinner—she can meet a real cop, too." To Eldon, he added, "We'll get Misha married off sometime."

Mike grinned. "See you after work. Larkin, this stuff about the magnet and the nails is real interesting. . . . And I hope I'm not gonna read this conversation in the newspaper."

"Not if I get to be in on the arrest."

"Okay—if there is one," Mike said. "Got to look at this a little more closely first."

"What if Renner splits?" George said.

"He's like Larkin," Mike said. "He's not going anywhere until this weather lifts. And we aren't going out there after him, either. Why don't you pray for him or something?"

"That's for sure," George said.

"George prays for everybody. See you at dinner." Mike pulled on his raincoat and rushed out to his car.

"I'd better call Klinkatshut and let them know where I am," Eldon said. He used George's phone to place a collect call to the *Aurora.* Eldon felt a pang of homesickness as antiquated mechanical relays clattered on the line like Salvation Army tambourines; the same vintage equipment was still in use by the Greater Muskrat People's Rural Telephone Cooperative near Port Jerome.

Anita's phone rang several times. Cassandra answered: *"Aurora,* the weekly journal of a free Alaska. Editorial department or advertising department?"

"Will you accept a collect call from Eldon Larkin?" the operator asked.

Eldon heard the phone on the other end of the line fall to the floor with a bang. *"Mom! He's alive!"*

Anita came on and accepted the charges. "Eldon! I've been worried sick about you. So's Cassandra. Where are you?"

"I'm in church in Sitka," Eldon said. "And have I got a story for you."

"Church? What're you talking about? I was afraid you and that damn car were at the bottom of the strait—"

"It got me to Sitka, no problem. I thought you said you'd take it here without a qualm."

"Not in a storm like this!"

"I got here ahead of the weather. And I'm staying over tonight."

"Okay. Keep receipts."

"No need. I have a place to stay."

"You do?" Anita grew suspicious.

Eldon couldn't resist. "Yeah. I met this redhead."

George guffawed.

"I heard that," Anita said. "Are you in a bar?"

"I'm in church. Honest."

"That was a bartender," Anita said firmly.

Eldon repeated this to George, who howled with glee. "That is a Russian Orthodox priest," Eldon said.

"One with quite a sense of humor," Anita said.

"Amen," Eldon said. "I'm at St. Michael's Cathedral and I'm spending the night at the priest's house."

"You make odd friends." Anita was only half convinced.

"You're the one who hung out with an Indian chief," Eldon said. "This is Mike Atkov's twin brother."

"The red-haired trooper—oh!" Anita said. "Of course. You had me going there, Eldon."

"On the job for the *Aurora,* that's all," Eldon replied.

"I miss you," Anita went on, and Eldon wondered if she'd been drinking. "I want you back here safe."

"Me, too," Eldon said.

"What's this story you've got? Cassandra told me about—"

"Not on the phone, okay? But it's good copy. Believe me."

"Ohh-kayyy. . . . You know, Eldon, I've been thinking about that little debate we had . . . the one about my standing in the community? I wonder if I don't worry too much, you know what I mean?"

"You shouldn't worry. You're a pillar of the community, no matter what." Oh, boy, Eldon thought. It should've been obvious—good copy is the way to an editor's heart.

"We've got things to talk about when you get home," Anita said in a sultry voice.

Eldon imagined Anita waiting for him with a glass of whiskey on a tray. In his fantasy, the tray was her only apparel. Then he heard "Lemme talk to him, Mom," and Cassandra came on the line.

"Eldon?"

"Yeah, hi, Cassandra."

"I'm glad you're all right, Eldon. I was worried. Are you warm and dry?"

"I'm warm and dry. How was your day at Maggie's?"

"Oh . . . it was okay."

"Well, good." Eldon sensed reticence in Cassandra's tone. She suspects that Maggie and me are up to something, Eldon thought. Can't have her telling Anita. To deflect the topic, he said, "I'll bring you something from Sitka."

"What I want you to bring me from Sitka," Cassandra recited carefully, "is records of Jason's property holdings. Make sure to get the names of any lien holders—"

"What did you say?"

"You've got to look for motive, Eldon."

"Who told you about 'lien holders'?"

"Jimbo." Cassandra giggled. "He says to 'follow the paper trail.' "

If this kid ever sees *All the President's Men,* look out, Eldon thought. But he knew Jimbo was right. A magnetized nail might point the finger toward Max Renner—but records showing financial dealings and insurance payoffs would solidly establish a motive for killing Jason Baer. Money—that had to be it. Eldon shook his head. How did Max ever imagine he could cover it up? It was all so obvious. The reasons for murder usually were. It was pathetic.

"Here's another message for you," Cassandra went on. "From Melissa. Who's Melissa?"

"Uh, Melissa Lafky—"

"Is she your girlfriend?"

"Uh, just someone I know—"

"Well, she says, 'Hope the big ones are biting up there, Tiger. Have I got a rabbit to pull out of the hat when you get home. Love, Melissa.' Are you *sure* she's not your girlfriend?"

"You'd like Melissa," Eldon said. "She does magic tricks."

"Wow. Can she really pull a rabbit out of a hat?"

"Probably. She knows some great card tricks."

"Well, she sounds like your girlfriend to me."

"Did Jimbo say anything else?"

" 'Bring back fresh salmon for my gout.' What's gout?"

"Something that's all in Jimbo's head. Let me talk to your mother."

There were shuffling sounds and some muffled discussion. Eldon heard Cassandra pounding up the stairs. Finally Anita's voice: "I see I have some competition."

"Me and Melissa? Hey, there's nothing between us," Eldon said. It was true enough so far—if only because Melissa had slipped out of a unique bet.

"Rabbits out of hats, eh? Melissa sounds as if she has clever fingers. Does she work for the *Sun*?"

"She's a prosecutor in Port Jerome. She's very sharp."

"This only makes me more determined."

"About the outdoors tab?" Eldon was enjoying himself.

"I'm a newswoman, and competition only gets me hot, uh, under the collar," Anita said. "I thought about the outdoors tab and then I thought about you writing the tab and then you out there in the Amphicar, braving rough seas and—well, I can't wait for you to come back."

"I'll be along as soon as the weather clears. And you're going to like what you get." Eldon's head whirled as he stared out the office window at the storm. When it rains it pours, he thought as rain hammered the glass.

The storm was still under way at dinner, which was served late because Mike didn't show up. Eldon met George's wife, Claire, a tiny, pretty woman with a merry smile and very large teeth, which made her head look smaller than it really was; and their children, each in some way a smaller edition of George, though neither had red hair. Eldon sipped hot tea and regaled the family with stories of Oregon journalism. Finally, they decided to eat. The main course was fish sticks. It reminded Eldon of many a Friday in his Catholic boyhood. There was fried rice and lots of fresh greens from the household garden, too.

He dug in with a will, finding that he was hungry. The good cheer of the family—George presiding and aptly fielding gibes from the kids, Claire asking solicitous questions about Eldon's past—made Eldon feel comfortable for the first time in Alaska. He realized with sudden relief that there was no alcohol on the table. Anita and Cassandra are in a weird situation, Eldon thought. And so's Maggie. I wonder if I'm helping things.

George was about to call the state police barracks to see what had become of Mike when the doorbell rang. It was Mike, dripping rain and looking weary.

They made room at the table, Eldon and George sipping coffee while Claire served Mike his dinner. Mike made only small talk until the kids wandered away. Then he said, "The nail doesn't check out. But you do, Larkin."

"What d'you mean—it didn't come from Max's store?"

"It may have come from his store, but there aren't any prints. It was a long shot, anyway." Mike flashed a grin. "But it's still magnetized. I like that part, from what you told me about Renner."

"What do you mean, *I* check out?" Eldon asked.

"I called Oregon to see if you were who you say you are."

"What the hell—?"

"I meet all kinds in my business. You blow into town, talking a line of patter, get yourself hooked up with a lonely woman, live off the fat of the land and pow! Someone gets shot dead and you're on hand."

"Potter said my story checked out."

"So now it double checks out."

"You called my newspaper?"

"No. I talked with a sheriff's detective, name of Art Nola."

"You did?" Eldon laughed. "What'd Art say? That I'm a fugitive from justice?"

"He said I could keep you if I wanted to. I told him to dream on." Mike stabbed his fork through a fish stick, swabbed it in tartar sauce, and bit off the end and stared at the white flesh inside the flaky brown crust. "That's when he told me about his dreams."

"Oh, God, his dreams . . . How'd you know to call Art?"

"Big brother's detective magazines. The doggie detective article mentioned him."

"What'd I tell you?" George said gleefully.

"Art belongs to a church that believes God communicates through dreams," Eldon explained. "You and he could have some interesting theological discussions."

"Lots of that in the Bible," George said.

"But Art thinks God sends him dreams to help him solve cases."

"Does it work?"

"Sometimes."

"Nola said to help you," Mike said. "He told me that he'd dreamed I was going to call. That was weird enough. And he knew I had red hair." Mike shook his head. "That was the really weird part."

"The Lord works in mysterious ways," George intoned. "If I hadn't written my article, you'd never have known about Nola. If Eldon hadn't covered the Oregon mummy story, I'd never have written the article. God's handing you clues to solving the Jason Baer murder."

"Well, burn you for a blasphemer," Mike said.

"God's big enough to take a ribbing from me, Misha," George said. "So how are you going to help Eldon?"

"I'm fresh out of tips. I need to knock around and find some."

George thought for a moment. "I've got one, then."

"What's that?" Eldon said.

"When the rain lifts and you head home, stop and talk with a couple of gold miners. They run a sluice box on a little island right on the way back to Klinkatshut."

Mike sputtered with laughter. "Those two!"

"Yeah, those two," George said. He left the table and returned with a local map. "Take this along. Here's the location."

Eldon took the map, eyeing Mike, who was trying to contain his mirth. "What do I ask 'em?"

"Whatever you think you should. They see it all come and go, know things nobody else knows, and what they know they seldom tell."

"Will they talk to me?"

"They will if you say I sent you—I think."

"Their names?"

"Ask them yourself," Mike put in. "They're real classic sourdoughs." Mike wiggled his eyebrows at Eldon and inhaled the rest of the fish stick.

"Okay," Eldon said warily. "What about the arrest?"

"I said you'll be the first to know," Mike said. "I'll get hell from the Sitka rag, but you got to me first."

"So there will be an arrest."

"Let's say that nail has got my hopes up."

"Listen—did Art say anything else? About that dream, I mean?"

"Yeah, he did. He said he dreamed about water."

"Water. Great. He's always dreaming about water."

"And a bird. A bird looking down into water and seeing its own reflection."

"Sometimes I wish God would use a telex," Eldon said.

The following morning was divinely clear—another of the crisp, vivid days that Southeast Alaska could throw up in the wake of nasty weather. "You ought to see Mandel's Glacier on a day like this," George said as he and Eldon walked to the Amphicar, lugging a can of gasoline between them. "The sun on the ice is glorious. The bay in front of the glacier is like a huge mirror. It's the kind of place where a blind man could take an award-winning picture—just stick your camera out and shoot."

"I mean to get up there," Eldon said. "Look, George, speaking as one pro to another—"

George chuckled. "You're ordained?"

"Reporter to reporter. You know what I mean."

"I'm flattered."

"You grind out the copy and that's what it's all about," Eldon said, "making words."

"Writing stuff for detective magazines?"

"Yeah, that, too."

"Then let me do some legwork for you on this. I've never worked on a real news story before. I've just pirated old stuff. This is *fresh.*" George said *fresh* the way Fiske said *good copy*.

"Do you know anything about property records?" Eldon asked.

"More about how we deal with 'em in Alaska than you do, I'm sure. Sometimes I help out elderly parishioners with property matters."

"You have to know what you're looking for."

"I can find it if you'll tell me what it is. I know how to check facts, and I've got contacts around here."

Eldon thought it over. George's aid would get him back to

Klinkatshut that much sooner—and the priest's network of contacts no doubt extended far. "Okay." Eldon explained what he was seeking. Then he added, "But not a word of this to those magazines of yours until after my story breaks."

" 'Seal of the confessional'—not to make light of it."

"We're not in confession," Eldon said.

"Would you feel better if we were? How long's it been since you've been to confession, Eldon?"

"I, uh—I don't know. Years."

"You're Catholic but the Orthodox version will do in a pinch."

"I know, Father."

"Some people build their whole lives around avoiding responsibility," George said. "I don't think you're one of those, though. I think you're trying to get your proper responsibilities sorted out. If you want to talk about it, let me know."

"Thanks, George. I appreciate that."

The Amphicar still glittered with water droplets from the rain. The jewellike effect banished Eldon's embarrassment and filled him with optimism. But as they topped off the car's gas tank, George said, "Remember what I told you about those women."

"Yeah. I was thinking about them."

"Grief manifests itself in strange ways sometimes."

"You mean Maggie?"

"It goes for Anita and Cassandra, too. And for you, too. They all may be making more of you than they should."

"I hope not." Eldon climbed into the car. "Thanks, George."

"Thank *you.*" George rubbed his hands together. "I'll get after those records. I think I'll pitch this one to *Confidential Detective Files.*"

Eldon laughed and started up the Amphicar. There are a lot of bereft women up here, he thought as he slammed the driver's door and threw the lever that sealed the door into place. Anita and Maggie and Cassandra, too. All Raven's widows, in one way or another. The idea disturbed him. Eldon turned the car around in the street, jumped the curb, and headed down into the water, sounding his horn as he drove through the harbor and out into Sitka Sound.

The vastness of the Alaskan wilderness was upon him again as soon as he was away from Sitka. The scale of things slipped his mind into a broader concentration. He put down the car's top and watched an eagle swoop low across the sound. He began thinking of the Baer case again. Ask the gold miners to show you some totem poles, Mike Atkov had said. The eagle traveled soundlessly with only an occasional beat of its wings, its image matching its speed in the waves. Art Nola had dreamed of a bird reflected in water. . . .

The eagle struck the water in a coruscation of spray. The spray shone like a rainbow for an instant, and then Eldon saw the eagle beating its way upward, a struggling salmon in its big claws. Now that's fishing, he thought.

Eldon made good time on his journey back to Klinkatshut. He saw few other vessels and then none. Now there were no signs of man except for an occasional jet contrail high in the blue sky. He unlimbered his fishing rod and whiled away the time casting from the car. He found he could sit sideways on the seat and steer with his elbow between casts. The sunlight and silence were lulling. After a time Eldon slipped into the fantasy that he was the only person in Alaska, a traveler from the future visiting primordial wilderness in his multipurpose time machine.

"Hellloooo!"

The voice jarred Eldon out of his reverie. He turned and saw a sight that almost convinced him that he *had* traveled back in time. A ragged little sourdough complete with a long white beard, slouch hat, and suspenders hailed him from a point where a weathered sluice box stood on the shore. Eldon glanced at the map. This was the place Mike had told him about, all right. He sounded the horn and reeled in his line, then steered for the point. The skinny figure waved and hopped around on the rocks.

Eldon gunned the Amphicar and headed into shore. The sourdough stood with thumbs hooked in his suspenders, chomping a corncob pipe. This one is right out of "The Ballad of Sam McGee," Eldon thought. I wonder if he can recite it? I wonder if he can read? As Eldon reached the shore he saw that the miner wore a leather cross-draw holster holding what looked like an antique cap-and-ball pistol. For wolves and bears, no doubt—but Eldon resolved to mind his manners.

"How-dy, stranger," the sourdough called as Eldon trundled up on shore and parked. His eyes were huge as tea saucers, aluminum gray with a thousand-mile stare. "Chilkat Charley's the name."

"Eldon Larkin, reporting for the *Aurora.*"

" 'The Weekly Journal of a Free Alaska'! Damn fine paper. M' wife and I read it whenever we can. Don't happen t' have a copy, do ya?" Charley's eagerness suggested that the miner and his spouse didn't get much company.

Fortunately, Eldon had a copy of the *Aurora* in the car. "Compliments of the editor."

"Say, thanks, pardner! You'll stay for some grub and some palaver? M' wife's a mighty fine cook."

Grub? Palaver? They talked like that in bad Westerns. "Uh, sure."

"What brings ya out here?" Charley asked. "Sellin' subscriptions?"

"No, Father Atkov in Sitka said to look you up—" Eldon stopped. Charley's beard was white but his hair was long and black and rather matted. The breeze ruffled Charley's hair, and Eldon saw that the beard was held on by flesh-colored makeup cement and wires that hooked over Charley's ears.

"Ol' Father George! As good a sourdough as ever popped nuggets outta the mother lode. What can I do fer ya?"

Eldon spoke slowly, watching the metallic gray eyes and the gun. "Uh, I'm a cheechako—"

"Wouldn't think it t' look atcha."

"Thanks. But I am. It's for a story I'm doing."

"Okay, stranger. Long's the padre sent ya. But first, grub."

Charley turned and led Eldon past the sluice box, a contraption that Eldon knew would make a fine picture for the *Aurora*. Eldon was still thinking about the false beard—and about the gun.

He thought about making a break for the Amphicar, but no—Charley would drop him with a single shot. Eldon's skin prickled as he imagined a pistol slug smashing into his spine between his shoulder blades. . . . What was Charley's wife like?

They passed a heap of mussel shells, gray-blue against the stony beach. "Those must be good eating," Eldon said, attempting conversation. Charley scowled at the midden heap and gave a stony grunt. So much for sane discourse, Eldon thought.

Charley led him across the rocks and a short distance into the trees. There stood a low log cabin with every storybook accoutrement of sourdough rusticity—mud-daubed walls, oiled paper over the windows, and moose antlers over the door. Smoke as pale as Charley's eyes drifted from the chimney. To one side was a low domed structure of brick and concrete. A kiln, surrounded by broken crockery.

Charley cupped his hands around his mouth and yelled: *"Nell! Cum'p-nee! Hey, Nellie!"*

The cabin door opened and a stately Indian woman stepped out. Nell stood six feet tall and wore braids and a long, beaded deerskin dress. Wampum necklaces swung around her neck, and she wore a beaded headband and a feather in her hair.

Nell rushed to them and caught little Charley in an embrace, lifting him off his feet and whirling him around. Charley landed on his feet and turned to Eldon. "Allow me t' per-sent m' wife, Nanook Nell. Nellie, this stranger is Eldon Larkin from the *Aurora* newspaper over in Klinkatshut. Father George Atkov sent 'im."

"Pleased to meet you, Mr. Larkin." Nell extended a hand. She had a bone-crushing grip.

"Hello," Eldon said. Nell's eyes were different from Charley's but no more reassuring. They were small and dark and seemed to jump around in Nell's head like little pieces of glittering flint. "We don't get many visitors," she said.

"I guess not. How's the gold mining?"

"Not enough to get along, but my husband can tell you about that. We support ourselves through pottery. Please come inside."

"Eldon here's a cheechako," Charley said.

"Impossible!" Nell said.

"Nell talks real refined, doesn't she?" Charley asked. "She was edjacated by missionaries."

"I try to set a good example for my husband," Nell said. "But come inside. If you're a friend of Father George's, you're a friend of ours."

The cabin's interior looked like a living history exhibit. All the furniture appeared handmade. There was pottery stacked everywhere—plates, bowls, covered butter dishes in gleaming glazes. A fire crackled in the fireplace. A kettle hung over the fire, bubbling with savory stew. A delicious odor filled the cabin. "Moose," Charley explained. "Shot it m'self."

"I've never eaten moose."

Charley nodded. "You're a cheechako."

"I want to be a sourdough, though."

Charley gave a high, raucous laugh. "T' become a sourdough ya gotta sleep with a grizzly bear!"

"You've never slept with a grizzly bear," Nell chided.

"No." Charley's voice was tender. "Just with you." Charley and Nell embraced and nuzzled with affectionate little sounds.

"Ahem," Eldon said.

"Nell, this man's *hongry*—and so am I! Why doncha rustle up some o' that grub? We're fer-gittin' our manners. Siddown, stranger!"

They sat at a plank table while Nell put out big hand-thrown bowls and carved wooden spoons.

"You made these?" Eldon asked. "They're nice work."

"Nell did," Charley said. "We sell 'em in Sitka. Only take 'em in when we hafta. City folks are peculiar."

"Yeah, they are. But I liked Sitka."

"Well, there's folks and there's folks in Sitka. Some are like Father George. His twin brother the trooper's all right, too. But mostly city folks are not our kind of folks. Act like they've never seen a sourdough or an Injun. Even the Injuns in Sitka act that way."

"Uh, yeah. . . . How long've you lived out here?"

Nell brought the kettle to the table and ladled out the stew. "Oh, four years now. We tried to make a go of it in Sitka but"—she shrugged—"we didn't get along."

"Had problems." Charley sawed hunks from a loaf of sourdough bread. "That's where Father George come in. I got jumped one night by some fishermen thought they'd have a little fun. Waal, I'm as ready for a brawl as the next sourdough, but I admit I wasn't doin' too well until the padre showed up. Then *they* weren't doin' too well."

"George *fought* them?" Eldon asked.

"He boxed in high school," Charley said. "And then Mike the trooper showed up, too, and those cusses *really* were seein' double."

"After that, we knew that we'd be better off on our own," Nell said. "Please eat."

Eldon took a steaming spoonful of stew, blew on it, and sampled it carefully. It had a rich, gamey flavor. "Hey, this is good. Can I have the recipe?"

"Oh, yes," Nell said. "Do you like to cook?"

That was Eldon's cue to launch into his well-worn cooking lecture, which he had developed to beguile prospective dates. It showed, he hoped, that he was sensitive. His specialty was fish, and as he talked he reflected that he had yet to prepare fish for Anita and Cassandra. He wondered about them. And about Maggie.

"It's rare to find a cultivated person out here," Nell said.

Charley snorted. "Fine airs for an Injun."

"Jason Baer was an Indian," Nell retorted. "And he was one of the best artists around."

"You know about his death?" Eldon asked.

Nell nodded somberly. "Oh yes. We have a radio."

"Danged newfangled gadget only brings bad news," Charley said. "Oughta chuck it in the water."

"Jason's murder is why I came out here," Eldon said. "I'm trying to find out who killed him and why. George said you could help me."

Charley and Nell looked at each other. "How?" Charley asked at last.

"He said you know just about everything that happens in these parts."

Nell gave a deprecating laugh. "That's overstating it."

"Even if we know it, it don't mean we can make sense of it," Charley added. "Depends on what it is."

Eldon decided to play a wild hunch. "How about totem poles?"

Charley and Nell looked at each other again, and Eldon knew that he had struck pay dirt. "Totem poles?" Charley asked. "There's a bunch o' old ones a little ways from here, at an old Injun buryin' ground. Don't reckon many folks know about it."

"Jason knew," Nell said firmly, and Eldon's ears perked up.

Charley sighed. "Yeah, it's true. Jason put up a totem pole of his own there a while back. Said it was a memorial. But he wouldn't say t' who."

"Will you take me there?" Eldon asked. "I want to see it."

"Well, I don't—"

"Father George sent him, Charley," Nell said. "He helped us. And so did Jason. We're eating, thanks to Jason."

Charley looked Eldon over. It was like being scanned by featureless radar reflectors. "Yeah," Charley said slowly. "There's a price on ever'thin' out there in the world."

"How did you know Jason?" Eldon asked.

"He helped us sell our pots in the galleries in Sitka," Charley said finally.

"Jason was kind to other artists," Nell said, "though he could be a rather scrappy man."

"Scrappy!" Charley said, false beard waggling as he chewed. "Hunh! Coulda used him in my corner dealin' with those fishermen."

"Father George was help enough," Nell said.

"You said Jason helped you out with the pottery," Eldon said.

"We're eatin', thanks to him."

"Did he ever ask anything in return?"

"That's a *reporter*-type question," Charley said.

"Reporter's what I am," Eldon said.

"Jason wasn't the sort you liked ta take favors from. Ya didn't want ta be beholdin' to 'im. Now, the pots was one thing. We fired ceramic masks fer 'im in return. . . . But he could be an easy man to hate."

"Charley!" Nell said sadly.

"How come?" Eldon asked.

"Usta just toy with us, idlelike. 'How'd you like some more visitors?' He knew how to git under yer skin. You was okay long's you could dig back—he'd given us the Sitka markets and we'd given him the masks."

"A potlatch," Eldon said.

Charley nodded. "Jason liked to play at upping the ante, like he had some big game he was trying to win. Long's you evened things off somehow, you were okay. But Jason warn't the kind of man I'd try to *top*. That could get dangerous."

"Maybe topping somebody is how he got killed," Eldon said.

"That's not bad thinkin', for a cheechako," Charley said.

"Well, what about yourselves?" Eldon asked, deciding to be bold. "How'd you get out here?"

Nell broke into a grin. "You mean, why are we dressed like this? Why don't we wear 'normal' clothes?"

"Well—ah—"

"These *are* our normal clothes!" Charley cried. "Never felt so normal as when we started wearin' them."

"So there was a beginning—?"

"If history has a beginning," Nell said. "You've heard of re-enactors?"

"Sure. They put on 'living history' exhibits, dress up and pretend it's some pioneer year."

"That's what we are," Charley declared.

"Uh, don't you need an audience?"

"We're not pretending!" said Charley, and he and Nell laughed merrily. "He's okay, Nelly," Charley said. "He doesn't let people push him around."

"That quality comes in handy in Alaska," Nell told Eldon.

"We're not just historical reenactors," Charley went on. "We're the best reenactors that ever was."

"Oh, Charley," Nell said. "You know you just got into it because you can't grow a decent beard."

"Didn't need one when I was an insurance agent!" Charley retorted. He and Nell laughed with real affection.

Eldon got the whole story as they ate. It came out in pieces, a tall tale filtered guilelessly through the fantasy—or was it the commitment?—that Charley and Nell were living.

Charley and Nell were soul mates from Minneapolis, he an insurance agent, she a registered nurse. They had stumbled upon one another at a living-history encampment outside St. Cloud, Minnesota. (" 'Charley,' she told me, 'you should wear a false beard.' ") They had paired up at once.

"After that, the workaday world seemed mighty tame," Charley said. "And it didn't even seem normal."

"I *still* don't see why they wouldn't let you wear your beard to work!" Nell burst out. "Your boss wore a toupee."

"Or why they wouldn't let you wear your purty Indian dress at the hospital," Charley replied. "Well, Eldon—I guess you can figure out that it eventually ended our careers. . . . And guess what? We didn't care."

"We took to the road," Nell said. "Living-history identities are a great way to hitch rides. Though we soon realized that traveling in cars wasn't for us."

"None of this *modern* stuff is for us," Charley said. "Pioneer pursuits is our style. Varmint trapping in Montana. Ridin' fence in Alberta. Sheep herding in Wyoming. Like our forefathers. Nothin' odd about it. Made ends meet."

"The past was a pure time," Nell said. "So why shouldn't the past be present? The Indian legends don't make much distinction between past and present, you know."

"We had to find somewhere that was still pure," Charley said. "They don't call Alaska the Last Frontier for nothin'."

"And so here you are," Eldon said.

"So here we are," Charley and Nell chorused.

Two more oddballs in Southeast, Eldon thought, camped on the edge of the world. He liked them.

Charley and Nell treated their old real-world identities as if those were the roles and their pioneer dress and this cabin the reality. Well, it *is* the reality now, Eldon thought.

"It's delicious stew," he said.

"It's nice to see a new face now and again," Nell said, "a friendly one."

"What about those totem poles?" Eldon asked as cheerfully as he could.

"Take ya there right now," Charley said.

Charley rose from the table and headed out the door, Eldon hurrying after. Charley made good time through the trees, and Eldon had to hustle to keep up.

They climbed over rocks and then went down into the trees again. There were no paths and the ground was soggy from the previous day's rain. At last, Charley held up a hand: "Here."

They stepped out into a clearing along a beach. Here stood totem poles so split and weathered that Eldon could hardly tell what they depicted. Other poles had fallen. The place clearly had been deserted for decades.

"Don't touch nothin'," Charley whispered. "Bad luck."

"Okay." Eldon stepped forward and something crunched under his feet. He looked down and yelped—it was a human femur, gray with age. Next to it was a row of human skulls.

"What the hell—?"

"Injun burial ground," Charley said. "Don't touch nothin', I said."

"I won't, I won't. Where's Jason's totem?"

"This way." They worked their way along the edge of the beach, Eldon keeping his eye on his feet every step of the way. They went into the trees and emerged into another clearing, and there it was.

The totem pole was magnificent—and not what Eldon had expected. It was T-shaped, an upright more than ten feet tall supporting a cross beam. Leaping over the beam were salmon, exquisitely detailed, and sitting at the cross was long-beaked Raven.

"Ridicule pole," Charley said.

"Who was he making fun of? Why'd he put it out here?"

"Jason wouldn't say. I reckon it refers to that fishing boat of his."

"How?"

"I think it has to do with that time up in the gulf when they lost that man. You know about that?"

"Mark Frame," Eldon said.

"Guess that was his name. Never met him."

"What's that got to do with the pole?"

"The man's *dead.* This is a *graveyard.* Ya git it now?"

"Oh. Like laughing in a graveyard, yeah. But at who?"

"See how the fish are all lined up? Pre-cise like? Now, there's only one feller in all Southeast who lines up fish that way."

"Max Renner. Of course—his store."

"Got fish stacked in there neater 'n a spinster's pincushions," Charley said. "And he's not a nice man—squeezed our credit many a winter. I'd say the Raven refers to Jason; that's his totem critter."

"Raven's laughing at something."

"Or maybe the joke's on *him.*"

"On Raven?" Eldon's mind was working. Baer blamed Max for their comrade's death and had insulted him with this pole. Renner finally had murdered Jason for revenge. Or to cover up something that they both knew. . . .

"How long's it been here?"

"Maybe three years."

"Anyone else come here?"

"Naw. Not too many folks know about the place, like I said. Not even Injuns come out here much."

"Jason put it up himself?"

"Nell and me helped him. That's how we know about it."

"I'm gonna take some pictures, okay?"

"Okay—long's you don't take a pi'ture of *me.*"

Eldon shot photos of the pole from all angles and then shot close-ups of the figures. "You gonna put this in the paper?" Charley asked nervously.

Eldon ignored him. He examined the figures on the pole's upright. They were familiar—then he recognized them: he'd seen some of the same patterns in drawings in Jason's studio.

Here was the face of the woman with hair like waves . . . here was a curious lightning pattern that Eldon had never seen on another totem pole—at least not a traditional one . . . here was a gaping, long-faced white man gripping a horseshoe over his chest. Eldon examined the carving. Little things might become big things in the long Alaska winters, but he could not imagine someone as self-absorbed as Max Renner caring about a totem pole standing in a remote Alaskan graveyard. Certainly not killing someone over it. He'd be in his store maniacally lining up nails, not visiting far-flung islands. Yet there remained the magnetized nail that Cassandra had found.

"Did Jason tell you what this pole's about?"

"No . . . got some guesses, I suppose."

"Such as?"

"Jes' as soon not guess, if it's all the same to ya."

Eldon tried another tack. "Did Jason ever come back to the totem pole? Or did anyone else come to look?"

Charley let his breath out softly. Eldon sensed he'd come to a decision. "A boat come around here not long ago."

"A boat."

"A troller. We saw her creeping up the channel at night, lights out, engine cut way back. Real late—it was dark. Figured at first that it was a poacher—bear, deer, whatever. Steered clear of 'em. Local folks add to their larders whether it's huntin' season or no, and I don't like botherin' strangers with guns when they don't bother me.

"But we never heard any shots. Not a poacher. Unless it's someone doin' some shady fishin', I thought. Finally I crept out here for a look, found the strangest thing . . ."

"What's that?"

"Boat was standing just offshore—*there*—shinin' a spotlight on the totem pole."

"Totem pole rustlers?" Eldon asked. "That thing's worth money—it's an original work by Jason Baer."

"Nope, just shinin' the light. Like they was just lookin' at it."

"No one came ashore?"

"Nope."

"Who was on the boat?"

"Couldn't see. The spot was in my eyes."

"Name? Registry numbers?"

Charley shook his head. "Couldn't see 'em. Might've been covered up."

"Would you recognize the boat again?"

Charley shrugged. "Looked like a lot o' boats."

"Did you tell anyone about this?"

"Why? They wasn't doin' anything *wrong.* They warn't trespassin', and spotlightin' totem poles ain't illegal. It's not like spotlightin' game."

"Did they stay long?"

"Not long. Just drifted past."

Max's boat, Eldon thought. Who'd be the wiser if he sailed it here? It was easy to imagine Renner, drinking and brooding, examining the ridicule pole and coming to the decision to eradicate its creator.

He glanced at Charley. There's something he's not telling me, he thought, but I don't know how to prod him. Maybe another time. "Let's go back."

"Seen enough?"

"For now. I might come back and see you again."

"Yer welcome if ya do. Enjoy yer company. Yer an edjacated man."

"I was never here in the first place, though. Best stew I never ate." Eldon chuckled.

Charley winked. "Gotcha."

"One thing—you don't like visitors."

"Got that right."

"You're friendly enough to me."

"Tarnation, you come in straight on, blowin' yer horn, like some kinda cruise liner. A lone cheechako I can always handle." And Charley patted the pistol in his waistband, grinning as he fixed Eldon with a gray aluminum stare.

11

Charley and Nell waved good-bye to Eldon as he drove into the water. They were a picturesque sight, like something in a nineteenth-century gold rush photograph. No, Eldon thought, like something on a lobby card in a 1940s movie theater.

Beside him on the Amphicar's front seat were gifts—three small bowls for Anita, Cassandra, and Eldon. Eldon in return had given Charley and Nell several choice fishing flies from the collection studding his hat. Fishermen prized flies from other regions. He could always tie more, and the gift was suitably modest. Just a few days in Alaska had taught him that casually topping someone in a potlatch wasn't prudent.

The longer he poked at it, the clearer it was becoming—Max Renner was Jason's killer, motivated by greed and the bizarre potlatch ideology that seemed to grip the wilds of Southeast Alaska. Twisted, mutated, it incubated in the Panhandle's rain, growing for at least a few into resentment, a game of one-upmanship swollen out of all proper proportion in the long lightless winters and the long summers under the white sky.

But that couldn't be all of it, Eldon knew. Life in Southeast Alaska was not a continuous potlatch. Panhandle dwellers might abide on the edge but they lived usual lives. They had jobs, families, aspirations, debts. . . .

Debt. Eldon could smell it in the way Max drank and in the way he coveted everything in his store. Proving his theory hinged on George Atkov. If George came through, Eldon would have his scoop, Mike Atkov would have his arrest, Ed Katlean would bless Eldon's fishing, and Anita would fall into his arms. Maybe Maggie would, too.

But now it was time to do what he'd come to Alaska to do.

Eldon aimed the Amphicar straight down the channel and lashed the wheel with a short length of rope. He assembled his fishing rod, attached a fly, and baited it with salmon eggs from a jar he'd brought along. He worked the soft red spheres onto the lure's hooks and began casting to the sides and stern.

The sky was so wide and the air so clear that it was like launching the fly into outer space. Eldon started on the driver's side and worked his way around, casting on target each time. He let out plenty of line, trailing the lure in the water before he reeled it in.

The strike was sudden when it came. Eldon had just cast off

the passenger side. The king hit just as the lure touched the water. The rod bowed as if dragging an anchor. The fish jumped and Eldon caught his breath—a huge arching silver column that twisted in the air and plunged back into the water. Eldon let out some line. The fish was much larger than the king he had taken on his first morning here. How was he going to land it? The salmon whirled into the air again, fell back, and cut across the Amphicar's wake, curving back toward the stern.

Eldon checked his course. He could see Klinkatshut ahead, mirrored in the water. Faint plumes of blue chimney smoke drifted in the air like gauzy curtains. A few human figures moved among the houses and along the dock. Eldon saw a huge white shape on the beach before the clan house. Woody.

A small figure walked beside the great dog. Cassandra. Eldon hit the Amphicar's horn with his elbow, keeping a death grip on the fishing rod. Girl and dog hopped and waved. Woody's barks drifted out over the water, thunderous even at this range. Cassandra sprinted up the beach, followed by Woody, doubtless to tell Anita of Eldon's return.

Eldon sailed along the line of the beach to the dock. Maggie was on the dock—there was no mistaking the blowing blond hair. Eldon sounded the horn. "Big fish!" he yelled. "Help!"

Maggie ran down onto the gravel beach next to the pier. Eldon cut the props and let the car's momentum drive him onto shore. Maggie vaulted into a sitting position on the car's hood. "Eldon." She leaned over the windshield, grabbed Eldon's face in both hands, and gave him a long, deep kiss.

Welcome back, Eldon thought, bent halfway over the windshield and still clutching the fishing rod, which bounced and flexed with the king's struggles. He knew he was being publicly claimed. Maggie's hair fell around his face, and for a moment Eldon was transported into an ethereal realm where—

"Eldon!" It was Anita.

Eldon pulled free to see Anita glaring over Maggie's shoulder. She was stone-cold sober, too—he could tell by the angry sparkle in her eyes. They were focused for cutting, like industrial diamonds. "Uh, hi!" Eldon said. "I've caught a really big fish—"

"Maggie! You—you . . . I ought to kick you out, Eldon—"

"I'll take him if you throw him out!" Maggie said with a laugh.

"The hell you will, Maggie Frame! He's got copy to turn for me and he's going to do it, too, if I have to stand over him at the typewriter. He won't get a damn thing done at your digs except, except—"

Eldon's face heated with shame. At least Cassandra wasn't around. He started reeling in the salmon. "I've got to have some help with this fish!" Anita and Maggie turned their eyes upon him. Now I'm going to die, he thought. "Does anyone have a net or a club?"

Onlookers began to gather, lounging on the pier, leaning on totem poles or pausing as they lugged big plastic buckets of fish. There was even someone watching from the water—Kate Taylor, grinning from her two-seater kayak.

Eldon reeled the salmon in past the kayak. Kate paddled after the fish toward shore. Suddenly, Anita tripped Maggie and threw her flat on her back on the gravel. Maggie broke her fall expertly and kicked. Anita fell and half-rolled away, then scooted back at Maggie on her elbows. Eldon watched, astonished, as they twined legs and began to leg wrestle, growling and struggling as each sought to flip the other.

Anita and Maggie rotated crabwise, legs locked, calves tensed, grimacing. This is . . . splendid, Eldon thought. For the first time in his life, two women were fighting over *him*. He wanted to grab his camera and record the battle, but he had his hands full trying to land the salmon.

Kate ran her kayak ashore and stepped out. "Pay attention to business, Eldon!"

Eldon reeled the salmon in. It was almost five feet long, he saw, as it jumped and struggled on the beach. Kate brained the fish with her oar.

"That's a fifty-pounder at least," a man said in Eldon's ear as he climbed from the Amphicar. It was Chief Katlean. "And you've got those two right where you want 'em. You'll make a sourdough yet." Katlean pronounced it "shower-dough."

Maggie flipped Anita. Anita snarled and grappled again. Maggie somersaulted. The two women sat up and regarded one another, breathing heavily and brushing hair from their eyes. Eldon started forward, but Katlean clamped a hand on his shoulder.

"I'd let 'em have it out," the chief said. "My money's on Anita."

Eldon grabbed the salmon under the gills and hoisted it, staggering across the beach to throw it across the Amphicar's hood. The chief grabbed Eldon's hat and sailed it to the ground between Anita and Maggie. "He's a fisherman," Katlean said. "Settle it fishing."

Anita reached for the hat but Maggie got it first. "Deep-sea fishing." She twirled the hat on a finger. "I've got the boat."

Anita and Maggie looked about to go at each other again.

"That fish is nothing," Maggie said. "Wait'll I take you out on my boat."

Anita grinned wolfishly. "Come home and I'll cook it for you."

"I cook better," Maggie said.

"Come to dinner," Anita told her poisonously. "You can make the salad."

"I won't let him out of my sight," Maggie retorted.

Katlean patted Eldon's shoulder. "Nice going. I'll want a report. Stop in tomorrow—if you can still walk."

"I want to give half this fish to Kate," Eldon said.

"Good man."

"But will she eat it?"

"Old Kate falls off the veggie wagon every now and then."

"Thanks. Your chariot awaits, ladies," Eldon said. "And gimme my hat." He snatched the hat from Maggie's finger and stuck it firmly on his head.

Anita and Maggie brushed themselves off and climbed into the Amphicar. Once Eldon got the car under way, they started laughing with weird delight.

"They'll talk about that for weeks!" Anita said.

"Shocking conduct of a leading editor!" Maggie said.

"Gigolo scandal!" Anita said.

"Just a minute," Eldon said. "I'm earning my keep!"

"More than you can say about a lot of the men around here!" Maggie said, and she and Anita roared with laughter.

Well, it's better than being punched in the mouth, Eldon thought as they drove past the houses where the fighting still went on.

"I'm cooking tonight," Eldon said. "You two don't have to raise a finger. I'm doing Gourmet Seduction Dinner Number Three."

"Ooooh," Maggie said.

"What's that?" Anita asked.

"You'll see," Eldon said. In fact, he had no idea what it was, but with a fresh fish like the one he had to hand, how could he go wrong?

"Cassandra told me about the nail," Anita said. "What did you find out in Sitka?"

"After dinner," Eldon said.

At Anita's house, Eldon cleaned the fish, cut off some steaks for broiling, put the salmon's lower half in the refrigerator for Kate Taylor. He prowled through Anita's larder and whipped up a baste of melted butter, Worcestershire sauce, and grated onion. He prepared a cucumber salad and heated a loaf of sourdough bread. Anita had no wine on hand—a pity! Eldon thought—but there was, of course, bourbon. On impulse, he drizzled bourbon over the sizzling fish. Shortly they were toasting one another over what the chef had to admit was one of his best improvised dinners.

"This is amazing," Anita said.

"It's nothing, really," Eldon said.

Maggie took a bite of salmon. "Is that what you found out in Sitka? Nothing?"

"Hardly." Eldon glanced at Anita. "I might as well tell you both about it—Maggie was there when Cassandra found the nail."

Eldon described his meeting with George and Mike Atkov. "I'm waiting for George to get back to me on the record search. You were Jason's agent, Anita. You told me business was off."

"You can only raise so many totem poles so fast."

"Was Jason in debt?"

"I was his agent, not his banker," Anita said. "The money was going somewhere—but I'd have known if he owed someone really big."

"He didn't say where?"

"Wouldn't say where."

"Drugs?"

"Come on."

"He had commissions down in Oregon—"

"Cash flow, Eldon, cash flow. That money was down the road. Haven't you ever spent the week counting off the days to your paycheck?"

"Every week," Eldon said. "But Jason owned a plane. Had a house. He was working on a masterpiece—"

"Owning a plane up here's like owning a car or a boat," Anita said. "Jason needed it for business, so he had one. Overhead. Like my commissions."

"So maybe it was the overhead that got him," Eldon said. "What do logs for totem poles cost?"

"They didn't cost Jason anything," Anita said. "He used to pick them out himself, in the forest."

"He must've been into someone for money," Eldon said. "Like you said, it was going somewhere."

"Then why would they kill him?" Anita asked. "They wouldn't be able to collect."

"There's the nail," Maggie said. "Max."

"The store," Eldon said. "Jason may have been leaning on Max for dough, cutting into the store's margin."

"He'd know better than to sink the store, then," Anita said.

"That depends, doesn't it?" Maggie said.

"Dammit, Maggie, Jason was a canny guy," Anita said. "If Jason needed money, he wasn't going to kill the golden goose."

"Wouldn't he?" Maggie asked.

She didn't like Jason, either, Eldon thought. She said she admired his work, but that's different from liking somebody. Nobody really liked Jason. And if someone I didn't like kept tapping me for money, and it kept pushing my head under, kept endangering something I loved and controlled—like a store—and the winters were long and dark enough, I might—

Control was Max's whole reason for being, Eldon thought, and he was in complete control within the narrow confines of his store. He even stacked the nails in there. "Can you see Max arguing with Jason? Or trying to slug it out?"

"No, of course not," Maggie said.

"Well, maybe they did argue. In fact, they probably did. Max gets the worst of it, maybe even gets pushed around a little. So Max doesn't confront Jason again. He gets a rifle and guns him down, from a safe distance."

"How would he know when to ambush him?" Maggie asked.

"Jason worked outside a lot in the good weather," Anita said. "Everybody knew that."

"Max picked a night when he knew Maggie was at the Button Club," Eldon said. "It was perfect."

"Jesus, he might've shot me, too—" Maggie said.

"No," Eldon said. "He had to keep things under control."

"Except for the nail," Anita said. "Why was he walking around with it in his pocket?"

"He'll never admit any of this," Maggie said. "He'll say he was framed."

"Then we don't have a story yet, do we?" Anita asked.

"Not yet." Eldon said. "But if George turns up a paper trail—"

"Then we'll have him!" Anita said. "How a wanton killer robbed the heritage of a free Alaska—"

"Save that for the editorial page," Eldon said. "We don't have anything until we have an arrest. And Mike Atkov's moving in."

12

Dinner was a triumph—if triumph included Maggie and Anita eyeing each other as they chewed and Cassandra chomping happily, speculating with elaborate nonchalance on the Baer murder case. Cassandra had been chatting with Fiske on the telex—why doesn't her mother lock the office? Eldon wondered desperately—about journalism's grislier aspects. Jimbo was recounting some of the most gruesome news stories of his Methuselan career—the blowtorch murder, the last scalping in Oregon (Klamath Falls, 1954), the pyromaniac boy and his homemade bomb gone awry, and murder by elephant. Cassandra repeated these tales at the dinner table with a nine-year-old's dreadful relish.

Eldon, chilled at first, realized that Cassandra was dealing with the horror of Jason's death in the same way as he. She might've started dissociating when her father beat up on Anita, he thought, or maybe when they got divorced.

Eldon wondered how young he himself had been when he had discovered the protective tactic of distancing himself under pressure. Maybe the time when Billy Vogel punched out his front teeth in grade school; he wore caps and knew that if he ever covered Billy's murder, he would write it up as a humor feature.

Eldon had first been really aware of dissociating as a teenager, when he had largely tuned out the idiotic culture of high school in favor of fishing and books. Girls, of course, he had yearned after, with little success. He wasn't plugged into the letter-sweater scene, he just wasn't suave enough. . . . Now he had two women sparring for his favors. It makes me feel like a piece of beef, he thought. It feels good.

Eldon's and Anita's fingertips touched as he collected the dinner plates. He felt sparks. He felt more sparks when he collected Maggie's plate. Cassandra snickered. Did the kid suspect? Cassandra could hardly control herself. At last she succumbed to gales of childish laughter, and Anita ushered her off to bed.

As soon as Anita and Cassandra had left the room, Maggie stepped up to Eldon and kissed him. "I can't wait to get you off into the woods."

"I thought we were going fishing."

"That salmon tonight was tremendous. If you can catch a fish like that, trolling off the back of an Amphicar, wait until you see what you can catch from my boat."

Anita returned. "Hope you're behaving yourself, Maggie."

"I was just complimenting Eldon's cooking. Most men around here won't lift a finger in the kitchen."

"How many Gourmet Seduction Dinners do you know, Eldon?" Anita asked.

"Oh, dozens," Eldon said. "It all depends on the ingredients on hand—blonde, brunette, redhead—"

"Well, you've got a blonde and a brunette," Maggie said and kissed Eldon.

Anita pushed Maggie aside and kissed Eldon, too. Eldon slid one arm around Anita and reached for Maggie. Anita said, "Yes, it was a very good dinner. I'm throwing you out now, Maggie."

"Gonna work off a few calories?" Maggie asked.

"Sure are—down in the office. Got stories to write and edit and layouts to do. There's still an outdoors tab to get out."

Maggie regarded her. "She's not kidding, Eldon."

"Well, the news comes first," Eldon said.

"Keep an eye on her."

"Oh, I will. I'll keep an eye on you, too."

Maggie grinned and blew him another kiss. "I know you will. Bye."

"Hussy," Anita said after Maggie had left. "And with my daughter in the house, too. You're a pig."

Eldon had never heard anyone actually use the word *hussy* before. "What'd you want me to do? Knock her down? You invited her to dinner."

"You are one slick operator, Eldon." Anita's eyes were shining. "You come on like a lost kid, but you've got a girl in every port."

"Well, hardly—"

"You've got that lawyer in Oregon, and there's me and there's Maggie and your Gourmet Seduction Dinners—" Anita was clearly warmed with bourbon—and by what she perceived as Eldon's sexual and culinary enterprise. Her eyes and voice took on that feral quality once more.

I'd better change the subject before I'm a pig again, Eldon thought. "I was late getting back from Sitka because I stopped along the way."

"Got yourself an Indian gal out there in the forest?"

"You don't know the half of it," Eldon said. "Have you got an inventory of Jason's totem poles?"

"I have a list of all the works he sold. Why?"

"Let me see it."

Downstairs in the office, Anita got a fat manila folder from a file cabinet. Eldon opened it and ran his finger down the list—several pages of totem poles, masks, ornate boxes, and other art objects that Jason had created over the years. He had been prolific. The totem poles were described by size, imagery, and location, and there were photographs of many of them. There was nothing on the list like the totem pole that Chilkat Charley had shown Eldon.

"Is this everything Jason made?" Eldon asked.

"Probably not. But if it's not listed, it wasn't sold."

"There's one of Jason's totems on an island not far from here that's not on this list. Do you know about it?"

"No. Where is it? That thing's valuable."

"A couple of crazy sourdoughs showed me on the way back from Sitka. I don't think they'd let you take it away."

"You're sure it's Jason's work?"

"He brought it there and put it up," Eldon said. "An unusual piece—a crossbar with leaping salmon, laughing Raven on top."

"It doesn't ring a bell. I want to see it."

"I took pictures—"

"Gimme the camera." Anita took the Rolleiflex and headed

for the darkroom. Eldon started to follow her in, but she stopped him with a hand on his chest. "You'll joggle my elbow." She was all business now.

Eldon paced the floor while Anita developed the film. At last, she opened the darkroom door and called him in. "Take a look."

Anita was examining the strip of big, square negatives through a hand magnifying glass as it hung drying from a nylon line stretched across the darkroom. "It's Jason's work, all right. A ridicule pole, by the looks of it."

"That's what they told me. But how can you tell?"

"Well, by its . . . wit, I guess you'd say. This is a very witty piece."

"That's what they said about Warhol's three beer cans in a row."

"Same difference," Anita said. "Crosspiece-style totems aren't unknown. This one's a parody of a ridicule pole at Wrangell, the Three Frogs totem—a crosspiece with three frogs on it. It's quite well known."

"What's the Three Frogs totem make fun of?"

"A chief of the Shakes clan erected it to shame the Kiksadi clan. He said they didn't pay the upkeep of three Kiksadi women who married three of the chief's slaves."

"I don't get the joke."

"Frog is the Kiksadi crest."

"Did they pay?"

"Opinions differ."

Eldon studied the negatives. "This is valuable, right?"

"Jason Baer carved it."

"And Jason's totem subjects were frequently things that were on his mind, as we know."

"Yeah—"

"Then it just might be a reference to money troubles, if you think of Jason as the slave and the salmon as referring to Max's fishing boat."

Anita nodded. "Those 'crazy sourdoughs' showed it to you?"

"Mike Atkov steered me onto 'em."

"Is Mike going to . . . arrest Max?"

"I think so. But not yet. I persuaded him to let me line up my ducks before he does."

"Eldon, this is gonna be *good copy!* I'm proud of you!" Anita hugged him, then broke off. "Just a minute—what's the totem pole doing out there?"

"There's more," Eldon said. "There's a boat that comes in there now and again at night, and whoever's aboard spotlights that totem and broods on it."

"What boat?"

"A troller. That's all they know."

"A troller," Anita said. "Max still owns a piece of that troller."

"Maggie works it now, mostly, doesn't she?"

"Sure. But Max still owns a piece, still takes it out."

"We'll have to ask around about the boat's comings and goings."

"Eldon, I just thought of something!"

"What's that?"

"Max might *own* that totem pole."

"What? How?"

"He and Jason were business partners. If Jason's estate is in debt—then artwork might have to go to pay off debts. He'd have a claim. And revenge."

Eldon nodded. "Max *wants* the pole, simply to sell. Doesn't care if it makes fun of him or not."

"Dammit—this isn't solid, is it?"

"No. Gonna need a paper trail. That's what I've got a source in Sitka working on. Mike Atkov's brother, George. The 'bartender' you were worried about. He's a well-connected guy."

"You work fast, Eldon." Anita slid her hand along Eldon's shoulder and gently gripped the side of his neck. "Now—what's between you and my friend Maggie?"

"Nothing."

"Nothing?" Anita squeezed harder.

"Ow! Honest. Well, a couple of smooches. But you got to me first."

"Gonna stay first, too, buddy." Anita kissed Eldon long and lasciviously. Then the telex exploded into activity. Anita leaped up. "That damned machine will wake the dead—"

They went to the telex and watched the message type out:

> ELDON
> WHERE IS STORY
> GOUT ACTING UP HURRY WITH SALMON
> FISKE

Eldon typed a reply:

> JIMBO
> KEEP WATCHING THE WIRE
> GONE FISHING
> ELDON

"You're quick, Larkin," Anita said. "I like that. Let's see just how quick. Into the bedroom."

Eldon forced himself not to run for the bedroom. He gathered Anita into his arms and began humming the "Blue Danube" waltz. They danced awkwardly into the bedroom, where the humming stopped and the grappling began. The first thing Eldon found he had to undo was Anita's shoulder holster. It was under her bulky pullover. It was somewhat more complicated than a bra, but Anita slipped smoothly out of the rig. She placed the gun and holster on the floor and pushed them under the bed. "Now I'm unarmed."

"Why do you wear that damn thing at home?" Eldon asked as they dropped onto the bed.

"Might meet a bear." Anita rolled atop Eldon and showered him with kisses.

Eldon pulled her shirt off over her head. Anita wasn't wearing a bra and didn't need one.

Eldon fought to hang onto his concentration as he helped Anita out of her clothes. Something important was forming at the edge of his mind, and he didn't want to lose the thought. He kept grasping the threads of the concept and trying to pull them together. But he lost his train of thought completely when Anita yanked open his shirt, popping off several buttons that made little spattering noises as they bounced on the floor. "I'll sew 'em back on." Anita attacked Eldon's belt.

Afterward, Eldon drifted deliciously and finally recovered the germ of his idea. "About that Indian girl in the woods—"

Anita lifted her head from Eldon's chest. "So there was one!"

"If you like 'em six feet tall." He told the story of Charley and Nell. "They said they helped Jason put up the totem pole about three years ago. Can you remember anything important back then that happened between Jason and Max?"

"Three years ago? No—unless you mean that was when Jason started paying other people to ship the poles."

"Why?"

"He stopped delivering them himself after they lost Mark Frame overboard in the Gulf of Alaska. He never said anything about it. He just—"

"Jason and Max never fought?"

"Hand to hand, you mean? No. Kind of funny that they didn't. Jason was always practicing with this punching bag, but it was just swagger."

"The punching bag at his house? I saw it. Go on."

"I told him to stop, he might damage his hands. Anyway, it made me uneasy. But he just laughed."

"And?"

"He used to make these drawings of people he was mad at and fasten them to the bag and hammer them until they were shredded. It was kind of a hobby of his."

"Drawings of whom?"

"Of all sorts of people. There was a really good one of Ed, I remember. And—Max."

"When?"

"Right after Mark was . . . oh, no."

"Let's have another look at those negatives."

"I'll get them." Anita swung off the bed and padded out into the office. Eldon enjoyed watching her go.

He switched on the reading light when Anita returned with the negatives and the magnifying glass. "Take a look at the designs on the upright," he said as she slipped back under the covers and snuggled up. "Do any of them look familiar?"

Anita peered. "That one looks like Max."

"They could be anyone."

"Eldon, he had a drawing of this design up on the punching bag one day. I remember."

"One more bit of circumstance. It's still not evidence. We have to wait for George to call from Sitka."

Anita was silent. Eldon slowly stroked her thigh.

"This is awful," Anita said at last. "We're about to pin someone for murder—while I'm here naked in bed with you—"

"Ain't journalism a great profession?"

"I feel as if we're holding an inappropriate celebration."

"Think of it as a wake. Jason would be pleased."

"He probably would be. He'd think it was funny. He was jealous of you, you know."

"What?"

"After you turned in that night in Ketchikan, I called Jason's hotel, just to make sure he wasn't lying in an alley somewhere."

"What'd he say?"

" 'Lucky white boy.' "

"Nasty son of a bitch."

"He always thought of white men as richer and luckier than him. He thought they would be remembered and he wouldn't be."

"That's stupid."

"He figured they had more money than they knew what to do with if they were buying his art, stuff they didn't even understand." Anita's eyes suddenly flooded with tears.

Eldon gathered her into his arms. "It's okay. I've been callous about all this."

"No, you've been very strong," Anita said. "I don't know which is worse—that Jason was murdered or that it was Max that did it."

"Why don't we try to get some sleep?" Eldon said, stroking Anita's hair.

"I don't guess George Atkov is going to call at this hour."

"I sure hope not," Eldon said.

"So we have some time on our hands." Anita wiped her eyes and turned to him. "George is not gonna save you tonight. No sirree."

13

The telephone ringing in the office awoke Eldon the next morning. He knew it must be late. Anita had slipped back to her own bedroom in the early hours. Eldon's muscles were sore and his knees felt rubbery when he staggered up from bed toward the office, remembered that he was naked, and staggered back to the bed to yank on his pants.

He heard Cassandra's thunderous plunge down the stairs. The ringing stopped: "This is the *Aurora,* the journal of a free Alaska. News or advertising? . . . *Eldon! It's for you!"*

"Okay . . . okay. Just a minute—"

"How d'you say that in French?"

Eldon lurched into the office. "Gimme the phone, *s'il vous plaît.*"

"Say 'please.' "

"I just did." Eldon grabbed the phone. "Eldon Larkin."

"Stop the presses, Eldon—this is George Atkov. I think I've found what you need."

"Great! What've you got?"

"Well, I started out by having my friend at the title company check out Max Renner's store. Max owned the building and took out a couple of extra mortgages. Jason Baer held one of 'em."

"He was a partner in the store," Eldon said.

"So far, so good," George agreed. "Next step—where'd Jason get the money to invest in the store?"

"From selling totem poles."

"Right," George said. "But that made me wonder if there were liens against Jason's business. I checked to see if Jason was incorporated, and so he was. Then we looked for liens against his company—and there were some." George rattled off the names of several lending institutions. "Some of these are years old, so he must've taken them out when he was getting established. There also was a mortgage on Jason's house."

"Go on."

"I said that the liens were old," George continued. "They'd been refinanced, in fact. And this guy was supposed to be a successful artist, one of the hottest in his field. But Jason wasn't as flush as he wanted people to think."

"Keep talking."

"Loans mean you're in debt."

"He was in a slump on the art market."

"I kept checking," George said. "Next stop was personal property records. Such as boats. Jason was part owner of a troller, with Max Renner and a man named Mark Frame."

"I know that, too. Frame's dead."

"He is? That's interesting. I was able to tie one of those liens to the boat. It was a personal loan but effectively a lien against Jason's share of the vessel; he used the boat as collateral. The boat's not a corporation. So his partners wouldn't necessarily know."

"Jason was skimming the profits from the boat," Eldon said.

"That's how it looks," George said.

"Max Renner told me Jason was leaning on him for money," Eldon said. "He always took his cut from the store, even when he should've been sinking it back in."

"Jason was pushing the store under to shore up the boat and was using the boat to shore up something else."

"And Renner found out," Eldon said.

"Probably the same way I did," George said. "These are public records."

"Yeah. Max has that clerkish bent and he'd kill to save that store."

"So that's all there is to it." It was a statement, not a question.

"That's often all there is to it," Eldon said.

"I know, Eldon, I know. Merciful God."

"This is great work, George. You may have missed your calling at that."

"I know."

"Have you told Mike?"

"Thought I'd let you know first."

"Thanks. And listen, George—when you write your *Confidential Detective* article, you can rely on me. Quotes, photos, whatever you need."

"I may hit you up for an interview and some pictures," George said. "They'd pay pretty good for that."

They agreed that George would mail copies of the records to the *Aurora* by special delivery. Mike will be out here with handcuffs sooner than you can whistle up a sled dog, Eldon thought as he hung up the phone. I've got to get cranking. "Anita!"

She came downstairs. "Yes?"

"Let's publish an extra."

"D'you know what that'd cost?"

"Spoken like a true publisher. But this is worth it."

"Why?" Cassandra wanted to know.

"Do you remember how to say 'fly-fishing' in French?" Eldon asked her.

"This is about Jason, isn't it?" Cassandra said.

"Say 'fly-fishing' in French."

"Pêche à la mouche."

"Very good. I think you should go outside and practice your fly-fishing. *Maintenant, allez dehors et mettez en pratique votre pêche à la mouche.* Your mother and I are about to get very busy."

Cassandra considered it, glancing from Eldon to Anita. "Okay." Her eyes held that Fiske-like glitter. She got her fishing rod from the corner and looked back as she opened the door. "You're a busy pair anyway!"

"What's that supposed to mean, young lady?" Anita demanded as the door slammed. She gave a rueful chuckle. "You're very good with her."

Eldon shook his head. "We have to be discreet. I don't mean about us. I mean about this story." He told Anita what he had learned from George. "We should be ready to hit the streets with a special edition when there's an arrest."

"Now it's obvious that Max did it, isn't it?"

"Well, that's up to a judge, but with the financial connections and the nail from the store, I think Max has some explaining to do."

Anita reflected for a few moments. "Max Renner . . . one of my own neighbors. But Jason was my neighbor, too." She gave a wan smile. "This is *good copy.*"

"That's the way to think!" Eldon said, adding to himself: You go crazy in this business if you don't.

"Wouldn't it be something if we could get Max to admit it?"

"Here's what we do," Eldon said. "Set up an extra with a big hole on the front page. I'll write a story detailing Jason's financial problems and his links with Max. We'll top it with the arrest and roll the presses."

"I like it—I think. Suppose there's no arrest?"

"Nothing's lost," Eldon said. "That becomes the front page of your next regular edition. And I convert the story into one about Jason's financial problems when he was murdered."

"Eldon, how'd you like to stick around and become editor of a newspaper? You play this game better than I ever will."

"No time to talk about that now," Eldon said brusquely. "I've got to turn some copy."

By Eldon Larkin
Special to the *Aurora*

SITKA—Leading Alaska totem pole carver Jason Baer had money troubles when he was murdered at his Klinkatshut home.

Baer had borrowed heavily against his already mortgaged house and against a fishing boat in which he was a partner, according to property records in Sitka and Juneau.

State police refused to comment on possible links between Baer's debts and his murder. But Baer's sales agent, Anita Povey, confirmed that demand for the artist's work was in a slump. Povey is publisher of the *Aurora*.

Max Renner, who owned a store in Klinkatshut in partnership with Baer, said the artist had dunned him for money in recent months. . . .

Eldon described the situation as fully as he was able on the basis of what George had told him. When the special-delivery packet with the documents arrived from Sitka, he would go back and fill in the gaps.

After he had roughed out the story, Eldon marked "draft" on each page of the copy and put the story away. Then he went downtown to find Chief Katlean.

Katlean sat in his office, wearing his nose ring and tinkering with a dusty television set. Woody lay curled up by the office door next to a metal basin of drinking water. The dog thumped his tail at Eldon and whined.

"What's the matter with him?" Eldon asked.

"He's cold," Katlean said. "Can't you feel the chill in the air?"

"Uh, not really."

"Me, neither," Katlean said. "But Woody's very sensitive to cold. He can always tell. Know what he'd do if I took him to Hawaii?"

"Run and play on the beach."

"Nah, he'd curl up tighter and try to get even warmer. He'd bury himself in hot sand. Now—what've you got for me, Eldon?"

"It's Max."

The chief put down his pliers and said quietly, "Figured."

"Figured? Then why didn't you go to the cops?"

"I didn't have anything but a guess. A chief damn well better not talk that way to cops about his people. Not without evidence. That's where you came in."

"I'm your hit man."

"You're an outsider. You're not on anyone's side but your own."

"I won't frame anybody, you mean."

Katlean shrugged. "If you want to put it that way."

"That's why we're going to wait for the state police before we publish."

"Sure, sure. Expect that you would."

"Well, I don't quite have the evidence yet. It's coming in the mail. Now, why did *you* suspect Max?"

"The tension between Max and Jason was thick enough to cut with a blubber knife," Katlean said. "It got really bad right after I announced the potlatch." The chief smiled slowly. "The pressure was on then. Jason didn't know how to match me."

"Chief, you're a bastard."

Katlean kept smiling. "And why is that?"

"You timed the potlatch. You waited until you knew Jason couldn't match you."

"Right. I saw my chance when the totem pole market slumped. A potlatch starts when you announce it, not when you hold the festivities."

"Did you hope one of 'em would kill the other?"

"No." Katlean's smile faded. "I never figured that. I just wanted to make sure Jason would never make a comeback in tribal politics."

"That nose ring means a lot to you."

"I'm a better chief."

"Now Jason won't be making any kind of comeback at all."

"And too bad, too. He really could carve. That's why I aimed you at this whole mess."

Eldon pulled out the roll of negatives. "These may be a little hard for you to make out—"

"I can read negatives. Picked up the knack back when Anita and I were—well, gimme." Katlean unrolled the negatives and held them up to the light, peered, then pulled on a repairman's headband mounted with a set of jeweler's loupes. He swung one of the lenses down before his eyes and guffawed. "A ridicule pole! Pretty good one, too. Jason's?"

"Yeah. Listen, take a look at the carvings on the upright. Do they mean anything to you?"

Katlean looked. "Damned if I—you know, I've seen these before. The images, I mean, not the pole."

"Where? How?"

"I can't place 'em. But I've seen 'em."

"Have you been over to Jason's studio?"

"We weren't on speaking terms."

"Did you know about his punching bag?"

"Some of his girlfriends, you mean?"

"No, I mean a real punching bag. He used to tape pictures on it and go at 'em—"

e Katlean snorted. "Bet he drew dirty pictures to beat off to, too."

"He might've drawn a picture of you, Chief."

"That's about the only way he'd get a shot at my jaw," Katlean said. "I had the reach on him."

"If we can figure out what the images represent, we may find the killer."

"You said it was Max."

"Yeah—but was it only Max?"

Katlean looked at Eldon and massaged his ringed nose. "Go on."

"Look, Jason was shot with a rifle. Then someone pushed the totem pole he was working on over on top of him. Was it the same someone?"

"Why wouldn't it be?"

"He'd've had to cross water to administer the coup de grâce," Eldon said.

"So?"

"So that's complicated. I keep thinking there was an accomplice. Or someone who tricked Jason out into the yard."

"You make it sound like the town's crawling with killers."

"Might be," Eldon said. "It's certainly crawling with Jason's enemies. Or people who felt uneasy about him."

"They wouldn't kill him just because they felt 'uneasy.' "

"No, but they might cover up."

"Unnnhhh . . . I *really* don't like this now."

"A fishing troller visited the site of that ridicule pole," Eldon said. "I think it's Max's troller. But how many of them are there around here?"

"Several. What's the name of this troller?"

"Don't know. It only puts in at night."

"Who told you this?"

"Crazy old sourdough lives out on the island."

"Charley and Nell?" Katlean laughed. "They *are* crazy!" e

"It doesn't mean they aren't telling the truth," Eldon said.

"Those two've been mixed up for so long they can't tell the smoke from the mirrors."

"How many boats?" Eldon asked stubbornly.

"Several," the chief repeated.

"Then we start asking crewmen questions."

"Not gonna find that many around—it's the season. The biggest sockeye run in the world's about to happen up in Bristol Bay. And anyway, you wouldn't need a crew. One person could handle the boat himself, if he knew what he was doing."

"Or two."

"Yeah, or two. . . . Look, Eldon, how'd you like a knighthood?"

"Do Alaska Indians have knights?"

"Not really. I'll dream something up."

"I just want to go fishing. Why d'you want me to drop this?"

"Isn't it easier to let the state troopers scoop up Max and make him confess?"

"I asked you a question."

"I don't want to rile the village up any more than it already is."

"You want the accomplice to walk, you mean."

"No! I don't want my man to have been the one to finger him, that's all. Looks too much like a purge of the opposition. Nothing's gonna disrupt my potlatch. If the cops do it, that's another thing."

"I'm not your 'man.' "

Katlean held up the negatives. "Let's go over and ask Max what these figures mean."

"Tell him that we know he did it?"

"I'm the chief. He killed one of my people. It's right that I lay the charge before him."

"He'll bolt."

"Where to? He can't fly."

"He could take a boat. He has a rifle—"

"Max got his man," Katlean said. "He doesn't want to kill *us*. He doesn't need to kill anybody ever again."

"Let's wait for the cops anyway."

"I'm going over there, and you're coming with me," Katlean said with a grin. "Know why? Because you want a story. You want to be in on it. That's why you agreed to do this in the first place, didn't just go somewhere else to fish. And of course, there's the beautiful Anita—"

"I hope that doesn't bother you."

"Been doing your homework, I see. No, it doesn't. That's over. I promised my wife. No more good-time girls for me. A chief's gotta walk clean. And it got messy, she being Jason's agent." Katlean's voice turned a little wistful. "Lots of fun though, isn't she?"

"The drinking bothers me."

"Me, too." Katlean stood up. "Let's go see Max."

They went outside. Woody squeezed himself out the door after them. Eldon's heart sank as they walked along the gravel street toward Max's store. The building was locked and dark.

"He's flown the coop," Eldon said.

Katlean merely grunted and peered in the window. "Relax. We'll find him."

"What do you mean? He's gone—"

"Every now and then Max takes time off to binge. Come on."

Katlean led Eldon up the street and around the corner, past houses where Eldon heard sounds of raised voices. The fighting seemed to be nonstop. "It's how you tell if someone's home," the chief said with a grin.

Here, surprisingly, was a sidewalk. It stretched down one side of the street, buckled and pitted by repeated freezing, past a shabby wooden garage and a small, weed-choked lot piled with crab pots. The bright pink stars of Alaska roses shone amid the unkempt growth. Eldon saw WORKS PROJECTS ADMINISTRATION etched in one of the concrete slabs beneath their feet. They picked their way down the sidewalk to a gray cottage with a peaked roof and a porch. Here the sidewalk ended. Katlean climbed the porch and knocked. No answer.

Eldon had a horrible thought. "Suppose he's dead in there?"

"Whatcha mean?"

"Suppose he killed himself?"

"Out of remorse? Abandon his store? That's a good one."

Katlean banged on the door again. No answer. The chief peered through the window. "Nothing out of place in the living room. Let's check the back."

They worked their way around the house, peering in the unshaded windows. But there was no one to be seen, only sparse furniture, all of it as neatly arranged as if in a barracks, Eldon thought as he peeked into the bedroom. The bed was made with hospital corners, the plain blanket so tight you could bounce quarters on it. The closet door was ajar. Clothes hung within, neatly arrayed.

"Well, he's not in there," Katlean admitted. "But if he left town, he did it naked. It doesn't look like anything's missing."

"Where'd he go? Why's the store closed?"

"That's a good question. Let's go down to the pier. Check the boat."

They walked back down the sidewalk, Woody trundling after. Eldon was certain Renner had bolted. But to where? He had an awful thought: Suppose Max had fled in the Amphicar? He could be in Sitka in a few hours, catch a flight out—

But the Amphicar was still parked on the beach. They made their way back through Klinkatshut toward the fish-processing plant. The workers on the outdoor slime line were in a lull, hosing off the bloody stainless-steel tables where they gutted the salmon and throwing leftover fish eyeballs at one another. Katlean asked after Renner, but no one had seen the storekeeper. "Kind of odd," said one man in a blood-smeared apron. "Max is usually down here pronto to get fish for the store."

"Maybe he's gone out in the boat," Eldon said.

"Maybe," the chief said. He asked the man in the apron, "Hey, Larry—has the *Just My Luck* been in here to unload?"

"Sure."

"Maybe Max was aboard?"

Larry shook his head. "Just saw Maggie Frame."

They headed down to the pier. Eldon's heart was racing. He wanted to hurry events along. A feeling of desperation was starting to engulf him; he could feel the story slipping away. I'll have a story even if Max has run, he told himself. They'll issue a warrant for his arrest.

The troller was there, her outriggers up and a couple of Indian crewmen hosing down the deck. They hadn't seen Max, either.

"He's still around town somewhere, then," Katlean said. "That boat's his only transportation off the island."

"Well, he could've taken a smaller boat, couldn't he? I made it to Sitka and back in the Amphicar."

"Yeah. I don't think he took a kayak."

They worked their way among the boats, but all were accounted for—either known to be out fishing or moored nearby. No one had seen Max—or missed him.

"Not a guy with a lot of friends," Katlean said. "Spent his time in his countinghouse."

"He said he used to get out more—"

"Not so much after they lost Mark Frame. That changed things for Max—and Jason, too."

"Not to mention Maggie."

"You know, Maggie came through better than I expected. At first she completely fell apart. I figured that was the end of it—we'd ship her out for a basket case. But she came back tougher. People do."

"They don't stay tough if they can't eat," Eldon said. "What do people do for groceries if Max doesn't turn up and open the store?"

"They'll jimmy a window and take what they need, leave the money on the counter. Stop worrying. He didn't go out with one of the boats. So he didn't fall overboard and drown. He didn't steal a boat. He doesn't know how to fly a plane. He's still on the island, passed out in the bushes somewhere."

"What if a bear finds him?"

"Stop talking like a cheechako."

Eldon was silent. Katlean was probably right. Max couldn't know that Eldon was onto him, so he wouldn't have run, unless—

"Unless he realized that he'd dropped the nail," Eldon said aloud.

"What?" Katlean asked.

"Never mind. You're right. Let's split up. I'll take the north side of town; you keep filtering around down here."

"I'll look in the clan house," Katlean said. "Guys sleep it off in there sometimes."

"Be careful."

"*You* be careful. I've got Woody."

"Yeah, Woody's a real killer." Eldon thumped Woody's ribs and moved off up the street. He wandered through the village, glancing into alleys and behind bushes, asking this person and that if they had seen Max Renner. No luck.

He worked his way toward Klinkatshut's outskirts and found himself heading for Maggie Frame's house—back toward the scene of Max's crime. As Eldon entered the woods, he reflected on the stupidity of hunting for a man with a rifle. But the more he thought about it, the more he thought that Katlean was right. Max wasn't lurking in the woods with a rifle. He was off somewhere, drunk, ready to be scooped up whenever Mike Atkov arrived with a warrant. Nevertheless, Eldon walked through the brush and not down the middle of the road.

He walked until he heard the discordant bells, like ice cubes tinkling in a swirling punch bowl. Eldon moved quietly in the direction of the chimes, walking parallel to the road among the trees.

Soon he saw the house. He stopped and slipped behind a tree, waited, and then moved off at a right angle to the road, trying to get a view of the rise where Cassandra had found the nail. Nothing seemed amiss at the cottage; the wind chimes twirled and glittered in the sun. Ah—there was Maggie, digging in her garden. She wore jeans and a pink halter top. She had tied a kerchief over her hair.

Eldon delayed starting down to the house, enjoying playing the peeping Tom. He crept forward a little and crouched behind a bush. He leaned forward, pushing the foliage aside for a better view—wait! What was that? A bear? Something rustled the bushes nearby. Eldon instantly poised for flight. He sniffed the air. No odor. Must be his imagination. He waited, his pulse racing a little, then returned to watching—

"Boo!"

Eldon screamed and launched himself reflexively forward, lost his balance and toppled into the brush. Cassandra hopped out of the bushes, laughing.

"I've been following you, Eldon! You're spying on Maggie!"

"No. No, I wasn't. I was looking for—"

"For what?"

"For something I dropped."

"What'd you drop?"

"Nothing. I—"

"Jimbo says you like spying."

"If you keep bothering Jimbo on the telex, he won't get his work done. Then Ed and Marcia and Ambrose will have to do it."

"Who're they?"

"The other reporters at the *Sun*. You'd like Ed. He's tall and rather funny. You'd like Ambrose, too. He's short and funny. He looks like a tree stump—"

"Jimbo wants to know what you've found out," Cassandra said implacably.

"Never mind that for now. What are *you* doing out here?"

Cassandra gave an elaborate shrug. "Came to see Maggie."

"At least you're away from the telex. Let's go down."

Maggie had heard Eldon's shout and stood watching from her garden. "So that was you. I see you survived the night. Hi, Cassandra."

"Hi," Eldon said. "Thought we'd drop in."

"Want some coffee?"

"You make great coffee. Love some."

They went inside. Cassandra got a cookie from the cookie jar and began strolling around the living room, elaborately nonchalant. Eldon asked, "Had any visitors today?"

"Like who?" Maggie said. "Are you jealous?"

Eldon glanced at Cassandra and decided to forge ahead. "Like Max Renner."

"Why would Max come here? What's going on?"

"We can't find him. The store's closed and his house is locked up. Ed Katlean thinks he's drunk somewhere."

"Did you look on Jason's island?" Cassandra asked.

"What?" Eldon asked. "Why would he be over there?"

"He used to go over there and drink with Jason," Cassandra said from in front of the fireplace, where she was gazing at Mark Frame's rifle. "Grown-ups don't think kids *notice* things. Well, kids do."

Maggie gave Cassandra a stare, as if she realized that her flirting was not going over the child's head. Cassandra is going to have to learn some tact when she gets older, Eldon thought.

"We can take my rowboat over there and check," Maggie said.

"Might be worthwhile," Eldon said.

They went down the path to the water, over the rise where Cassandra had found the nail. Nothing seemed different. Eldon kept an eye peeled for footprints but saw only a couple of little ones that had to be Cassandra's and the marks of Woody's huge paws.

"Has anyone disturbed the rowboat?" Eldon asked when they reached it.

"It's just like I left it," Maggie said. "Cassandra, why don't you go on home? Eldon and I had better do this by ourselves."

"I want to come," Cassandra said.

"Well, I don't think you should—," Maggie said.

"I want to come!" Cassandra repeated.

"It's okay with me," Eldon said quickly. *"Mais, il faut que tu sois silencieuse, d'accord?"*

"What's that?" Cassandra asked.

"I said, 'You'll have to be quiet, okay?' "

"Okay."

As Cassandra climbed into the front of the rowboat, Eldon whispered to Maggie: "She's really upset about Jason's death.

Might do her good to go back there again, work through it."

"It's okay," Maggie whispered. "I'd sure like to get you alone, though."

"Oh, you sure will." Eldon raised his voice to normal volume: "Sure, I'll row. Let me get in and then you push off."

They got under way, Eldon rowing. The crossing took only a few minutes. They tied up at the boat ramp and ducked under the yellow crime-scene tape that still fluttered across the ramp.

Cassandra kept glancing back at Maggie and Eldon as they walked up the path toward Jason's house. Finally she dropped back and let Maggie pass her, with Eldon still bringing up the rear.

Jason's house was closed up, the front door tied off with crime-scene tape. The house seemed empty as a movie set. They went around to the backyard. The totem pole that had crushed Jason lay where the cops had rolled it, its designs canted but still staring up at the sky. Cassandra wandered around the yard, poking into things, giving the adults a wide berth. She ducked into the work shed and emerged carrying a long chisel. She held it like a sword.

"Careful with that," Eldon said.

"Jason borrowed this from us," Cassandra said. "I'm taking it back."

"Okay." Eldon knelt by the prostrate totem pole and examined the designs—fish, waves, stars and sun, the inverted man, a salmon and Raven at the pole's top. "A sea totem," he said.

"Unconventional," Maggie said. "He always was. He was taking the craft somewhere new, that's for sure."

"Do these images mean anything to you?"

"Huh? Well, I think they're—pretty personal. The inverted man's the imagination, of course, and I think it must represent Jason's own imagination. The fish could mean anything—Alaska, prosperity—"

"The man's falling into the deeps," Eldon said. "He had money troubles." Eldon ran his hand over the pole, imagining how it would look painted. "I wonder if he wasn't getting at something when—"

A sharp snap interrupted him. Eldon looked up to see Jason's back door swing open and Cassandra flourishing the chisel.

"So that's why you wanted the—what the hell are you doing, Cassandra?"

"You wanted to look for clues."

"The police aren't going to be too happy."

"I didn't break it, just snapped it open."

"Where'd you learn that?"

"Brownies."

"I never learned how to pick locks when I was a Boy Scout," Eldon said, trotting over.

Cassandra handed him a handkerchief. "Don't touch anything. Fingerprints, you know."

"Are you going in?" Maggie asked.

"Yeah—might as well."

"What are you looking for?"

"Max."

"Max? The place is locked up."

"Signs that Max has been here. Signs of something missing. You two wait out here."

"No," Cassandra said. "I'm scared. I want to come with you."

"There's nothing to be scared of," Maggie said. "I'll stay with you."

"I want to stay with Eldon," Cassandra insisted, clutching the chisel.

"Oh, okay," Eldon said. "But don't touch anything."

They crept down the hall, looked through the kitchen and the living room. The police, of course, had inspected the house—cushions and other small furnishings were disarrayed, and there were sprays of fingerprint powder on tables and other surfaces.

Cassandra crept along with her chisel ready, looking all around. I wonder if letting her in here was such a good idea, Eldon thought, and he asked, "What're you so scared of?"

"It's creepy," Cassandra said, "like a haunted house."

"Yeah, I guess so." Eldon reflected on the curious paralleling of empty, locked buildings—Max's house and store and Jason's house. You could make a totem pole motif out of it, he thought.

The bedroom had hardly been disturbed. The bed remained unmade, the punching bag still hung in the corner. The night-stand drawer was halfway ajar and splashed with fingerprint powder. Using the handkerchief, Eldon slid the drawer open. Jason's fifth was still there. It had been dusted for fingerprints and replaced. Honest cops up here, he thought.

There remained only Jason's studio. Eldon had decided to purloin the folder of totem designs and notes. Would they match up with anything on the ridicule pole? We'll see, he thought. Eldon saw that something was amiss the moment he entered the room. The pastel drawing of the woman's face was missing from the easel. And the folder of drawings on graph paper was nowhere to be found.

Cassandra came in, stuffing a piece of paper into her pocket. "What are you looking for?"

Eldon shook his head and checked the window. Locked. It was somebody who had a key, he thought. Max wouldn't have had a key—or would he? Or maybe it was the police. . . . Mike didn't mention any drawings—but he did tip me off to the ridicule pole. He must know its significance, but he can't just hand me the information—this is an active investigation. He'd probably tell me if I asked point-blank, though. Or refuse to comment, and then I'd know for sure.

"Let's get out of here," Eldon said. "What was that you put in your pocket?"

"I'll tell you later. How do you say 'Let's get out of here' in French?"

Oh, let the kid play detective, Eldon thought as they headed into the hall. "Uh, let's see. *Partons d'ici* or *filons d'ici.*"

"Well, which is it?"

"Depends on how familiar you want to be."

"We're friends, aren't we?" Cassandra sounded a little anxious.

"Friends would say, *'Fichons-nous le camp,'* " Eldon said as they reached the living room.

Cassandra smiled and repeated the final phrase.

"Very good." Eldon paused for a last look around. Several of Jason's record albums were not quite as Eldon remembered them—right where Jason had stashed another bottle of liquor. He pushed the albums aside and peered into the space behind. The bottle was gone. No fingerprint powder here. The cops didn't take it, he thought, or they'd have taken the other one, too. A hopeless feeling stole over him. Now he could never put the puzzle together. Max was here after all, Eldon thought. He stole those drawings and took off.

14

Eldon was dejected as he rowed Maggie and Cassandra back to the main island. Max's flight was a story but not the story he wanted. Cassandra kept asking him what was the matter. He started telling fishing yarns, about the big black bass he'd unexpectedly caught on Sackett Lake and the Zen cast with which he'd once won a fly-fishing duel. Of course, those things had happened in Oregon, which only made him think of home and of Melissa and Fiske. He grew more depressed.

Maggie watched him with a curious smile. "You need to go fishing, Eldon."

"Been fishing."

"Not deep-sea fishing."

"This is hardly the time."

"This is exactly the time. Hanging around Klinkatshut will not help you find Max. The salmon are running. This'll perk you up."

Eldon thought about it as he guided the boat into shore. "Okay. When?"

"Hell, right now," Maggie said.

"I need my gear—"

"I've got the gear. Unless you're afraid of getting seasick."

"I never get seasick." It was no idle boast; Eldon might have an uncertain psyche, but he had a cast-iron stomach.

"I want to come!" Cassandra said.

"That's a nix," Maggie said firmly. "Too dangerous. I'll take you when you're older."

"Eldon needs protection!"

Maggie laughed as the boat scraped on shore. She climbed out and pulled the boat onto the beach. "I'll take good care of him. Now head on home."

Cassandra started to climb out of the boat. Then she stopped and surprised Eldon: she kissed his cheek. "Be careful, Eldon."

"Uh. Sure. Thanks. Tell your mom not to wait dinner."

"Okay," Cassandra said with a sigh. She swung out of the boat and headed into the forest.

"She likes you," Maggie said.

"Needs a father. I'm not it."

"You're better at some things than you know, Eldon."

"I wouldn't be any good at it, that's all." Eldon listened. "Your chimes are silent."

"No wind. Means there'll be a gentle sea."

"That's a laugh."

"Glad to see that you're realistic," Maggie said. "Come on."

Eldon climbed out of the boat and followed Maggie up the path from the beach. He came up abreast of her and tried to slip his arm around her waist. Maggie slipped free. "Concentrate," she told him. "We're going fishing."

"Ah. I didn't know you were a fanatic."

"Fishing-boat skippers only come in a few kinds, Eldon—mostly drunks, drug dealers, and fools. And fanatics."

"That's why you've got to get a good skipper," Eldon said.

"I'm going to *be* the skipper. It'll just be you and me."

They paused at Maggie's house while she retrieved windbreakers and rubber boots. Eldon wandered around outside, toying with the wind chimes. They tinkled faintly under his touch but the air remained still. They were in myriad designs—steel tubes, ceramic flowers, wooden clappers, bells of all sizes and descriptions. One with Alaska Indian motifs caught Eldon's eye—Raven's head with strings of salmon hanging down for chimes. Eldon was studying it when Maggie came back.

"These were Mark's. I guess they'll fit you. There are deep-sea rods aboard the boat. Sometimes Max takes out charters."

"Thanks." Eldon took the clothing carefully. "Is this wind chime Jason's work?"

"Yeah. He gave it to my husband, back when they were partners."

They started up the path.

"Were you teaching then?" Eldon asked.

"No. I had the certificate but there weren't any jobs, except seasonal at the processing plant, and that's not exactly a living. Mark kept us afloat, fishing, different deals, like the thing with Jason."

"What was he like?"

"I think you'd have liked him. Mark liked to read—and not just tide tables." She looked at Eldon. "I think that's why I like you."

"You must, to leg-wrestle Anita for me. Look—what's between you and Anita, anyway? You act like you're trying to get back at each other for something."

Maggie's eyes twinkled. "Very perceptive."

"So what is it?"

"We're almost to the boat."

They had reached Klinkatshut's center. People strolled in the streets—or rather, some strolled and some reeled, smelling of liquor. A group of boys, white and Indian, had a basketball game under way under a hoop bolted to a telephone pole. Three old Indian men sat in a row on the porch of Max's locked-up store, passing a bottle back and forth in a paper bag. All three wore grimy denim pants and jackets and broken baseball caps. Eldon thought of the three blind mice. The visor of the baseball cap worn by the man on the end was half torn off and hung down over one eye. The old man pushed it back when he took his turn at the bottle. Why bother with a bag? Eldon wondered.

The boat was moored by the pier. A troller, Eldon thought. Maybe *the* troller. "Hey, Maggie, ever been over to some of the other islands?"

"Sure, been all around 'em. Why?" Maggie pulled open the deck hatch and knelt to inspect the engine. She twisted off the oil cap and checked the oil level with a dipstick.

"There's a work of art on one of 'em—a totem pole of Jason's?"

"Really? Where?"

"Up the channel. On that island where the crazy old sourdoughs live."

"I haven't been up there," Maggie said. "Give me that gas can, please."

Eldon pushed the gas can across the deck. "They say a boat like this one came to visit."

Maggie grinned. "It may be this boat but it's not me. I've had about as much of Jason's art as I can take."

"I didn't mean you. I meant Max." Eldon brought her the gasoline can, helped her lift it to fill the tank. "How often does he take this boat out?"

"When he wants to. We don't check in and out with each other. We try to keep coordinated during the fishing season."

"Like now."

"Yeah—Max can be a bit sloppy about that, which you might agree is something of a surprise. He wants to buy me out, you know."

"I didn't know. Why don't you sell?"

Maggie tilted the gasoline can back to level and returned it to Eldon. "It'd be like selling my last piece of Mark."

"I guess so."

"Max and Jason were aboard when he was drowned. They lost him, Eldon."

"Well, that's a little hard—"

"Everybody's responsible for each other on these boats—even the boats where the skippers are drunks or drug-dealers or fools. Or fanatics. Especially on those boats. I lost Mark. And you know, when Jason was killed, it was like I lost another part of Mark. I thought my husband was gone, but it was as if he'd been divided into three, into this weird trinity that consisted of Mark and Jason and Max."

They reached the pier and clambered aboard the boat. It was a twenty-footer, weathered by years at sea, everything about it worn. But the equipment was in good shape—the ropes new, the joists oiled, no rust on the fittings. Eldon could smell the hold.

He walked aft of the big square stainless-steel refrigerator behind the pilothouse and pulled up the wooden hatch cover. The fish stink rose up to him as he looked down into the hold. He could see the stains of blood, slime, and scales washing in the bilge below. This was a working boat, all right. Eldon let the hatch drop and went forward to the pilothouse. There was a little shortwave radio mounted on the ceiling over the wheel and a radar unit to one side. A nautical compass floated in a glass bubble. Good; they had a fair chance of getting out and back without getting lost.

"Fishing rods are in the forward locker," Maggie called, still inspecting the engine.

The locker was mounted crosswise on the deck in front of the pilothouse. Eldon opened the hasps and pulled up the lid. Boy, oh, boy, he thought, those are real deep-sea rods. They made his graphite fly rod look anemic. He ran his hands along the rods, imagined them bucking in his grip with some monster of the deep at the end of his line. If I catch a really big king salmon, I'll have the bastard mounted, Eldon vowed. I'll hang it up in the *Sun* newsroom behind the news desk, and I'll be able to look at it every time Fiske calls me back there to give me an assignment. And every assignment will be easy because I caught that fish.

Maggie started the engine and came forward. "Thought you'd like the looks of 'em. The harnesses are in the cabin. We've got hooks, bait, the works. Let's cast off—"

Someone was calling from the pier, over the sound of the engine. "Hey! Eldon! *Hey!*"

"Shit," Maggie said.

Eldon looked up to see Anita on the pier, dressed for ocean travel in hooded jacket and rubber boots.

"Hi, there," Maggie said. "Cast us off forward, will you?"

"Hell, I'm coming aboard," Anita said.

"Aboard my boat?" Maggie asked. "I haven't invited you."

Anita jumped aboard. "Sure you have."

A flush ran up Maggie's cheeks. Anita nodded toward Eldon. "I need to keep an eye on my employee."

"If you're going to deadhead, you can pull your weight." Maggie stepped behind the wheel. "Cast us off."

"Aye, aye." Anita cast off the hawsers. The boat backed away from the dock. Eldon saw Cassandra standing at the far end of the pier. Anita waved.

"Will she be all right?" Eldon asked. He still wasn't used to this custom of letting kids run loose.

"She has any number of other kids to play with, any number of houses where she can walk in and they'd treat her just like one of their own. I expect we'll find her eating supper with Ed's family when we get back."

"She doesn't want you to go."

Anita looked stern. "I am not going to have my daughter running my personal life. It's a jealousy trip and I'm not taking the bait."

"Uh, you're the boss. I'm not coming between Mama Bear and her cub, though."

"Don't worry, you're not. It's not up to her to approve or disapprove of what I do."

Eldon waved to Cassandra as they swung around and headed up the channel. "Wait'll she's a teenager and tells you the same thing."

"That's gonna be different. I'm her mother." Anita looked stubborn and handed him a life jacket. "Now—what were you two planning to do? Elope."

"No. Something more important. Go fishing."

"I can see that. I mean, what were you doing together at Jason's house? I had to find out you were over there from Cassandra."

"I'll tell you later. I was going to tell you." Eldon put on the life jacket and took another aft. Maggie stood at the wheel, hair blowing in the breeze, mouth set in a line.

Eldon handed her the life jacket. "I'm looking forward to this," he said.

"Thanks." Maggie's voice was a little tight. "Sorry it can't be a private party after all—"

Eldon glanced around the deck. The little craft wasn't his idea of a place to get intimate, anyway. And there was a higher calling—fishing. "We'll have a private party when we get back. Now, about the fishing gear—"

"Anita can show you how to set it up." Maggie slipped on the life jacket and snapped its clasps.

"Okay. I can probably manage."

"Bait bucket's over there in the stern." Maggie steered into the channel's current and they picked up some chop.

"Should've brought some sandwiches," Eldon remarked. "I get hungry when I go out."

"I don't." Maggie gave a stiff smile and pushed her hair back to expose the Dramamine patch behind her ear.

"You're pretty brave," Eldon said.

"Alaska breeds women of iron, Eldon."

He assumed they were going up the long channel to Sitka. But Maggie knew a shortcut that took them swiftly through the archipelago's myriad islands and into the open sea. Soon, they were heading out into the Pacific, land receding and green water all around them. If the seas were gentle, that was always a relative term, Eldon reflected. In fact, the weather was picking up. The boat pitched and bucked. The motion made the mast seem to pivot like a gyroscope fixed on an unseen point in the sky. It didn't bother Eldon—or, he was glad to see, Anita. She joined him as he braced himself at the forward equipment locker and pulled out the fishing rods.

Eldon noticed the bulge under Anita's parka. "You strapped?"

"Always."

"Christ. Help me mount this reel."

They got the rods assembled and the lines strung, baited their hooks, and got ready to cast from opposite sides of the boat. Eldon looked back at Maggie. Her face was pale. Eldon hoped he wouldn't have to take over the wheel, although he knew enough elementary seamanship to keep control and get them home. He hoped Anita did, too. The sky was still clear, even if the sea was no longer gentle. Eldon turned to the rail and made his first cast.

The rod was far heavier than a fly rod, and the boat moved like a living thing. He couldn't aim as he would from a rowboat or a stream bank. Instead, Eldon tried to move in synch with the boat as he cast; it seemed to put extra throw into his cast. Maggie still grimly held the wheel, lips set. Eldon knew that she had her gaze locked on the horizon as a fixed point. Just what did she think of doing out here with me, if she gets seasick like that? he wondered.

Anita was holding her own, if casting rather clumsily—somewhat to Eldon's surprise, since she had been skillful enough fishing in the stream. Deep-sea fishing didn't seem to be Anita's forte. Eldon had imagined that everyone in Alaska was a master salmon fisherman; but that was like imagining everyone in Switzerland was a master watchmaker, or that everyone in India wore a turban and charmed cobras.

Anita got a strike. Eldon saw the rod bow. Anita braced her feet and hauled, just as the boat plunged into a green sea canyon with the sickening drop of an elevator. Then they were traveling upward again as cold water sprayed over the deck. The boat rocked and then the waves opened once again. The ocean seemed to fall away beneath them, and for a moment they were in free fall. They hit the water with an impact that was like belly flopping onto concrete and then were once more heading up into the sky. Eldon gave an exhilarated yell. This was fishing!

"I've lost him!" Anita yelled over the noise of the water. "I lost the damn rod!"

"At least we didn't lose you!" Eldon yelled back. He didn't know if Anita heard him. He cast once more. Eldon stole a glance at Maggie and felt guilty that he was working up an appetite. Maggie looked like a chalky statue. Her hair was plastered around her face by the spray. Eldon reeled in his line and went to the pilothouse. "Go do it. I'll take the wheel."

Maggie opened her mouth to argue, made a froglike croak and headed for the rail. She bent over, heaving for several minutes while Eldon steered, then pushed herself up and staggered back to the pilothouse, wiping her mouth. "Sorry—go on back to your fishing."

"Let's head back. You look awful—"

"Go back to your fishing."

"You're the skipper."

"Damn right." Maggie clamped her hands on the wheel and clenched her teeth. "And you're going to enjoy yourself."

Eldon went back to the rail and cast again, pitying her. There was nothing he could do. And this was nothing, barely brisk weather. Eldon thought of Jason and Max and Mark Frame fighting to stay afloat in the Gulf of Alaska, one of Jason's totem poles lashed along the deck. At that moment, the boat went bow-first into a wall of water and for an instant Eldon was blinded and deafened by cold. Icy brine burned in his eyes and nostrils. Then they were in clear air and he was drenched.

Anita took refuge in the pilothouse with Maggie. Eldon's skin prickled with excitement as he saw his chance to play the man. Maggie seasick, Anita's rod gone—it was up to him to land a big one and salvage the voyage. He hurried to the stern and cast from there, letting the wind and the boat's motion carry his line out in a long, swaying arc that vanished into the sea. The ocean was like a pitching floor, lethally fragile; it could swallow you with one step, the way it had swallowed Mark Frame.

This is how Maggie faces up to it, he thought. It's like paratroopers going up to jump again after somebody gets killed. Just then something hit Eldon's hook. It felt like a freight train.

He yelled as the line started running out like a hissing cable uncoiling from a speeding car. Eldon hit the lock and the line stopped with a slam. The rod bowed so fiercely that Eldon feared it would snap. Now I have got me a fish, he thought exultantly, the biggest king salmon in the world.

Maggie brought the boat around, turning toward starboard in the beginning of a curve that would loop them back toward shore. Eldon had the illusion that the fish was the fixed point and that he and boat were turning on the pivot. He looked up, saw the mast swinging across the sky like a metronome; now the boat's deck seemed to be pivoting under him while the fish orbited the boat. Eldon set his jaw and stared down the bend of the rod. The moment of vertigo passed, and the world narrowed down to the line and the green, angry sea.

He had hooked something enormous. He had visions of whales, sea monsters, salmon the size of submarines. Maybe it *was* a submarine. Eldon started cranking in his line. It felt like an automobile on the other end—one going full speed in reverse. How was he going to land it? He abandoned pride and yelled for Anita.

Anita popped out of the pilothouse, scrambled across the deck, and grabbed on to the rod. They pulled together. The fish was still fighting, zigzagging across the boat's wake. The boat was pitching fiercely. They fell down another green chasm in the ocean, and Eldon caught a glimpse of his quarry through the spray—a huge, blunt torpedo shape.

"That's no salmon," Anita cried. "Looks like a halibut!"

"I'm cutting the line," Eldon said. "It's too big to land."

"Hell it is," Anita said. "This is Alaska. Haul it in."

"But what happens when we get it—"

"We can take care of that," Anita said. "Maggie! Cut speed."

Eldon cranked the reel, dragging the fish in by brute torque. His wrists burned like hot iron. He almost had it to the boat now. The fish was swinging back and forth in the water on the end of the line like the clapper in a bell. The boat's motion died. Maggie stepped up, ready with an ax. She had a cold look in her eye—her gaze was locked on his and Eldon thought for an instant that she was going to brain him and not the fish. Then Maggie saw something behind Eldon's shoulder and lowered the ax. He shook off the wild thoughts and yanked.

The halibut burst from the sea, hit the gunwale, and flipped thrashing into the boat. Eldon stumbled backward. Then something came over his shoulder and he had just an instant to focus on it—Anita's arm with the Magnum pistol in her fist. There was a roar in Eldon's ear that he felt more than heard and a flash of heat and light and the stink of gunpowder mixed with salt water. The halibut slammed flopping to the deck with a hole in its brain.

"Well done, Eldon," Anita said, lowering the pistol. Her voice seemed far off since Eldon was now deaf in one ear.

"Pretty solid marksmanship," Eldon said weakly.

"Yeah, I'm good. It must weigh two hundred, two-fifty. Just a peewee."

Maggie was breathing slowly and heavily, still holding the ax. Her face was still pasty. Finally she put the ax down. "Put the gun away, will you?"

"Do you have a rag?" Anita asked. "I've got to wipe it down. The salt water."

Maggie tossed Anita a rag, then went to rev the engine.

"Lots of fishermen carry big-caliber pistols," Anita explained as she polished her revolver. "Comes in handy."

"Yeah," Eldon said, "you might run into a bear." His ear was ringing fiercely now. At least the eardrum's still there, he thought. "What do we *do* with it?"

"Leave it lie till we get in," Anita said.

"It's bleeding all over the deck. Let's put it in the locker."

"Okay. It's your catch."

"You killed it."

"Merely the coup de grâce." Anita slipped the revolver back under her coat.

So what if it's not a salmon, Eldon thought. It's the biggest fish I ever caught. He debated whether to mount the fish or have it canned and shipped to Oregon. Anita unlocked the refrigerator—and screamed. The scream cut right through the ringing in Eldon's ear. Anita jumped away from the locker, her face as white as Maggie's, and Maggie looked out from the pilothouse, her face stricken.

Eldon stepped to the locker. Horror went through him like an electric shock. Crumpled inside, rimed with bloody frost, was Max Renner's corpse.

15

"He was dead when he went in the locker—pretty near," Mike Atkov said.

"Pretty near?" Eldon said. He felt seasick now that he was back on dry land, safe in the *Aurora* office.

"He was knifed," Mike continued. "He bled to death in there. He didn't freeze to death."

"There was blood on his knuckles."

"Mostly from trying to stanch the wound."

Eldon made another note. "How long was he in there?"

"Overnight," Mike said, amused. "This is weird. I question you, then you question me."

"You solve the murder, I write it up," Eldon said.

"D'you have to put this in print?" Mike asked.

"Are you crazy? Of course I do." Eldon put down his pen and rubbed his eyes. His hearing had nearly returned to normal. "So Renner didn't kill Jason."

"What makes you say that?"

"You want to make it 'no comment'?" Eldon asked. "Renner killed Jason. Now someone's killed Renner, to shut him up."

"Put the pen down," Mike said. "Thank you. This is off the record. I think the same person killed them, even if the MO is different."

"And what was the MO in this case?"

"A fish-gutting knife in the kidneys. Up close and personal. Different from a rifle, you have to admit."

"Signs of a struggle?"

"No."

"Then it was someone he knew."

"Everybody knows everybody around here. But you're thinking fast, Larkin."

"Let's go back on the record," Eldon said.

"Let's not," Mike said. "Let's just talk."

"Okay, okay," Eldon said. "Two people killed Jason. I think this was the accomplice. Somebody pushed that totem pole over on Jason. I don't think it was the same person who shot him. It's just too complicated. One person lured him out into the backyard. The second person shot him. Then the first one pushed the totem pole over on him, to finish him off."

Eldon thought about how best to bring up the missing folder of drawings without suggesting that he'd been back to the crime scene. "Listen, we know there's money involved in this."

"George did some pretty good legwork," Mike agreed with a scowl. "For you as well as for me."

"Professional courtesy, one journalist to another," Eldon said. "Now, since we're off the record here, do me a favor and tell me if any of those financial leads checked out."

"What the hell. My brother'll never give me any peace if I don't tell you. Here it is, but you won't like it. The financial leads don't check out."

"What d'you mean?"

"I mean that there's no one who Baer owed money to that would gain a thing from killing him. If he can't carve totem poles, then he can't pay off his debts, right?"

"What about insurance?"

"Baer didn't have any."

"What about the boat?"

"Ms. Frame is now the sole owner."

"Well, what about her?" Eldon amazed himself with the cool way he said it.

"Not a possibility, though she owns a rifle, a .30-06 with a scope."

"It was her husband's."

"My colleague Potter asked to look it over, and Ms. Frame was glad to oblige. No way it's been fired recently. In fact, it didn't look as if it'd been fired in a few years."

"Mike, did your people take any works of art from Jason's house? For evidence?"

"Huh? No. Why?"

Aha. "Uh, Anita wanted to know. She's Jason's agent. His estate's agent now. It would be money tied up in the evidence room, you know."

"Only relevant thing like that would be the totem pole we found him under, and it was too big to move. We'll go back for it. The crime team already went over it for traces."

"Did they find anything? Fingerprints? Handprints? Footprints where someone dug in their feet when they shoved?"

"No—just that the victim was alive when the log landed on him."

"He just lay there and waited for the totem to fall?"

"Well, he wasn't conscious. But the chest wound wasn't fatal outright. The log finished him off."

"So he might've lived if he'd gotten help."

"Yeah."

"Jesus, that's cold-blooded."

"That's why we think it was personal. Now, who had something personal against Baer?"

"Not me, that's for sure." Eldon grinned.

"No, but his agent might've."

"Anita? She couldn't't've—"

"How do you know? Were you sleeping with her that night?"

"Uh, no."

"For that matter, were you sleeping with her *last* night?"

"Uh, yeah."

"So you both have an alibi for Renner's death."

"Yes, we do. Stop trying to muddy the waters—"

Mike smiled briefly. "What with Renner a murder victim, we were able to get a warrant quick to search his house. Guess what we found." e

"Oh, a bunch of magnets, all stuck together," Eldon said.

"We found a .30-06 with a telescopic sight," Mike said. "Tucked away under the floorboards. Recently fired. We still don't have the slug that killed Baer for a ballistics match, but I think we've got our murder weapon."

"I want to go on the record," Eldon said.

"Okay, everything we discuss hereafter is on the record."

"Don't fuck around with me, Mike. I want the rifle."

"Okay, you've got it. Go file your story."

"That still doesn't take care of the accomplice."

"No, it doesn't," Mike said. "But it takes care of Renner. He owed Baer. And he couldn't pay. But the money wasn't the reason. Renner was a control freak, but Baer was controlling *him.* Nothing a control freak hates worse than being controlled. It makes him feel out of control."

"This isn't wrapped up until we find who killed Max Renner."

"Renner's dead because a lot of people owed *him* money and he finally pissed somebody off. We're going through his books right now, and sooner or later we're going to find a grocery account that's big enough to warrant murder."

"Max got killed over *groceries?"*

"What's the matter with you, Larkin? You're a reporter. I'm a cop. We've both seen people killed over *nothing."*

Eldon was silent for a moment. Actually, most of the murder victims he had seen had been killed for perfectly good reasons—or reasons that had been important to their killers, anyway. Never for nothing. Groceries was a perfectly good reason to kill somebody. But even as he told Mike, "You're right," instinct told him that Jason's death and Max's were intertwined.

Eldon wrote in his notebook while he thought. At last he asked, "Say—did you find anything of Jason's in Max's possession? Works of art in his house, anything like that?"

"No."

"Just curious. It would've made a nice touch for my story."

"You and George are a couple of vultures."

"Picking the bones is how our work gets done," Eldon said. "Thanks for going on the record about the rifle."

"Sure, hell, roll the presses."

" 'Mad Sniper Took Totem Artist's Life.' " Eldon grinned. He felt like galloping out the door.

By Eldon Larkin
Special to the *Aurora*

KLINKATSHUT—The murder of a Klinkatshut storekeeper has deepened the mystery surrounding the killing of Alaska Native artist Jason Baer. State troopers revealed this week that the rifle they believe was used to kill Baer was found in the storekeeper's house.

Max Renner, who owned the Klinkatshut general store, was found dead in a deck refrigerator aboard a troller of which he was part owner. He was stabbed and dumped into the refrigerator, where state troopers said he swiftly bled to death.

Investigators revealed that Renner was the prime suspect in the sniper killing of Baer, who was found shot and crushed beneath a totem pole he was carving. They believe Renner killed Baer using a .30-06 rifle recovered from the storekeeper's house because Renner owed the artist money.

Who killed Renner is still unknown.

Police refused to comment on speculation that Renner had an accomplice in Baer's slaying, who then turned on him and killed him. Nor would they comment on the idea that one person may have done both murders. . . .

"God, that was horrible," Anita said, lacing her coffee with bourbon.

"Drinking won't make it any less horrible," Eldon said.

Anita ignored him. "The rifle was the proof. We should've gotten the proof. Max would be alive now if he'd been arrested."

"How would we have gotten the rifle? By breaking in to Max's house?"

"Ed could've taken you in. No one would've known."

"Great. My fingerprints all over just when Max turns up dead."

"They wouldn't think you'd done it. No motive."

"There's such a thing as tampering with an investigation," Eldon said. "I've already tampered enough."

"Like how?"

"It's what I was doing at Jason's before we went fishing. I didn't want to say anything in front of Cassandra or Maggie, and then I never got to tell you."

"What?" Anita swigged her spiked coffee.

"There's something missing from Jason's house—a folder of rough drawings that was there the day he was killed. I saw it. But when I went back, it was gone."

"The cops took it."

"I don't think so."

"Max, then."

"They didn't find them in Max's house. I asked."

"What were they?"

"They looked like totem pole designs," Eldon said. "I wanted to show them to you, see what you thought of them. I think Jason used to fasten them to that punching bag of his."

"Hmm. Have a drink, Eldon."

"Just listen. I got to thinking the designs might be important after I saw the ridicule pole."

"Why? How do they connect?"

"If the designs that Jason was pounding on his punching bag are the same as the ones on the pole, then we're a step closer to figuring out who the pole ridicules—to who visited the pole at night."

"Do you think they are the same?"

"How could I tell?" Eldon asked. *"You* could tell."

"They must be important if the folder is missing," Anita said. "Who's got the folder?"

"Whoever killed Max—and Jason," Eldon said. "I've got to put out more feelers. And I've got an idea."

"What?"

"Make prints of those shots I took of the totem. I'm going to talk to old Kate."

Anita took a final swig of coffee and headed for the darkroom, then stopped. "Suppose *she* killed them?"

"I'm willing to believe anything at this point," Eldon said. "Did either of them owe her money?"

Anita looked thoughtful. "Not that I ever heard. But Kate carried some big grocery tabs at the store."

Kate lived in an old Airstream trailer on a slope overlooking the town. As he approached, Eldon sniffed an unmistakable fragrance—broiling salmon.

Kate was unabashed at having been caught falling off the vegetarian wagon. "The fisherman. Come in."

"Thanks." The trailer was tidy if meager, full of cast-off furniture carefully repaired with duct tape and nylon fishing line. Provisions were stacked everywhere. Eldon felt as if he had entered a spaceship lined with canned goods. It was a little like Max Renner's store but in a way that only showed how crazy Max had been. The store was like a bizarre museum; Kate's trailer looked as if someone actually lived in it.

He heard faint shortwave voices, saw that an old Army radio receiver without a case sat on a rolltop desk, vacuum tubes glowing. The radio's face peeked out of a cave of canned goods. A string of sausages hung from a doorknob. Cans of peaches stacked atop the television set framed a portrait of John F. Kennedy on velvet. A rifle with a scope hung on the wall—a handsome burnished thing that looked as if it had seen plenty of use. Kate had opened the windows while she cooked. Eldon could see the distant glare of Mandel's Glacier.

Kate trundled out mismatched mugs and a pot of coffee and set a tin of vanilla cookies on a coffee table before Eldon. Eldon sampled the coffee and shuddered. It was instant.

Kate offered a can of evaporated milk.

"Black's fine," Eldon said.

"The fisherman," Kate repeated, watching him drink. "Thank you for your gift. I'll remember you at the potlatch."

"Oh, that's okay. Couldn't have landed it without you. It was a lot more fish than I could ever eat."

"That's why you're a good fisherman," Kate said. "But you didn't expect to catch what you caught out on that boat."

"No." Eldon patted a No. 10 can of stewed tomatoes that rested on a coffee table. "Guess you don't have to pay him for these now."

Kate returned a cold stare. "No, guess not. But I think I have to pay you for what you brought."

"You can help me out." Eldon pulled out the print of the totem pole as he wondered if Kate's grocery account had been big enough to justify murder. And she was a crack shot. Had Max bribed her to shoot Jason in exchange for supplies? It wouldn't seem so petty in the teeth of winter. Or had Jason pushed his luck too far with her, say by paying just enough of Kate's bills to keep her afloat? She wasn't young and pretty but she had influence in the tribe. "What does this totem pole say?"

Kate studied the pictures. "I've never seen this pole. Jason's work?"

"He carved it, all right. It's on an island nearby. It's a ridicule pole."

"How are you so sure?"

The question caught Eldon off guard. "That's what people say. I want to find who it's making fun of."

"Maybe the killer, right?" Kate flipped through the pictures. "You know, totem poles don't tell stories the way white people do, with a beginning, a middle, and an end. They just suggest stories."

"Yes, I know."

"It's good that you still think you have things to learn. Eating meat hasn't made you crazy yet."

"Sometimes I wonder."

"So anybody can make up his own story about a totem pole," Kate said. "Every totem pole is lots bigger and taller than it seems to be."

And heavier, Eldon thought, remembering Jason lying dead beneath one. "Yeah. There's the part we see and the part we imagine. Go on."

"Very good, you think fast for a cheechako. Now, remember the story about the Daughters of the Fog?"

"The good-looking women at the head of the salmon stream? Sure." Eldon took a cookie.

"So what do you think the pole says?"

"I was hoping *you'd* tell *me.*"

"Three salmon in a row," Kate said. "Salmon fishing."

"In a real neat row. Max Renner."

"Maybe, yeah," Kate said. "Salmon are the wealth of the world. Food for all the people. Power over the sea. A gift from Raven."

"Raven's sitting up there atop the pole," Eldon said.

"And what did Raven do?"

"Raven did a lot of things. . . ." This reminded Eldon of catechism class as a child, on Wednesday afternoons and on Sunday mornings after Mass, all the Catholic kids who went to public school. Hundreds of numbered questions and answers to be learned by rote. "Raven created the world," Eldon said. The answer simply popped out.

Kate nodded slowly. "And who had wealth?"

"Not Raven. Raven was always poor." A thought struck Eldon. "Raven was Jason's totem creature—"

"Yes," Kate said. "But how could that be? Jason was rich."

"Raven had power," Eldon plunged on. "And Jason had power. He was an artist, he had the power of creation, like Raven."

"Salmon are wealth," Kate reminded him. "Salmon are a gift from Raven."

"And if you have power over the salmon, you have power over the people—" Eldon took the pictures and looked at them. "Max owned the store . . . but Jason owned Max. . . . Is that what the totem pole means, Kate?"

"Maybe this totem's no big deal—"

"Yeah, yeah, like that potlatch everyone's spent a year preparing for—no big deal." Eldon flipped through the pictures. It was like studying Tarot cards, all right. I do not find the Hanged Man, he quoted to himself. Fear death by water. But Alaska was no wasteland. . . . "Here's a tumbling man. He's holding a box. The tumbling man is the imagination. But what's in the box?"

"Everyone knows that story."

"Will you tell it to me?"

"In the beginning," Kate said, "all the light in the world was kept in a box by a man who lived at the head of the Nass River. He guarded it closely. Raven tried every trick he knew to get into the man's lodge house and steal the box. But the man always outsmarted him. Raven decided to seduce the man's beautiful daughter. But the man guarded his daughter too well. Finally,

Raven turned himself into a hemlock needle and slipped into her water, and the daughter drank the needle and became pregnant, which is how Raven came to be born into the household.

"Now, the man loved his grandchild and gave the baby whatever it wanted. One day, the baby cried and cried. It would not be comforted. So the man gave the baby the box of light to play with. Raven seized the box and flew up the smoke hole of the man's lodge house. Raven let the sun and the moon and the stars out of the box, and they flew up to heaven. And Raven enjoyed his new world full of light."

Eldon took another cookie. "But the man on the totem is falling away from the light—away from the salmon, which represent power and wealth."

"Go on."

Eldon fumbled in his mind for what he knew about the case. He tried to bring the images together. "Jason drank too much, and his business wasn't going well. The tumbling man's a drunk. But the tumbling man also represents the imagination. And the box is full of light—" He laid the photographs out in a row. "The ocean, the salmon in a row at the top, Raven the trickster, Raven the thief. This is about Jason's drinking. It's about his debts. It's the story of Max and the store and the fishing boat, isn't it?"

"Could be," Kate said.

"Why not say it straight out?"

"Because I don't know, Eldon. You can't say 'don't know' in the white man's court. The white man thinks it's possible to know everything. Thinks he *does* know everything." Kate poured herself some more coffee. "No offense."

"I know a little bit," Eldon said.

"What do you know?"

"That Jason didn't have many friends. Just wealth. He was

putting that wealth somewhere I don't know about. And when the wealth began to slip, he turned meaner. Nobody liked him—he demanded too much. Anybody around here might've killed him.

"People liked Max even less. They owed him money the way they owed Jason in potlatch and there was no way to pay. And Max owed Jason. And Jason got meaner. And finally Max killed him—the police found the rifle."

"I heard."

"But who killed Max?"

Kate smiled, and Eldon felt a chill. "Could've been anybody," Kate said.

"No," Eldon said, and took another cookie. "It was somebody in particular. Somebody who owed Max more than money. Or somebody who Max owed." Eldon remembered something that Max had said. He picked up the photo that showed the tumbling man. "What's in the box?"

"Come to the potlatch and you may find out," Kate said.

Eldon went down the path from Kate's trailer thinking that he had eaten too many cookies. A cold breeze was blowing and rain threatened. The whole sky seemed to be in motion. I'd better lay this out for Katlean, Eldon thought. Half the town could've done in Jason and the other half, Max. But Max had been knifed at an improvident time, too soon after Jason's murder. Anyone with sense would've waited. Did sense come into it? Yes, it did. Neither murder had been a crime of passion. Both had been calculated.

Max must've been killed on or near the boat. Klinkatshut's not the kind of place where you walked down the street with a bleeding body over your shoulder. It was someone with access to the boat—

Maggie.

Eldon nearly stumbled as the thought flashed across his mind. Then he recovered, realizing that it couldn't be so. Maggie had been elsewhere when Max was killed—the people at the fish cannery had said she hadn't taken the boat out in weeks. And Maggie got seasick. Eldon had to smile at the thought of a seasick murderer. Then he wondered, what am I smiling about?

Eldon saw the Klinkatshut clan house as he walked down the path. There was a huge white clump on the porch. Good. Where Woody was, Chief Katlean was. He wanted to tell Katlean that he was donating the halibut he had caught to the potlatch. Hell, maybe Katlean killed Jason and Max, Eldon thought, though he's the last guy with any reason to.

Woody sprang up, barking happily as Eldon approached. "Good boy." Eldon tried to flank the big dog, but Woody wheeled after him, delighted with the game. He barked again and lunged. Eldon grabbed Woody's muzzle overhand and shook it gently. This, he knew, was the alpha dog's gesture of domination. "Good boy!"

Woody apparently didn't know the sign. He leaped again and bounced Eldon off the clan house wall. Woody pinned him and licked his face, nearly smothering him.

"Who's there? Hey, Woody, get away." Katlean stepped through the doorway. He wore his nose ring. "You gotta knee him, Eldon. I'm trying to break him—"

"Of jumping," Eldon finished. "He's too fast for me. Kate Taylor was too fast for me, too."

"Couldn't she tell you what that damn thing means?" Katlean grabbed Woody's collar and pulled him off Eldon.

"I got a course in subjective reality," Eldon said. "I need facts and figures. I want to look at Max's books. I want to see who owed him and how much."

"The state troopers are way ahead of you," Katlean said. "They've got the books."

"How much did *you* owe him, chief?" Eldon asked.

"I like your style, Eldon, you never give up." Katlean was unconcerned. "I didn't owe him anything, as a matter of fact. Got a good round of TV repair work, thanks to the salmon run. People had money to pay me and I had the money to pay Max. Happens that way every salmon season. Max hated me for it, too—I could see him computing the lost interest as I counted out the money. Hunh! I should've held out. If I'd known someone was gonna kill him, I'd have saved my dough. . . . Finding him kind of cast a pall over your fishing trip, I bet."

"You know that halibut I caught? I'm donating it to the potlatch."

"That's damn generous," Katlean said seriously. "You don't have to do that. You're a chee—a visitor. Exempt."

"I want to." Eldon had expected Katlean to be delighted, not just solemnly surprised.

"Come inside," Katlean said. "I want to show you something."

The lights were on and the table and folding chairs were set up before the great screen. There was something black on the table. Eldon saw that it was a carved wooden box, perhaps a foot across and six or seven inches deep. It was locked with a small padlock. The box was splintered on one corner—no, gnawed.

"I found it this morning," Katlean said. "Woody was chewin' on it. The big dummy knew he'd done wrong—he was hiding in a corner with it, or I'd have found it like I was supposed to."

"Like you were supposed to?" Eldon asked.

"Max Renner left this for me, here in the clan house. I'd've found it when I came in here looking for him, if Woody hadn't carried it off."

"Well, what's in it? Open it."

"No can do, Eldon. It's a potlatch offering. Got to wait."

" 'Do not open until Christmas'? We've got a double murder case here, chief—"

"Can't screw up the mana." Katlean pulled out an envelope and handed it over. "Before you tell me off about Indian superstitions, read this."

The envelope contained a short typed note. *Chief Katlean—Jason Baer instructed me to deliver this box to you in the event of his death. It is not to be opened until the potlatch. To do so will void the promise contained herein. Read Jason's promise aloud to the people. —Max Renner.*

The name was typed, not signed.

"So what?" Eldon asked. "Why should you do anything for Jason, dead or alive?"

"Because I take the potlatch seriously," the chief said. "And because there isn't any key. Maybe Woody swallowed it. Everyone would see that the lock's been broken."

Eldon sighed. "I see."

Katlean looked gleeful. "This has to be a setup. Jason didn't have any love lost for me. Neither did Max. Point is, Max got hold of this box—maybe Jason really did turn it over to him before he was killed. This is as if Max were preparing for something. Max knew he was in trouble, or he'd have brought the box to the potlatch himself."

"If he'd feared for his life, he'd have gone to the police."

"Not if he'd killed Jason," Katlean said. "No, sirree, Eldon, I think that what this box contains is insurance. Something Jason had on somebody. If we open it at the potlatch, we just may unmask Max's killer."

16

The potlatch began late in the afternoon two days later. Eldon looked out the window of the *Aurora* office and saw a steady trickle of people going in the direction of the clan house.

There were Indians and whites, men and women, in braids and baseball caps, beards and shaggy hair, plaid shirts and anoraks, a parade of Southeast Alaska life. Some carried picnic hampers and coolers, strolling as if on their way to a church social, while others were empty-handed. Some walked with the unsteady gait of dedicated afternoon drinkers. Eldon watched one giant white man in grubby denims, with a huge brown beard down his chest, leading a thin little woman and several small children. He lurched along while the children scurried after. The woman, unsteady herself, bumped around among them like a disoriented mother duck among her ducklings.

"Out of work," Anita said.

"What's in the baskets?"

"Food for the potlatch. And things people intend to give away."

"Like what?"

"You'll see. They don't have to be big things."

Cassandra bounded down the stairs. "Let's go!"

e Eldon was glad that the prospect of the potlatch had cheered Cassandra up. "Afraid they'll run out of presents?" he asked.

"They're not allowed to run out! A potlatch is better than Christmas—you don't even have to be *good* to get somethin'!"

"Anything in particular that you want?"

Cassandra made a show of thinking about it. "Mmmm . . . another Barbie doll."

Eldon had hoped she would want a set of fishing flies. Oh, well. "Think you'll get one?"

"Naw. That's not the kind of stuff they give. But it'll be fun. Wait till the dancing starts! *Good copy!"* Cassandra shot back upstairs.

"She loves the drumming and dancing," Anita said. "And wait until you see the masks."

"It's okay to take pictures?"

"Sure. And get a shot of Ed in his rig."

"Don't give away the newspaper."

"Not a chance. I'll give away some advertising, though. If you're canny at a potlatch, you eventually get back a lot more than you gave away, and with interest."

"Too bad for Ed that Jason's not around, then," Eldon said.

"It's a relief, in a way. That could turn ugly. Potlatches can run up huge debts of honor that people can never pay off."

"What about Jason's family? Could Ed out-potlatch *them?* Didn't Jason have any relatives?"

"None that still talked to him. They're not in Klinkatshut, anyway. They're scattered all over the Panhandle."

"Hmm." Eldon got his notebook and camera while Anita slipped a wad of advertising gift certificates into her coat and went to get Cassandra.

Eldon remembered something that sheriff's Detective Art Nola had told him back in Port Jerome: that a murderer sometimes attended the victim's funeral or visited the victim's grave. Art said murderers and their victims knew each other in at least half the cases.

Jason's killer knew him, Eldon thought. And suppose it was Ed Katlean. Going ahead with the potlatch, which he had timed so as to get even with Jason, would be a great way to deflect suspicion. So would setting a reporter to investigate the case. Just make sure the reporter is kept busy writing features about quaint Indian crafts and that there's really nothing for him to investigate. . . .

e Eldon gave a start as Anita and Cassandra came downstairs.

"Something wrong?" Anita asked.

"No, no. Just thinking."

They joined their neighbors. Darkening clouds marred the w blue sky. Cassandra skipped ahead as they strolled down into the village to the clan house, where Woody sat by the door like some enormous snowball Cerberus, barking and wagging his tail. Cassandra ran and threw her arms around the dog's neck. "Hiya, Woody!" Woody rose, lifting Cassandra's feet off the ground as the girl swung from his neck.

Eldon dodged Woody's happy attempts to leap on him and slipped into the clan house behind Anita. A fire burned in the central fire pit, and a delicious smell filled the air. Salmon steaks set on alder sticks were baking around the fire's edge, spread open to the heat like pink wings.

People milled around talking, a sense of gaiety building already. Most wore ordinary clothing, but some wore traditional d robes and headdress. Anita explained that those in costume would help distribute the gifts. Eldon spotted Kate Taylor, resplendent in a red button robe with a great eagle on the back. The old woman seemed to glow and, again, Eldon was struck with a sense of timelessness. He heard a sudden patter of rain on the roof.

Timeless or no, an electric buffet for the food had been set up along one wall. People were lining up and loading paper plates. Cassandra made a beeline for the chow. Eldon decided to do the same.

There were traditional and modern dishes, steaming in

stainless-steel tubs. Eldon's mouth watered as Anita pointed them out. There was baked king salmon fresh from the fire. And broiled steaks from Eldon's halibut. There was wild duck with onions. There was, to his amazement, brisket of bear. There were huge Alaska king crab, spiny and red, their long armored legs hanging over the edges of steel serving tubs.

There were steamed fiddlehead fern tops; Eldon knew from Oregon that fiddleheads tasted like asparagus. There was salmon soup and chilled whipped raspberry soup. There was fresh hot sourdough bread. There were whipped potatoes with brown gravy on the side, canned square-cut green beans, frozen succotash, and sliced-up cylinders of jellied cranberry sauce that showed the ribs of the cans. Eldon saw people unloading still more canned goods from their picnic baskets.

Eldon piled his plate with food, working his way down to the apple pie and coffee cake set out beside tall steel coffee urns and brimming punch bowls. Anita steered Cassandra to a bowl filled with iced red punch. There was pale punch in another bowl. "The red is fruit punch," Anita told Eldon. "The pale stuff is spiked."

"How do you know?"

"That's the way we do it here." Anita thrust a paper cup of the pale punch into Eldon's free hand.

The three of them sat on a riser near one of the house posts, balancing their plates on their knees. Eldon sipped his punch. It was strong stuff. I'd better watch it, he thought. Anita gulped half her drink before she started eating.

"I haven't had a feed like this since the Sons of Eiden Hall back in Port Jerome," Eldon said. "And they were Finns."

"This is the food potlatch," Anita said. "The stuff potlatch starts after."

" 'Stuff' potlatch?"

e Cassandra laughed around a mouthful of food. "That's when they give away the *stuff,* cheechako!"

Drumming began. People continued eating and talking. Woody squeezed through the door and wandered about cadging scraps.

"Some places, potlatches are a lot more formal," Anita said. "Sit-down affairs with tablecloths and silverware and even printed invitations. It depends on the tribe. With the Klinkatshut, one part of the celebration just melds into the next. I'm going to get some more punch. The party's young."

Cassandra watched Anita go. "My dad gave away our newspaper once."

"He did?" Eldon asked. "To who?"

"To Chief Katlean. But the chief gave it right back."

"He was smart," Eldon said. "Nobody in their right mind wants to own a newspaper."

"Well, then Daddy gave it away again."

"Yeah? To who?"

"To Jason Baer. And Jason gave it to Max Renner and Max gave Daddy his boat. But then Daddy gave the boat to Maggie's husband, Mark, who drowned later. Only he couldn't."

"Who couldn't what?"

"Daddy couldn't give the boat to Mark because Mark and Max already owned the boat. But he gave the newspaper to Mom."

"Did your father ever fight with them?"

"He and my mom fought a lot," Cassandra said. "Did you fight with your wife? Mom said you used to have one."

"Oh, she did?" Eldon said. "No, we really didn't fight. Maybe *not* fighting was our mistake."

"What?" Cassandra stuck a white chunk of crab into her mouth and chewed it, considering. "What?" She gave him her gimlet-eyed look.

"Never mind. Don't let your food get cold."

The drumming speeded up, reached a crescendo, and stopped. The track lighting dimmed and talk died back in the hall. Woody gave a thunderous bark.

Ed Katlean emerged from behind the great screen across the front of the hall as if the dog had announced him, no longer an ordinary man but a splendid chief. His red robe glowed in the light from the central fire. Its myriad buttons sparkled. Katlean's Eagle headdress gave him two more eyes. That nose ring must be killing him, Eldon thought.

The chief extended a hand toward the fire. "We thank the salmon for coming to our table. We thank the Great One for making this happen."

Katlean stepped aside. Dancers emerged from behind the screen in robes and fantastic wooden bird masks.

One dancer wore a feathered robe and a mask with a bright hooked beak. He swept his arms out and danced in long, graceful swooping movements.

"That's Eagle," Cassandra said.

The second dancer wore a shaggy fringed robe and a mask with a beak almost five feet long. This dancer kept his arms cocked beneath the mask to hold it up. "That's Raven," Cassandra said as the dancer began a stooped, rhythmic shuffle. "Raven made the world."

"Ness Raven," whispered a new voice in Eldon's ear.

He turned, a little startled, to see that it was Maggie Frame. She squeezed his hand in the darkness: "Hiya."

"Hi there." Eldon tried to squeeze back but Maggie drew her hand away. Her smile gleamed in the darkness.

The dancers circled and dipped to the rhythm of the drumming while the rain outside, which had picked up steadily, added its own dull thrumming to the beat of the dance. The circling was dizzying and somehow enormous.

"The ring of existence," Maggie said. "Raven and Eagle circling the great world."

There was applause when the dancers finished. Talk rose again, and the flow of people back and forth to the food and drink resumed. Two men knocked back paper cups of pale punch, set them down, and started punching each other. Each one got in two or three good socks. There was no sound to the fight but the smack of fists on flesh; then their friends pinned the fighters' arms and hustled them out of the hall.

"Now the gift-giving starts," Maggie said.

Kate and the others in robes began to carry out boxes and piles of folded blankets. This, Anita explained, was the beginning of the stuff potlatch. Cassandra giggled with pleasure.

"Ed's family has been preparing for months," Maggie said. "The women have been reweaving robes and blankets, and the men have been making some of the crafts. Ed's put some of his own money into it, too."

"What are people going to give *him?*"

"You'll see. Token things. They don't need to top him. It would be an insult to top him, under these circumstances."

Lines formed and the people in the hall began receiving their gifts. Things began passing from hand to hand. The robed people handed out blankets. The people who accepted them handed things back—knives, canned goods, a red hunting cap with earflaps tied up on top. There was happy talk, an occasional exclamation or laugh and once or twice a frown. It seemed less formal even than gift-giving at Christmas; yet there was a formality to it that carried overtones of serious obligation, like something Japanese.

Eldon moved through the crowd, taking pictures and getting names. People were matter-of-fact, even friendly, as if he were taking pictures at a family party. Eldon envied the villagers—they had a sense of belonging that he hadn't felt in a long time.

Now the talk grew louder, more boisterous. Eldon saw someone empty a good-size kitchen pot of fresh spiked punch into the punch bowl. Anita and Maggie went over and refilled their cups, glancing at Eldon and then grinning at each other as they spoke in low voices. There was something appealingly feral in their expressions. Eldon's heart speeded up as he hoped against hope.

Katlean began calling out names. These were people who were singled out for the honor of receiving individual gifts. They seemed all to be solid citizens, mostly middle-aged Indian men and a few whites. Probably the big contributors to the chief's election campaign, Eldon thought wryly.

At last, Kate brought out the carved, locked wooden box and handed it to Katlean.

"Now we have a gift from Jason Baer, who's dead," Katlean said. "It came to me through Max Renner, who's dead now, too. You think about those guys, you think, 'They met bad ends,' and so they did. You think about Jason and me, you think, 'Jason and Ed didn't get along.' That's right, Jason and Ed didn't. But this is Chief Katlean talking now, and the potlatch is the place to open this box."

Katlean held out the box and walked around the front of the audience, showing off the lock. A silence fell over the room. Finally, Katlean drew a pair of pliers from beneath his robe and broke the lock. He raised the box lid to reveal an envelope. He opened the envelope. Inside were two sheets of paper.

"It's a message and a map." Katlean stood silently reading, lips moving slightly. The chief's eyes widened and his lips stopped moving. His eyebrows came together as he read the paper again. The crowd stirred, murmured. Woody gave a single bark.

"Shuddup," Katlean told his dog.

There was faint laughter from the audience.

Katlean waited for the titter to die. "Jason's left us a bequest.

It's fitting for a potlatch. First he tells a story—the story of how Raven lost his beak."

The crowd stirred and murmured. "I will read the letter now.

" 'One day Raven went out looking for an easy meal,' " the chief read. " 'He found some fishermen and decided to steal the bait from their hooks. He was feeling very pleased with himself when his beak caught on one of the hooks and came right off.' "

"Everyone knows that story," Anita whispered. "What's he getting at?"

" 'The fishermen took Raven's beak home because it was such a curious object,' " Katlean continued. " 'Raven assumed human form and went to their house, wrapped in a blanket to cover up the hole in his face. He said that he might be able to identify the strange thing. When the fishermen gave it to him, Raven clapped the beak onto his face and flew away.'

" 'Raven was a trickster. But we all know that Raven could be generous, too. He gave mankind the salmon and the rivers. So like Raven, I'm leaving you a gift as I fly away: a trust fund that will pay the tuition to the University of Alaska of any child from this village who qualifies for admission."

There was an awed silence and then applause. Suddenly the crowd burst into conversation.

e *"That's* where his money went!" Anita said with a gasp. "He was putting it all into the foundation. And he never told anybody—"

"Quiet!" Katlean roared to the crowd. "There's a catch!"

Everyone fell silent as Katlean read on. " 'And like Raven, I'm going to play a trick. You have to do something for me. You have to erect my favorite totem pole overlooking Mandel's Glacier. It stands on an island near here, map enclosed. You can't miss Raven and the jumping salmon. . . ." Katlean's voice trailed off; Eldon had the impression that there was something he didn't read aloud. " '—Farewell, Jason Baer.' "

"Good copy!" Cassandra squealed as the room erupted in a babble.

"He means the ridicule pole." Eldon stood up, aimed the camera and shot a flash picture while Katlean's hand was still in the air.

Anita turned to Eldon, her eyes shining with emotion. "That noble man! He never told anybody about it—"

"He was bleeding Max, too," Eldon said. "It got him killed—"

"This is the tab's lead story, not the potlatch—"

Cassandra tugged Eldon's sleeve. "This is your potlatch present, Eldon—a great scoop!"

Katlean was still staring at the paper. The muscles in his jaw worked. Reporter's instinct galvanized Eldon. He pushed his way through the crowd to Katlean. "What's wrong, Chief?"

"Jason played a trick, all right. Woody and I have to carry the totem pole up there ourselves—on our backs."

17

"This is right out of Amundsen and Scott," Eldon said.

"They went to the South Pole, not the North Pole," Cassandra said scornfully. "We learned that in school."

"Well, the chief's not going to the North Pole, either." Eldon was exasperated. It was cold and wet on the glacier. He was dressed warmly, in borrowed clothes that made him look pounds heavier than he already was. Crampons were locked to his boots.

It had been a glorious voyage to Mandel's Bay. A flotilla of Klinkatshut vessels including the Amphicar, Maggie in the troller, and Kate Taylor in her kayak had borne half the town's population into the great deep bowl where the glacier emptied. The sun shining on the glacier and the icebergs had been a tremendous sight, the ice glaring white and the sky and water vivid ultramarine against the black, snow-streaked mountains. Eldon had never seen colors of such purity. The immensity of the setting and the clarity of the air had exhilarated him.

But his mood had deteriorated with the weather. A rainstorm was closing in, and now the sky was the color of dirty steel. Up close the glacier was dirty, too, and it wasn't flat: its surface was corrugated, made of sharp sheets of ice sticking upward, something like a compressed accordion bellows. The sheets were formed by the constant creep of the ice. Its endless, unfathomable pressure flattened and pressed and lifted the ice as the glacier made its stubborn, mindless journey to the bay.

The ice was shot through with grime—bits of dirt and stone. But down inside were glints of sublime color, delicate greens and blues. Trapped light, Eldon thought. I wonder how far down it goes.

Katlean adjusted his nose ring. Bulky in his winter garb, walking stiffly on his crampons, the chief checked the harness that hitched Woody to the sled. The big dog barked and danced eagerly. Woody's paws were protected by canvas boots lest he slash his pads on sharp ice. Katlean checked their bindings while others tightened the lashings on Jason's totem pole. Eldon tried to jot a few notes but found that his gloves were too thick. He pulled off his gloves, stuck them under an armpit, and opened up the Rolleiflex to take a picture. Here's one for the wire service, he thought.

"I want to take the pictures," Cassandra said.

"Why not?" Eldon handed her the camera. "That's *'Je veux prendre des photos'* in French," he said.

"Merci," Cassandra replied. She sighted through the viewfinder

and snapped off a shot. "I'm sad," she said as she advanced the film.

"Why? This is good copy."

"You haven't caught the killer yet."

"Max killed Jason—"

"So who killed Max?"

"I didn't think you cared about Max." Eldon instantly regretted saying that. "Sorry. Look—that just makes this story better, you know what I mean? People will be more interested because they're still wondering who killed Max. Without that, this is just a fat man dragging a log up a hill."

Cassandra dissolved in giggles. "Woody's doing the dragging. Hey, Woody! Good dog!" Cassandra ran through the crowd and shot a close-up of Woody.

Anita stumped up, walking carefully on the rough glacier surface. "Here's the route map. He'll traverse the face that way and work his way up the slope. The rock promontory where the totem pole's supposed to stand is somewhat farther on."

"Any chance we can get there by tonight?"

"No way. We have to camp."

"Half the town's along to watch, to make sure the lawyers can't say that Ed didn't actually do it," Eldon said. "What can go wrong? We'll hold another potlatch afterward."

"I wish TV was here," Anita said. "But they'd have to fly the film out—"

"Who needs competition?" Eldon asked. "So much the bigger scoop for the *Aurora*."

" 'The Weekly Journal of a Free Alaska,' " Anita recited with a faraway look in her eyes, as if planting the totem pole near the top of the glacier would open a fissure between Alaska and the rest of the United States. "That totem ought to be Alaska's national shrine. I'm going to write an editorial. We can still go ahead with that special edition—"

"Um." Eldon was calculating the money he could make selling photos of the "Katlean expedition" to the wire services. At twenty-five bucks a crack, he could make a dent in his travel expenses. Even Fiske might spring for a shot or two.

The thought of money brought him uneasily back to Cassandra's words: He hadn't really gotten the scoop. He hadn't really earned his keep or his fishing trip. The revelation that Max had killed Jason Baer seemed tepid in the dark wake of Max's murder. Just when you think the work is done, there's more work, Eldon thought. Reporters often got out of the office late. If you want regular hours, work in a bank, as Fiske always said.

On the other hand, reporters didn't have to hang around the office, like bankers, or even wear ties. And while a banker might find himself caught up in the excitement of the occasional bank robbery, a reporter got a broader range of adventures to cover, such as this trek up the glacier. Eldon had already done an interview with the chief and sent it out over the wire. Now all he needed to do was cover the expedition and the triumph.

Jason's letter had not specified that Katlean had to erect the totem pole single-handed. There were plenty of people standing by to help with that, so success seemed assured. Had that been Jason's oversight or had the artist sincerely intended that his promise of generosity to the village become reality? No, Eldon decided, Jason just couldn't bear the thought of Katlean failing to put up his totem pole.

That same egocentric stubbornness had brought Jason to grief. Jason had pushed Max too far, perhaps had even known that he was pushing him; yet his pride in having power would not let him stop. And somehow, Jason's folly had killed Max, too.

Eldon quit woolgathering and came alert. Katlean slipped on his harness and stood next to Woody, ready for action. This was a good angle—dogsled events were a dime a dozen in Alaska, but this time the man would pull, too. Katlean clasped his hands clumsily over his head in the sign of "the winnah." Cassandra scampered up with the Rolleiflex and snapped a picture. Good enterprise in that kid, Eldon thought: she'll go far in the trade.

Eldon saw two familiar figures in the crowd—Chilkat Charley and Nanook Nell, swathed in enormous fur coats. Charley wore a bearskin coat that made him look like a hairy toadstool. Nell, graceful in a fox fur number, carried a first-aid bag. They stepped along together in homemade snowshoes, ignoring the stares. Someone hooted—too close. Katlean whirled and flung a handful of ice in the man's face, snarled something in a voice too low for Eldon to hear; the man backed off, hands open, nodding hasty agreement. Cassandra took a picture of Charley and Nell, then sprang onto the sled and straddled the totem pole: "Mush!"

Woody barked, Katlean threw his shoulders forward. Man and dog got under way as the crowd laughed and applauded. There was a crunching noise as the sled trundled over the ice.

Eldon crunched along after, part of the ragged line of people that followed the sled like the trail of some ragged comet. It was clumsy going. But Anita grasped his hand and steadied him, and hand in hand they trudged up Mandel's Glacier.

"I should've brought an ice ax for you," Anita said, "or a ski pole."

"We'll get there," Eldon said, puffing. "I just hope Katlean doesn't have a heart attack or something."

"Ed's chubby but he's tough. The glacier doesn't scare him. He has remarkable stamina." Anita looked around. "What a turnout! This is the spirit of a Free Alaska. This tops the potlatch as the story of the year."

Maybe it tops the murders, too, Eldon thought. "Where's Maggie?"

"She's up at the camp, helping with the cooking."

Helpful Maggie! The thought of camp and a hot meal waiting at the end of a long, cold trek filled Eldon with resolve. And there would be a snug night in a warm sleeping bag. A pity that he would have to behave discreetly. Eldon entertained himself with thoughts of slipping away somewhere after dark with Maggie or Anita. The glacier under the moon and stars would make a splendid, romantic view. And suppose there was a summer aurora?

Romance would have to wait. A cold wind swept across the ice and brought Eldon back to reality. He turned his full attention to his trek. "Gonna rain, sure enough—"

"Surprise, surprise," Anita said. "We'll hole up in camp until it stops. Here—have a candy bar."

Anita passed Eldon a Snickers. He chomped into it gratefully. The sun broke through the clouds for a moment, and dazzling light swept across the ice, lighting up the line of figures and the mismatched pair toiling with the sled. Eldon looked uphill and saw eagles riding the thermals across the glacier face. He kept climbing. Suddenly the sun was gone.

They crunched along all afternoon. It got down to putting one foot in front of the other; climbing a glacier, Eldon reflected, was a lot like life. He tried to keep a steady pace, planting his feet carefully. It would be great to be able to drive the Amphicar up here, he thought, but you'd need treads on the damned thing.

During a pause, Eldon made his way up to the sled. "Howya doin', Chief?"

"I'm okay." Katlean was leaning against Jason's totem, sipping hot tea from a Thermos Cassandra had brought him. The chief looked tired. He was breathing heavily and his face was flushed. A clear drop of sweat hung from the tip of his nose in front of the ring.

"Are you sure?" Eldon asked, peering.

"I'm okay."

"Sing out if you need help."

"That would void the bequest," the chief said doggedly. "I'm not letting my village down."

Or letting Jason out-potlatch you, Eldon thought. "No chest pains?" he asked. "No pains in your left arm?"

"Oh, fuck you, Eldon. I'm all right."

Eldon grinned to mask his worry. "I won't put that in the paper. We'd get calls about 'bad taste.' "

Katlean glanced up the slope. "Not that far to camp."

"Figure you can make it the rest of the way tomorrow?"

"If the weather holds. Woody's enjoying himself, aren't you, stupid?"

Woody hopped and barked in his harness, happy marshal of the parade. Cassandra placed a big steel basin on the ice and filled it with water from a plastic jug. Woody lapped thirstily, water streaming from his muzzle.

"I'd better check his boots," Katlean said and turned away.

The breaks had been about ten minutes apiece, but this one lasted twice as long. Finally, Katlean got back into harness and started up again. The temperature was dropping. The look of the sky grew heavier as the swirling clouds gave way to a pervading metal color. At last the rain started—a fine, cold, misting spray. Eldon drifted back to walk beside Anita and watched the butt of the totem pole as it bumped along the ice. It looked like the upright of a cross being hauled up a forsaken and frosty Calvary.

"I'm worried about the chief," Eldon told Anita.

"He'll make it," Anita said grimly.

"I wonder if *I* will," Eldon added.

"No choice—unless you want to spend the night in the open."

"Thanks anyway."

"Where's Cassandra?"

"There she is, talking with Charley and Nell."

"They're the ones who showed you the pole in the graveyard?"

"Sure did. They're harmless. A walking history lesson."

"I want to meet them," Anita said. "I'm going up there for a while. I can keep a closer eye on Cassandra."

Eldon nodded and kept crunching along, head down against the rain.

The procession crept across the glacier all through the afternoon. The pace was agonizing. After a while, some of the men started pushing the sled, helping Katlean and Woody along. Eldon wasn't sure if their impromptu aid voided Jason's bequest, but he decided not to mention it in his stories. He kept wondering if he would have to write Katlean's obit. The chief was bowed almost double, arms swinging. Woody pulled with shoulders bunched, head straight out, and tongue hanging, lurching over the ice like a huge hairy tank. They were in a particularly rough area now, heading for the edge of the glacier and the woods where the camp had been set up. Eldon could see campfire smoke and people waiting on the edge of the ice.

Eldon looked up the snowfield. The glacier wound back into the black mountains like a dirty white pelt. Glacier and mountains contrasted like the back of an immense skunk. The promontory where the totem pole would stand was lost in rolling fog. I'd hate to spend a night out in this, Eldon thought—and then he heard a crash and a yell from ahead and knew that Katlean had had a heart attack.

Then he saw that it was something just as disastrous—the rear of the sled suddenly lurched down out of sight. Yells of "crevasse" reached Eldon's ears. He visualized the chief, Woody, and the loaded sled, not to mention Cassandra and her camera, plunging into a bottomless blue ice chasm. Heart pounding, Eldon scrambled across the ice.

He reached the sled sweating and nearly exhausted. It sat

canted on the glacier, front runners off the ice and the rear wedged in the crevasse. Katlean was squatting beside the sled with a disgusted expression. Anita and Cassandra waited with others nearby.

"You don't look so good, Eldon," Katlean said with a growl. "Chest pains?"

Eldon fell to his hands and knees. "Okay, I take it back. What happened?"

"See for yourself. The ice under the rear runners gave way. The crevasse is about six feet deep. Make a good grave."

"Can we get it out of there?"

"Oh, sure—at least I don't have to do *that* myself. But we have to be careful. We don't know what's underneath."

"Uh! Shouldn't we spread out—?"

"Relax. This isn't *The Eiger Sanction*. I just don't want more ice to give way, drop the damn thing on somebody's foot."

Eldon crawled over and peered into the neon-blue gash. Katlean was right; this was merely an ice gully. The ice was solid enough. Too solid—the rear of the sled was firmly wedged. "We'll have to dig."

"I've sent up to camp for shovels," Katlean said. "Hey, Cassandra—got any more tea?"

Cassandra shook the Thermos. "All out. Sorry."

"Go up to camp and get some more," Anita told her. "Ask Maggie to fill you up."

Cassandra hesitated, her expression worried. Katlean grinned. "We're not gonna fall through the ice. Unhitch Woody and take him with you."

Cassandra looked more composed at that. "Okay." Anita helped her free Woody, who stepped up beside Cassandra with an air of authority. Cassandra gave Eldon the camera and started up the slope to the camp with the dog.

Eldon stared at the totem pole and shook his head. "We

wouldn't even be here if all this hadn't happened—Jason and Max dead."

Katlean gazed about them. "Yeah. The killer's on the trek with us, I can feel it. Indian instinct. Unerring. Especially when it's a small town and there's a limited number of suspects."

"I don't think it's anybody from Klinkatshut," Eldon said. "They'd have turned up by now. Somebody's story wouldn't have checked out. Or somebody couldn't have kept their mouth shut. Or somebody else would've overheard something, and that would've been that. I just haven't traced the paper trail far enough. Don't know if I can."

"Don't you want to be allowed to go fishing?" Katlean asked with a dry chuckle. "Someone had it in for Max, for sure. But who? A stranger couldn't have slipped into town without being noticed."

"Maybe he didn't," Eldon said. "Maybe Max picked him up in the boat."

"Where? How?"

"On the island with the ridicule pole. Or near there."

"Wouldn't Charley or Nell have seen them?" Anita asked.

"So they missed him," Eldon said. "But nobody in town knew about the ridicule pole—except Max."

"And maybe this unknown party," the chief said, "who knifed him and slipped out of Klinkatshut unnoticed. How?"

"How about a kayak?" Eldon asked.

That got another laugh from the chief. "Kate Taylor will love that one."

Eldon said nothing. He was thinking about Kate's grocery bills.

He shook his head. Was there a reason he didn't know about? His train of thought was interrupted by the arrival of the picks, shovels, and poles. I'm going to appreciate a hot meal and a fire tonight, Eldon thought as they set to digging. He started photographing the digging, shielding the camera from the rain as well as he could. Another good reason to be a reporter—he preferred taking pictures to digging.

Katlean and his helpers hacked the trench wider. Now they could shore up the rear of the sled. They prepared to lever the sled up.

The chief and others got hold of the sled, Katlean squatting with a strong grasp on a forward crosspiece. They counted to three and heaved. Counted to three and heaved. Counted to three and heaved. The sled came up and forward, out of the crevasse—

"Argggghhh!" Katlean toppled over in the snow, clutching at the small of his back. "Oh! God! Ow! I've thrown out my back—"

"Take it easy, Ed," Eldon said. "Somebody get Nell."

Katlean moaned. "I've pulled it bad."

The chief managed to sit up and leaned on one arm in the snow. "I can get up."

"Don't move," Anita said. "Wait for the medic."

Nell came crunching down the ice on her snowshoes, carrying her medical bag. She pulled up Katlean's layers of sweaters and examined him with strong fingers. "You've pulled the big cables, all right. You're going to have to take a few days off."

"No, dammit, I've got to pull—"

"You're a fool to try."

Katlean looked as if he expected Nell to try to stop him. When she didn't, he tried to stand and reach for his harness. "Ow!"

"See?" Nell asked. "Help him up to camp—he's done for the day. We've got a nice hard sled for him to sleep on."

"Damn Jason," Katlean muttered as Eldon and Anita got him to his feet and slipped his arms over their shoulders. "I'll top him yet. Arrgh!"

"I thought Indian braves scoffed at pain," Eldon said.

"That's Apaches or something! Ow!"

Katlean kept up a strained banter as they helped him up to camp. Now it was even colder, and snow flurries were whirling down, mixed with the rain. The wind picked up. And this was summer! Eldon didn't like the idea of sleeping out one bit, but he liked even less the idea of trying to make it down the glacier safely in the storm.

The prospects of surviving comfortably looked brighter in camp. Alaska's pioneering improvisational spirit had prevailed. Bright modern backpacking tents and canvas lean-tos were up and fires were blazing. The flames swallowed the snow flurries and the rain as cooks stirred big pots of soup.

"Plenty of potlatch provisions left over," Katlean explained as Eldon and Anita helped him sit down with his back to a flat rock. "This is Potlatch Chapter Two. In the morning, I'll drag that damn thing the rest of the way up the glacier without the dog. Owww . . ."

Eldon didn't think they were going anywhere in the morning. "Does it always snow in June?"

"It's not unknown," Anita said. "Don't worry, we'll be nice and warm tonight, though you and I will have to sleep separately."

"I'll freeze!"

"No, you won't." Anita reached into her parka and pulled out a flask. "Cheers."

"Thanks, I'll pass," Eldon said. Anita looked at the flask thoughtfully and then put it away without drinking.

Where's Cassandra? Eldon wondered, afraid the child might wander off as the weather closed in. But there she was, behind Woody, peering at Maggie Frame. Maggie was peering back. The child's stare seemed more intense than the woman's; Cassandra looked like a predator and Maggie like the prey. Woody's ears were up and forward. Was the dog growling? Then Cassandra glanced toward Eldon, glared, and stole away.

Eldon shivered. Was it from the stares or just from the cold? That dog would make an amazing hot pad at night, he thought. Be kind of rank, though.

The mood in the camp was upbeat, for all that Katlean lay, or rather, leaned painfully in the middle of it all, a reminder that Klinkatshut was only partway to its goal. Eldon made his way through the crowd to Maggie, who held out a cup of soup: "I feel like a Red Cross nurse."

"Welcome to the Klinkatshut Arctic Expedition," Eldon said. "I am war correspondent Larkin, at your service. What was that between you and Cassandra just now?"

"What was what?"

"You both looked annoyed."

"Eldon, you're seeing things. . . . What are you going to write if Ed can't make it?"

"The truth, of course. Either he makes it or he doesn't."

"Suppose Ed has some help?"

Eldon hesitated. He had already decided not to mention the men pushing the sled. Omission was a slippery slope. "What kind of help?"

"I mean, suppose other people took the totem pole up there?"

"I couldn't overlook that, Maggie—c'mon."

"You could if you weren't here," Maggie said.

"But I am," Eldon said. "And even if I weren't, there's Anita. And Cassandra."

"So there are."

"Don't look so grim."

"Oh, I'm not," Maggie said. Her voice became a low purr. "How about slipping away for a little snowtime fun? I have a quilt—"

Eldon mentally licked his chops. "How about when we get home? I'm on my good behavior for this little trek. I'm afraid the boss is watching."

"You've got yourself in quite a fix, Eldon. Two women after you at once and a third jealous. You remind me of Jason."

"But I'm nicer. So who's jealous?"

"So you are nicer. Cassandra."

"Phooey!" But of course Cassandra was jealous. It made Eldon uneasy. It smacked of paternal responsibility.

"You sell yourself short," Maggie said. "You're really quite formidable."

"You should tell my ex."

"Why do you still care what she thinks?" Maggie said.

Maybe I don't, Eldon thought. But if I go on like this, I'm going to wind up an Alaska resident, married to the somewhat tipsy editor of the Klinkatshut newspaper, with a stepdaughter and a girlfriend down the road—and I'll never be quite sure how I got here. The only thing to do is get the story and get out.

He didn't think it meanly. He was scared. The weather made him feel off-balance. "I've got to find out who killed Max."

"Still chasing the scoop," Maggie said.

"Yeah."

"I said you were formidable."

"But I'm stumped."

"Want to tell me about it? Have some more soup and we'll sit down somewhere comfortable and talk."

Maggie picked up a rolled quilt and led Eldon over to a fallen log on the edge of the campsite. It was still afternoon, but the overcast made it seem as if night were falling. Snow mixed with rain still came down in a soggy swirl. The forest seemed to drift in rolling fog. Fog obscured the glacier. Eldon saw that they were sitting before a steep slope that pitched down into the clouds. The log might have delineated the edge of the world.

Maggie tossed the quilt over the log and they sat, looking out into the fog. Maggie slid over toward Eldon until their shoulders and thighs touched. "I'm never going to be able to use that fish locker again," she said. "I'll have to replace it. Jesus, Max in there like one of his own frozen fish—" She shook her head as if to clear away the memory. "Look, what's got you stumped?"

Eldon drank some soup, caught a slice of carrot in his teeth and chewed it. "Reporters follow the paper trail. There's some paperwork missing."

"Like what?"

"Like a folder of Jason's drawings. It was taken from his house. The cops don't have it. So Max must've taken it. But I don't know what Max did with it."

"Ahhh. And why would Max take it?"

"If I find it, I'll know why. It's got something to do with that totem that Ed's pulling."

"Maybe Max destroyed it."

"Destroyed *what?* It was just a sheaf of drawings. I saw some of them. Totem designs."

"Jason was always making totem designs," Maggie said.

"Who am I overlooking?" Eldon asked. "I know that Max killed Jason. I know why. What I don't know is what the drawings had to do with it—and who owed Max badly enough to kill him."

"Money's not the thing here," Maggie said thoughtfully. "Power's the thing. That's what Alaska's all about. Magic. Power."

"You ought to write tourist brochures. Good money in it." But sitting here near a campfire on the edge of a glacier, Eldon almost believed in the magic. He knew that Jason Baer had believed in it, that Ed Katlean and Anita and Maggie believed in it, that the town of Klinkatshut believed in it. Otherwise, why would half the town's population be out here in a storm, instead of home getting drunk, fighting, and watching two-week-old sports contests on television? With weather like this, I could get interested in baseball, too, Eldon thought.

Maggie slipped an arm around Eldon's shoulders and hugged him. There was a big knife on her belt; the scabbard pinched Eldon's hipbone. "Tell you what," Maggie said, "let's go for a walk in the woods."

"In this? You're kidding."

"I know a snug little cave just down the way."

"If we're doing it on ice, I want to get on top."

"That's why I brought the quilt we're sitting on." Maggie leaned in, licked Eldon's ear, and tightened her squeeze. The knife scabbard pinched harder. Between the scabbard and trying to balance his tin cup of soup, Eldon felt trapped. Maybe it was the gloom beyond the edge of the fire or Cassandra's stare, glimpsed at the edge of his vision, bright little feral eyes like a baby editor's—

Just then a shadow rose up from the fog's depths. A bald eagle burst from the mist, wings outstretched, coming straight at them. A big one. Eldon had time only to blink as the great bird flashed over his head. He jumped to his feet, dropping his soup, turning to see the eagle cross the camp like a silent spirit. It flashed over the ground, over the fire and over Chief Katlean's upraised face before vanishing with a single beat of its wings. Woody gave a single tremendous bark.

"Wow!" Eldon ran into the fire circle, glad to be free.

"That was a blessing!" Katlean cried over the babble of voices. "I'm gonna make it! My back feels better already!" He dug out his nose ring and clapped it on.

"A blessing on Eldon, too," said Nanook Nell. "It flew over him first, Chief."

"Cheechakos need extra luck," Katlean said magnanimously, and Eldon remembered that Eagle was Katlean's totem.

"Might've been Raven, in Eagle's form," someone warned.

"That was Eagle," insisted another.

"I'll take whatever grace I can get," Katlean said. "Come to think of it, I've never even seen a raven around here—"

"I didn't get a picture!" Cassandra complained.

"Just another of the great unshot news photos," Eldon told her. "You've got to keep alert. You just never know."

"You're not very alert," Cassandra replied icily. "Over there smooching with *Maggie."*

"We weren't smooching," Eldon said. Cassandra's face darkened. Eldon pulled her aside before she could blow up and hunkered down with her. "You're on assignment, taking pictures for the *Aurora.* Right?"

"Right," Cassandra said reluctantly.

"Good. That means you will act professionally at all times. No tantrums. Got it?"

"Got it—"

"You will not embarrass me in front of news sources. Got it?"

"Y-yes, Eldon." Cassandra sniffed back tears.

"And I will not paddle you in front of them, either. We have got to work together, okay?"

"Okay." Cassandra's eyes glistened. Eldon thought she would cry but then her expression perked up. "This is *good copy,* huh?"

"Yes. That eagle's going to be in my lead."

"I have something better," Cassandra replied.

"Oh?" Eldon was wary, hearing Fiske in Cassandra's tone.

Cassandra reached under her coat and flashed a folded piece of heavy, rough-grade paper. The paper was folded in quarters, and Eldon could not see what was on it.

"What's that?"

"Let's go for a walk." Cassandra grinned and handed Eldon the camera. "Reload that for me, willya?"

"Sure." They ambled across the fire circle in the direction that the eagle had flown, Eldon rewinding the film in the Rolleiflex and fishing in his pockets for a fresh roll. They leaned over beside a tent to shield the camera from the rain as Eldon opened it and removed the film.

Cassandra pulled out the folded paper again.

"What is it?" Eldon whispered.

Cassandra glanced around and then partially unfolded the paper. "One of Jason's drawings. Guess who?"

Eldon looked, was startled to see a realistic pastel crayon drawing of Maggie Frame. Eldon stared at the smudged image as a raindrop landed on the paper and cut a rivulet through Maggie's hair. "Where the hell did you get this?"

"From a folder I believe you're looking for."

"Where's the folder, dammit?"

Cassandra inclined her head to one side. "In Nell's medical bag. I slipped this out when she was taking care of the chief." Cassandra whisked the drawing out of Eldon's hands and back under her coat. "Better close up the camera, Eldon. It'll get wet."

Eldon snapped the Rolleiflex closed. "I knew those two were holding out on me but—"

"They didn't kill Jason," Cassandra said matter-of-factly. "Look at the *other* one." She handed him a second, smaller piece of paper. The fire cast highlights on Cassandra's features, and for an instant Eldon glimpsed how she would look when she was grown—like her mother, he thought, only more ruthless.

The second piece of paper was flimsier. It was a bill of sale for a Remington .30-06 rifle—made out to Max Renner. Eldon stared at the receipt. "Where'd you get this?"

"I found it in Jason's house, the day we went there," the child's voice was fierce. "Don't you see, Eldon? *Maggie switched guns.*"

Mike Atkov said Max shot Jason with a Winchester, Eldon thought. "Why didn't you tell me this before?"

"I wanted to be sure. A reporter has to be absolutely sure. I wanted to get the scoop."

"How'd you know I was looking for the drawings? I didn't tell you that—"

"You told Mom," Cassandra said. "That night she stayed in your room. You think kids don't listen?" Cassandra studied Eldon's features. "I'm glad Mom likes you."

Eldon took a deep breath. "Who gave Charley and Nell the drawings?"

"Maggie. Before we got on the boats. I saw. And she knows I saw."

Abruptly, the whole psychological sparring match between Cassandra and Maggie came into focus for Eldon.

"I suspected her as soon as I found the nail," Cassandra explained.

Eldon studied Cassandra. Was this a young genius or a budding paranoid? "You *suspected?"*

"I saw that Maggie's rifle was different."

"Different? How?"

"It was different from the one in the picture of Mark—it takes a pretty dumb kid not to know a Winchester from a Remington. I kept thinking about it. So I went back to Maggie's house and peeked in the window and checked."

"The day you surprised me in the bushes."

"Yeah." Cassandra chuckled. "There was a Remington hanging over the fireplace, not a Winchester. I told Jimbo about it on the telex. And your friend Melissa. They said to follow the paper trail." Cassandra paused. "Melissa's nice. D'you like her better than Mom?"

"Never mind that. Why didn't you tell me about this?"

"I didn't have proof. Not until I saw Maggie pass Nell the folder. Then I knew that's what you must've been looking for at the house." Cassandra looked around and drew closer to

Eldon. "I was afraid of her even when we went to Jason's house. That's why I had the chisel. That's why I wanted to stay with you."

Max stole the drawings from the house, Eldon thought. Maggie got them from Max. Max shot Jason and then Maggie killed Max—and swapped the rifles. Which means she knew that Max killed Jason. They were in it together.

"We can't say anything," Eldon said, "until we get back to town. Then I'll call the state troopers."

"Let's call them *now.*"

"We can't get down the glacier in this storm," Eldon said. "It's getting dark. We'd break our necks."

"Then we've got to stick together tonight, Eldon. Because of *her.*"

"Don't be afraid. Maggie can't do anything to us."

"Don't go off with her."

"Uh, no." Eldon realized that Max's body had been in the fish locker aboard the boat because Maggie had intended to dump it overboard. And me, too, he thought. She'd have killed me with the ax, claimed that a wave got me. But Anita turned up for the ride—and Maggie knew Anita always carries a gun. Eldon's knees grew spongy as he ran the scenario through his mind. "I'm going to sit down. Go stay with your mother. *Don't* say anything about this yet. I want to tell her myself."

"You wanta steal my byline."

"We'll share one." I'm safe now, Eldon thought. There's nothing Maggie can do with all these people around.

"My name goes first."

"Your name goes first," Eldon agreed.

He went to Katlean. A nylon lean-to had been erected above the chief, who sat in a sleeping bag with his back braced against the rock, watching the fire sizzle in the rain. He had removed his nose ring. The waning afternoon light made the storm's color a dark gray-green. Others had retreated under shelters of their own. Eldon heard low voices and the clink of bottles. Woody lay beside Katlean, nose on his paws, filling most of the rest of the lean-to and smelling rank. Woody whined in greeting as Eldon approached, and his ears twitched. Eldon had expected Woody to be exhausted after his long pull, but there was an air of tension in the big animal.

"Pull up a rock and a nice warm dog, Eldon," Katlean said. "Welcome to the royal progress."

Eldon sat down on piled hemlock branches. "How're you feeling?"

"I'm full of aspirin and Nell slipped me a muscle relaxant. I'll be ready to go in the morning."

"Don't bet on it, if this weather keeps up."

"It's all turning to rain. I intend to stick it out until we can get under way again. Being king has its responsibilities. No way I can chuck this in. Not and win the next election."

"Waiting another day would be better for your back."

"Can't hold my audience if I wait. If enough people see me put up the totem, I won't have to campaign next time. Who they gonna respect? Jason? No—me."

"I've identified Jason's killers."

Katlean started, then winced and dropped his voice. " 'Killers'? Who?"

"Max Renner and Maggie Frame. They killed him together."

"What? *Maggie?* I don't believe it—why? How?"

"And then she killed Max," Eldon continued. "We'll find out 'why' when we get home. I'm taking what I know to the state troopers. I want you to know in case anything happens in the meantime—and because you're chief."

"And how do you know?"

"A bunch of things just came together. But we can't nab her now."

Katlean glanced back out at the rain. "You're right. Not with my back. And nabbing's not our business. You're a reporter and I'm an Indian chief."

"Got a flashlight, Chief?"

"Sure. Here. Why?"

"I'm going back to look at the totem pole."

"Why?"

"More clues."

"Well, don't get lost. Follow the tracks. Better take someone with you."

"I'll be all right. I'll be back shortly."

Eldon slipped on his crampons at the edge of camp and started working his way down the icy glacier slope, keeping the flashlight beam focused on the dirty rut of tracks that led down to the totem pole. Out here on the glacier face the wind threw the rain in unrelenting sheets. There was little sense of distance or direction in the fog. Eldon felt as if he were wandering in an immense, cold, smoke-filled bottle. He pulled up his parka hood over his jungle hat and tightened the drawstring. That was better, although the hat was already soaked and the cold, wet hatband pressed tighter onto his brow. My next vacation will be somewhere warm, he decided, like Bermuda or Hong Kong.

The trail was all grit and mud and the occasional blue jag of light in the ice. Now and then the wind blew a gap in the fog, and he glimpsed distant crags and was conscious of the immensity around him.

Maggie had almost killed him. His stomach turned over a little as he thought about it. Eldon had had his life on the line before, but never at the hands of someone whom he *liked.* Talk about a spoiled vacation. . . .

There was the totem pole, lashed to its sled under canvas, chocks and poles wedged beneath the sled's runners to keep it from sliding away. Eldon trudged over and leaned against the sled for a rest. He applied his weight gingerly but the sled was firmly parked on the ice. A ride down the mountainside is all I need, he thought.

He pulled out the drawing of Maggie Frame and studied it. There was nothing resembling this drawing on the totem pole, but Eldon wanted to study the carvings up close, to compare them with the drawings in the folder. They're going to tell the story, he thought, and the totem pole's story is going to make sense when you match it up with the financial records. Maggie's in there somewhere—but why?

Eldon thought he heard a soft crunching of ice. He jerked his head up and looked around, listening over the beating of his heart. But there was only the racing fog and the boom of the wind. He waited, finally pulled back his parka hood and stripped the canvas back from the side of the pole. He knelt to study the images partially exposed there: sea images. . . .

There was a loud click and a cold metallic ring suddenly pressed against the nape of Eldon's neck. The muzzle of a pistol.

A pistol! Eldon realized in a rush of horror that he had gotten it all wrong. Only one person among them had a pistol. The killer was Anita.

18

"Raise yer hands real slow, podner."

"Chilkat Charley!"

"And you're a damn sneakin' polecat," Charley said. "Now git yer hands up! What're you doin' to that totem pole?"

Eldon raised his hands. They felt light as balloons. "I was looking at it."

A head popped over the log. Nanook Nell. "Looking at it? Why?"

"I think I know, Nellie." Charley frisked Eldon, took away his folding knife and whipped out Jason's drawing of Maggie. "We've found the thief as rifled yer bag. He was fixin' to steal the pole! Knew we couldn't trust 'im the second I laid eyes on 'im—"

"Father George wouldn't send us a person like that," Nell said.

"Oh, he's a real charmer," Charley insisted. "Fooled Father George, too. Hate t' hafta tell the padre, but if'n he knows, he'll feel better when they find the body."

"Wait!" Eldon barely got the word out. "Please don't kill me. I didn't steal the drawing."

"How'd ya git it, then?"

"From Cassandra—"

"Cassandra?" Nell asked. "You can't shoot a nine-year-old, Charley."

"What was the kid doin' in the bag?" Charley demanded. "Lookin' fer drugs? Kids today are all on drugs—"

"She saw Maggie give you the drawings." Eldon tried to strengthen his voice, speak with certainty and authority. "The police are looking for those drawings—Father George's brother, Mike the trooper." Well, that was stretching it. But Eldon knew Mike Atkov would want the drawings as soon as he learned how they tied in with the double murders in Klinkatshut.

The pressure of the pistol muzzle eased on Eldon's neck. "Why're they looking fer 'em? They're Maggie's."

"Is that what she told you?" Eldon asked. "Let me put down my hands. I won't try anything."

"Let him up, Charley," Nell said in a worried way. "We'll see what he has to say."

"Drop 'em slow and turn around," Charley said. "But keep sittin'."

"Thanks." Eldon lowered his hands, turned, and sat on the edge of the sled. Charley stood before him pointing his immense cap-and-ball pistol. Moisture twinkled on the long barrel. It looked big as a sewer pipe. Worse yet, Charley's eyes had that alarming blank aluminum quality. They were as shiny and featureless as unlabeled can lids. Eldon prayed that it was only a trick of the light. He could almost feel the big, soft .44-caliber bullet poking through his guts. Wetness from the sled soaked through the seat of his pants, reminding him of the tumble down the wet steps in Ketchikan that had brought him here. What a vacation, he thought. If only I hadn't taken that short cut through the alley—

Nell came around the totem pole and confronted him. Charley won't have to shoot me, Eldon thought. Nell will just pull off my arms and legs and head and throw me down the mountainside.

"Talk," Nell said.

"You're the ones who'd better start talking," Eldon said boldly. "You're hiding evidence in a murder investigation."

"Is that why the child stole this?" Nell held up the drawing.

"Yeah," Eldon said. "Max Renner took the folder from Jason's house, after he killed Jason."

"We know that," Nell said.

"You do?" Eldon's heart sank. He'd called it wrong—Charley and Nell were accomplices in murder, not dupes. He was done for.

"Maggie told us the whole story," Charley said. "She found the folder in Renner's store, after he disappeared."

"She said it was hers?"

"Jason wanted Maggie to have those drawings," Nell said. "She wanted us to keep them for her, but she couldn't get them to us until we came to town for the totem pole trek. Maggie's afraid that the lawyers wouldn't let her have them—that Anita

Povey would sell them, because she's Jason's agent."

"That's a drawin' of Maggie right there," Charley said. "We owe Maggie."

"How?" Eldon demanded, desperate to keep the conversation going. If he could get Charley to start yarning—

"It's not his business," Nell said tartly. "It's shameful."

"He's come this far, he'll find out anyways," Charley said.

"He probably will," Nell said with a sigh. "As Charley said, we owe Maggie—and her husband, Mark."

"But Mark's dead, so we just owe Maggie," Charley explained patiently.

"What happened?"

Charley snorted. "Nell's cookin'!"

"And your fishing!" Nell shot back. She turned to Eldon. "When we first were living off the land here, we learned some things about Southeast Alaska the hard way—such as, never eat the shellfish."

"Clams, mussels, cockles, scallops—they're all bad fer ya," Charley said, nodding fiercely. "They kin kill ya."

"Paralytic shellfish poisoning," Nell said. "PSP. It's caused by a microorganism. In Southeast, you stick to king crab or any kind of real fish and leave the bivalves strictly alone."

"Right!" Eldon nodded vigorously. "PSP! We have problems with that in Oregon, sometimes."

"Pretty smart fer a cheechako," Charley said. "We were cheechakos once ourselves. And maybe not so smart. Learned the hard way."

Was the aluminum glint starting to fade? Eldon hoped so. "You got sick from PSP?"

"We almost died," Nell said. "One of the reasons we loved our island is that there are whole shoals of mussels and clams. Charley used to bring them home by the bushelful. We were lucky for a while—"

"Nature's bounty, like pioneer times," Charley said, a trifle defensively. "An' while we were bein' lucky, we got to know Mark and Maggie. Their boat put in one time to fix a rudder problem. We got to be friends. They usta come callin' on their way in and out fishin' and sometimes bring us supplies."

"One day they arrived just in time," Nell said. "PSP had hit us. We were both laid out on the cabin floor—"

"Chokin'," Charley said in a strangled tone, starting to act it out. "Suffocatin'. First yer tongue starts ta tingle . . . then the tinglin' spreads ta other limbs, such as yer hands an' feet. Yer mouth gits dry and ya can't talk or stand and everything's swimmin'—"

"Don't wave that gun around," Eldon said.

"Mark and Maggie knew what it was at once," Nell said. "They got us to a doctor and saved our lives."

"Never thought I'd be glad ta feel someone stick their fingers down m' throat," Charley declared, raising the pistol's muzzle a little, so that it no longer pointed directly between Eldon's eyes. "Though I barely remember it. We owe Mark and Maggie. It's why we're helpin' Maggie now."

"Max tried to cheat her out of those drawings," Nell said.

"Max stole them from Jason," Eldon said. "And Maggie stole them from him."

There was a silence broken only by the sound of the rain. Charley's eyes blazed metallic once more, and Eldon tensed, waiting for him to pull the pistol's trigger. But neither Charley nor Nell moved. Eldon knew that wheels were turning in their crazy minds; the real world was seeping in, and they didn't like it one bit.

"What d'you think I'm out here getting wet for?" Eldon asked. "Do you think I want to rob Maggie?"

"What *are* you out here for?" Nell said at last.

"Let me compare the drawings in the folder to the designs on the totem pole," Eldon said. "There's a story no one wants told. It's on the totem pole. I want to dope it out."

Charley and Nell looked at each other. "He's a reporter," Charley said, as if that explained everything.

"Newspapers are one of the things we came up here to get away from," Nell said.

"The *Aurora*'s a good paper, though," Charley said. " 'The Weekly Journal of a Free Alaska.' I'm surprised the editor's young 'un is inta thievery."

We're about to start talking in circles, Eldon thought, and said, "I'm getting wet. Will you let me look at the pole? And the drawings?"

"I've got the bag right here," Nell told Charley.

Charley lowered the gun. "You'd better not tell us anything we don't want to hear!"

Eldon laughed. "I can't guarantee that—but I will guarantee a good story."

"Publicity!" Charley muttered. "I knew it!"

Nell opened the bag and handed over the folder. When Eldon opened it, she snatched Charley's broad-brimmed hat from his head and held it over the drawings to shield them from the rain.

Eldon threw back the canvas and studied the drawings, comparing them with those on the totem pole. Here was the woman with hair like waves and that curious lightning pattern and the man clutching the horseshoe to his chest. . . . "That's no horseshoe—that's a magnet! It's Max Renner."

Nell was looking over Eldon's shoulder. "But the carvings and the drawings aren't the same."

Eldon looked again. Among the set were more designs that weren't carved in the wood—an alternative narration, as it were, with Raven proud above all. These were realistic drawings—not totemic—and they showed Max pushing a long-faced, dark-haired man into the ocean.

"That's Mark!" Charley said. "Mark Frame."

Eldon remembered the photograph Maggie had shown him. And the rifle. "Jason even dated them—three years ago."

"That's Mark," Charley repeated. "And there's the man with the magnet—"

"Max Renner," Eldon said.

"Mark was lost overboard in a storm—he wasn't pushed," Nell said. "Why would Jason have drawn these? Why would Maggie hide them?"

"Jason drew them for blackmail," Eldon said with a sudden certainty. "One more piece of power over Max. Jason needed to keep the money coming, and this was one way he could pry it out of Max."

"What're ya talkin' about?" Charley asked.

"Now I know why Max killed Jason," Eldon said. "But I don't know why Maggie killed Max—"

"Maggie killed that storekeeper?" Nell put her hands over her mouth. "My God. How can you say that?"

"A little matter of switched rifles," Eldon said.

Charley was still holding the revolver. "I don't like the sound of this one bit. Father George's brother, Mike, he'll have to hear this. We can't settle it." To Eldon's great relief, Charley put the pistol away.

"Maggie gave us those drawings to keep for her," Nell said. "She saved our lives."

"If Eldon's wrong or crazy, there's no harm done," Charley said. "But I don't wanta hafta settle this." Charley shook his head. His fake beard sagged off one ear, sodden in the rain. "Damn world keeps creepin' in. Gimme my hat, woman. Let's go back to camp."

"Thanks." Eldon accepted his clasp knife back from Charley, pushed the folder into his coat, and got to his feet. They began trudging back uphill toward camp. Almost immediately they heard the sounds of a commotion and thunderous barking.

Charley peered through the fog. "What in tarnation now? They fightin' in camp?"

"That's Chief Katlean's dog," Nell said.

They staggered up the slope, tripping on the corrugations of ice. It seemed to take an eternity to cover the uphill distance back to the camp. Suddenly they saw the camp, like a ghost town in the clouds, figures moving around and Woody barking. The fire burned dimly.

Eldon could hear Anita calling Cassandra's name. He lurched into camp to find Katlean leaning grimacing against a tree and others rushing around in a frantic tangle of arms and legs and flashlight beams. Anita ran down to Eldon, cheeks wet with tears, frantic: "She's taken her!"

"What?"

"Maggie grabbed Cassandra and ran," Katlean said.

"Which way?" Eldon asked.

"We don't *know,*" Anita said. "They're both *gone.*"

Woody galloped around the campsite, bowling people over, and headed off barking into the darkness. "Woody," Eldon said. "Follow Woody."

He went after the dog's retreating figure, Anita right behind him. They stepped across the foggy snowfield, calling Cassandra's name and Maggie's. There were no tracks—the snowfield was too hard. Eldon saw something shine in Anita's hand. The Magnum.

"Put away the gun—"

"I'll kill her. She took my baby—"

"No. Put away the gun."

"The hell with you."

"I'm not going to argue. Keep following the dog." Eldon forced himself to think clearly. Maggie grabbed the kid just to get out of camp, he thought. But you can't move fast with a hostage. Maggie's going to dump her and run—where? We're out in the middle of the Alaska Panhandle—

The boats.

Eldon abruptly cut downhill. He knew he would vanish from Anita's sight in the fog. In his keyed-up state, the glacier seemed to rock like the ocean as he floundered across the ice. The fog was so thick that he half expected to slam into it as he ran. He ignored Anita's yells and kept going, zigzagging downward until he snagged a toe and fell headlong.

Eldon hit the ice with a slam and rolled. When he went over the cliff he couldn't even scream. He hit an outcropping and stopped. He lay breathing heavily, clutching the outcropping until he got his wind back. When he sat up shuddering, he saw that the "cliff" behind him was a ledge only a couple of feet high. Cautiously, he crept forward. He was on level ice.

But he was lost. Nothing looked familiar. Clouds parted momentarily to show distant gray crags that seemed to be moving, as if the glacier on which he stood was flying through outer space.

Eldon's teeth began to chatter. Calm down, he told himself. Move downslope to reach the water. But which way was downhill? Next time he might really walk off a cliff.

He listened but there was only the boom of the wind. The fog lifted slightly, hovering now like a low ceiling. In the distance lay indistinct green forest. The wind boomed again, a rhythmic sound like barking. . . .

Barking! *Woody!*

But which way? Eldon turned, listening to the echoes. The dog could be anywhere. He started in the direction he had rolled. That had to be downhill.

There was movement at the edge of his field of vision. Eldon wheeled to see an eagle glide into view, a salmon glittering in its claws. Katlean's eagle had been fishing! Art Nola had dreamed of a bird hovering over water. The water lay close—but where?

Eldon almost yelled the question in desperation when suddenly a black bird swooped in from the left, losing altitude to swing behind the gliding eagle and steal the fish. It was Raven—Jason's totem! Eldon felt a superstitious thrill as the two birds wheeled over the icy world. Eagle screamed and twisted after Raven and they both dived out of sight to the right. Dived *down*. The sacred birds had shown the way.

Eldon heard Woody's barking ahead, distinctly now. He followed the line of the slope, forcing himself to move deliberately. A sprained ankle or broken leg wouldn't help him now.

Then he saw them—Maggie backing downhill, holding a struggling Cassandra against her. Maggie held Chilkat Charley's enormous cap-and-ball revolver. A disheveled Charley, Nell, and a frantically barking Woody stood at bay.

Woody lunged and the gun went off. The big dog yelped in pain and fell. Maggie wheeled and disappeared into the fog, dragging Cassandra with her.

"Ran right into 'em," Charley gasped as Eldon rushed up. His beard hung askew and there was swelling under his right eye. "The dog went after the eagle and flushed Maggie and the kid. Maggie clobbered me and got my gun."

Woody whimpered. There was blood on the ice. Nell rushed over and peered at the wound. "Just grazed the shoulder. I can handle this."

"And we'll handle Maggie!" Charley started up.

Eldon collared him. "The hell we will. She has a gun—"

"She has the kid!"

"We've got to get the cops—"

"They'll be gone by then!"

He's right, Eldon thought. I don't care if Maggie gets away or not, but we've got to make her give up Cassandra somehow. Trade a boat for the kid. "We've got to cut her off."

"This is the way," Charley gasped. "The eagle came from down there."

Eldon and Charley plunged downward and abruptly found themselves below the fog line. It was like falling through a ceiling. Before them lay the foot of the glacier and Mandel's Bay, broad and white in the midnight sun, with the boats anchored and the canoes and kayaks and Amphicar on the beach. Eldon scanned the huge, windy vista with a sinking heart. He saw no one. Had they guessed wrong? Were Maggie and Cassandra still on the glacier? Or had they gotten here ahead of them? "Let's get down to the boats."

"How're we gonna stop her?" Charley asked when they reached the beach.

"Wait a minute." Eldon fumbled open his coat, nearly dropping the folder of Jason's drawings, and pulled out his knife. He got the blade open and stood there feeling ridiculous, a plump man on a deserted beach with a knife in one hand and a sheaf of drawings in the other and a companion wearing a phony beard. The boats stood like the equipment of some vanished time-travel expedition. Eldon felt very tiny.

There was a footfall behind him and a child's whimper. They whirled. It was Maggie, still holding Cassandra—and the gun. Cassandra looked exhausted, her face tear-stained. Maggie's face was flushed and wet strands of hair lay on her cheeks. Her eyes were hard and bright.

"You look funny, Eldon—but that's what I always liked about you. Now stop waving that knife." The revolver was pointed at Eldon's midriff. Rain sparkled on the barrel. Eldon felt a sinking-elevator sensation. Somehow the revolver's bore looked even bigger with Maggie holding it.

Charley growled and started forward but Eldon stopped him, measuring the distance to Maggie. He had faced guns before and knew he couldn't tackle her. He remembered the leg-wrestling contest between Maggie and Anita. Even disarmed, she could knock my block off, he thought.

"You okay, Cassandra?"

"I'm okay. But she hurt Woody." Cassandra's voice was small and tired, but her eyes were narrow and keen—alert for the chance to escape.

"Woody's okay. Maggie just grazed him." Eldon advanced cautiously. Charley moved a step to one side.

"You stay put!" Maggie shouted at the sourdough and cocked the revolver.

"Stay where you are, Charley!" Eldon said. "Maggie, let Cassandra go. You might as well throw it in. You can't get away."

Maggie backed up. Eldon followed. "You're going to have to let me stay with you here."

"Why? So you can get the scoop?"

"Well, yeah." Eldon forced a grin. "Don't take it personally—it's only business."

"It was only business between Mark and Jason and Max, too. That's why they pushed him overboard, to get control of that damn boat."

"I thought you said Mark was drunk."

"That just made it easier for them. But they did push him."

Eldon advanced another step. "If they wanted the boat to themselves, why didn't they get rid of you?"

Maggie backed up. "They didn't have to. I was broke—I wasn't teaching then. I needed the money. Jason would've let me stay on as a hired hand, but I wouldn't sleep with him. That pretty much tore it. Jason had to have it all—"

Eldon took another step. In a moment he'd be close enough to lunge. "It was just business to try and knock me off, too, I suppose. Who killed who? Might as well tell me—professional interest."

"Hold it right there, Eldon. Not one more step. Now drop that knife."

"Okay." Eldon folded up the clasp knife, put the folder of drawings down on the beach and the knife atop the folder to weight it down. "They're all yours."

But Maggie didn't move toward the bait. "Stop being so reckless, and I'll let you go back to that girlfriend of yours in Oregon."

"Not to Anita?" Say anything, Eldon thought. Buy time.

"You're not staying with Anita. You just came up here to go fishing. You're just a tourist."

"At least you didn't call me a cheechako," Eldon said.

"Eldon, you are between me and my boat. Get out of the way."

"First tell me who killed who."

"It was a comedy of errors, really. And you know, I didn't think Max had anything to do with Mark's death until—"

"Until *you* shot Jason." It dawned on Eldon suddenly. "It wasn't Max. That's why you switched rifles—put yours in Max's house and took Max's for your own, to get rid of the murder weapon."

Maggie sighed. "You are really good."

"Cassandra's doing, really. She found the bill of sale." Eldon tried to keep his eyes on Maggie's and not on the gun. If he looked at the gun he would fall to his knees and start pleading. But he could tell from the look in her eyes that soon he would start pleading anyway.

"Cassandra's a smart little kid," Maggie said. "I shot Jason, all right. A clear shot across the water. I knew Jason worked in his yard nights, and it was nice and light, so I just sat out there and waited. That was when Max stepped into the picture—literally. I didn't know he was over there arguing with Jason, in the house. About money. Jason went outside and started working on the totem pole. That's when I fired." Maggie grinned a little. "You can imagine how I felt when Max walked out of the house, across the yard—and pushed the totem pole over onto Jason."

"Why didn't you shoot him, too?"

"Good God, Eldon, what do you think I *am?* Anyway, I thought I was off scot-free. Except that Max figured out pretty quick who had to have fired that shot, tried to blackmail me—"

"He wanted money and sex?"

"The money was a lost cause. The sex—well, that was when I clubbed him with the fish."

"You planted the nail to frame him."

"Yeah. Lived right up to my name. I figured the cops would find it when they combed the area. I didn't count on Woody and Cassandra here. But I had my alibi. The Button Club. The girls would cover for me."

"They knew?"

"I think they guessed. You know how they call themselves 'Raven's widows.' Oh, Jason cut quite a swath. Jason was out of friends, Max never had any. . . . When he came to me about the drawings, I finally realized that he had to go. And you, too. Jesus, Eldon, what have I become?"

"Sole owner of the boat."

"I didn't care about the boat. I just wanted to pay them back for—"

"You were going to dump me overboard when we went fishing, weren't you? But Anita showed up and she had a gun."

"It wasn't the gun that stopped me." Maggie laughed ruefully. "I was too damn seasick."

A sudden squall swept down the glacier, strong enough to ripple water in the bay. The cold gust snatched off Charley's false beard and flung it at Maggie's face. She brushed it away with her gun hand, trying not to drop the revolver. Cassandra slipped her chin under the wrist across her throat and bit down hard.

Maggie yelled and Cassandra broke free, driving past Eldon in the sprint of her life. Eldon stepped into the line of fire. He and Maggie watched Charley gather in Cassandra and retreat up the beach.

Eldon turned back to Maggie. "Quit now. There were mitigating factors—"

"No jail," Maggie said flatly and pulled the trigger.

Eldon only had time to feel an electric spark of fear as the .44's hammer clicked down—and a wet ignition cap sputtered uselessly. A little spume of white smoke curled out of the back of the pistol. Maggie hurled the gun at Eldon and turned and ran.

Why didn't she cock it and fire again? Eldon wondered as the .44 thudded to the gravel near him. He focused on the thought as he took one step forward. Then his legs gave out and he fell to his hands and knees, momentarily paralyzed with fear. He looked up to see Maggie running down the beach, toward the Amphicar. He lurched up and staggered after her.

He didn't chase Maggie too hard. Half of Eldon wanted her to get away. The other half just wasn't up to catching her. And part of him was angry because she'd tried to kill him.

Maggie reached the Amphicar and climbed inside, yanked the door closed, opened it, finally forced it shut.

"Throw the lever . . ." Eldon muttered but his throat was too dry for him to yell—dry with fear and anger. He saw Maggie fumble with the controls in panic. The keys, of course, were right where Eldon had left them. The Amphicar started up smoothly. She'll go to ground on some island, he thought, and starve in the woods until Mike Atkov finds her. Or maybe she'll get away, hide out in one of these isolated communities, cut her hair, sign on to a fishing boat, walk away when they put in at some port in Canada.

Eldon kept trudging down the beach toward the Amphicar. Maggie drove into the water. The props engaged and she headed out into Mandel's Bay at the point of a wide white wake.

"Eldon."

Eldon turned. It was Kate in her kayak.

Eldon splashed into the water and clambered into the kayak's front seat. "Got another paddle?"

"You'll only overturn us. Sit still."

Kate started paddling, twisting the double-bladed oar. The kayak turned smoothly and arrowed after the Amphicar. The Amphicar receded, mirrored in the waters of the bay. "What the hell you gonna do if we catch her?" Kate wanted to know.

"I don't know. Can we catch her?"

"Don't think so. We can follow till she runs out of gas."

"We can at least get a glimpse of her course—"

It was then that the Amphicar faltered and started to list. Eldon yelled in horror as the driver's side door popped open. He saw Maggie make a futile grab for the door—and then the Amphicar turned turtle and disappeared in a rush of water and bubbles.

"She didn't seal the door—" Eldon managed.

Kate swore and paddled harder as Eldon crouched wide-eyed and gasping in the kayak. They reached the place where the Amphicar had disappeared, but Eldon saw only his own reflection in the icy, opaque water. He almost fell in. Maggie and the Amphicar were far below, heading for the bottom of Mandel's Bay.

19

Kate Taylor paddled back into Klinkatshut and called the state police. The next morning the Atkov brothers stood in a police boat that crisscrossed the sunny bay, searching for Maggie's body, George the priest alert with a reporter's pencil and pad, Mike the trooper peering into the water with hands clasped in a curiously prayerful attitude. But there was no sign of Maggie.

Eldon was thankful for that. He didn't want to be there when they brought up the body. Instead, he climbed the glacier to cover the end of the totem pole's journey. Katlean insisted on being harnessed to the sled, and if the chief made only a show of pulling, there were plenty behind the sled to push.

Anita had wanted to go back to Klinkatshut at once—but there was no Amphicar to carry them, and Cassandra wouldn't hear of it. She wanted to finish covering the story.

They watched as Jason Baer's ridicule pole was bolted together and prepared for raising. Woody, despite a bandaged shoulder, was eager to gnaw the pole. Nell and Charley—who without his beard looked for all the world like an ex-insurance agent—held him back while Cassandra busily shot pictures of the work.

Eldon reflected that Jason's largesse had come with a lot of grief, like Raven's tricks of old. He'd have to work that theme into his story. "I tried to warn Maggie about the door," he said.

"It's not your fault," Anita said.

"I could've said it louder." Eldon wondered if his throat really had been too dry or if he had whispered through a trick of the will. She killed two people, even if they were bastards, he thought angrily, and she tried to kill me. Would have, too—except that Charley's pistol misfired, except that she got seasick.

"She knew about the door," Anita said. "I remember she said once that the Amphicar was only good if you were fleeing arrest."

"Yeah." Am I a bastard? Eldon wondered. The only way to find out was to return to Oregon and pick up his life again. There was no way to find out in Alaska. He was too close to things here and the sky was too broad.

"I'm going home after this," he said.

"I know," Anita said. "Cassandra will miss you. So will I."

"Maggie was right. I'm just a tourist."

"Maybe. But you're not a cheechako anymore. You're a sourdough for sure."

"And I didn't even have to sleep with a grizzly bear."

Anita laughed. "I wonder who thought up all that crap? You've still got a couple of weeks of vacation. You have to stick around for the inquest—so you might as well spend them fishing. You've earned that. And it'll be good to have you."

"I've got some more tab features to write, too," Eldon said. "A deal's a deal." The writing would make him feel better. It always did. So would the fishing, that was for sure.

Eldon felt for a moment as if they were haggling across Maggie's corpse. Thoughts swam through his mind like fleet fish. I'd never go fishing again if that would bring Maggie back, he told himself. But it won't, the way revenge couldn't bring back her husband. So the hell with her anyway. She tried to kill me.

I think I will go to confession, as long as George is still here. And I still might see a summer aurora.

Woody barked. The sound echoed across the glacier like the thump of a great drum. Cassandra snapped a picture with the Rolleiflex as the totem pole went up and dropped into its hole, and Chief Katlean made a stiff and uncertain bow. They hammered chocks into the hole to steady the totem, and Jason Baer's last, ambivalent masterpiece stood firm, overlooking the shining sweep of Mandel's Glacier and the bay and the infinite, rainy forest beyond.